I0562730

A Millionaire
of Yesterday

E. Phillips Oppenheim

Contents

A MILLIONAIRE
OF YESTERDAY

BY

E. Phillips Oppenheim

CHAPTER I

Filth," grunted Trent--"ugh! I tell you what it is, my venerable friend--I have seen some dirty cabins in the west of Ireland and some vile holes in East London. I've been in some places which I can't think of even now without feeling sick. I'm not a particular chap, wasn't brought up to it--no, nor squeamish either, but this is a bit thicker than anything I've ever knocked up against. If Francis doesn't hurry we'll have to chuck it! We shall never stand it out, Monty!"

The older man, gaunt, blear-eyed, ragged, turned over on his side. His appearance was little short of repulsive. His voice when he spoke was, curiously enough, the voice of a gentleman, thick and a trifle rough though it sounded.

"My young friend," he said, "I agree with you--in effect--most heartily. The place is filthy, the surroundings are repulsive, not to add degrading. The society is--er--not congenial--I allude of course to our hosts--and the attentions of these unwashed, and I am afraid I must say unclothed, ladies of dusky complexion is to say the least of it embarrassing."

"Dusky complexion!" Trent interrupted scornfully, "they're coal black!"

Monty nodded his head with solemn emphasis. "I will go so far as to admit that you are right," he acknowledged. "They are as black as sin! But, my friend Trent, I want you to consider this: If the nature of our surroundings is offensive to you, think what it must be to me. I may, I presume, between ourselves, allude to you as one of the people. Refinement and luxury have never come in your way, far less have they become indispensable to you. You were, I believe, educated at a Board School, I was at Eton. Afterwards you were apprenticed to a harness-maker, I--but no matter! Let us summarise the situation."

"If that means cutting it short, for Heaven's sake do so," Trent grumbled. "You'll talk yourself into a fever if you don't mind. Let's know what you're driving at."

"Talking," the elder man remarked with a slight shrug of his shoulders, "will never have a prejudicial effect upon my health. To men of your--pardon me--scanty education the expression of ideas in speech is doubtless a labour. To me, on the other hand, it is at once a pleasure and a relief. What I was about to observe is this: I belong by birth to what are called, I believe, the classes, you to the masses. I have inherited instincts which have been refined and cultivated, perhaps over-cultivated by breeding and associations--you are troubled with nothing of the sort. Therefore if these surroundings, this discomfort, not to mention the appalling overtures of our lady friends, are distressing to you, why, consider how much more so they must be to me!"

Trent smiled very faintly, but he said nothing. He was sitting cross-legged with his back against one of the poles which supported the open hut, with his eyes fixed upon the cloud of mist hanging over a distant swamp. A great yellow moon had stolen over the low range of stony hills--the mist was curling away in little wreaths of gold. Trent was watching it, but if you had asked him he would have told you that he was wondering when the alligators came out to feed, and how near the village they ventured. Looking at his hard, square face and keen, black eyes no one would surely have credited him with any less material thoughts.

"Furthermore," the man whom Trent had addressed as Monty continued, "there arises the question of danger and physical suitability to the situation. Contrast our two cases, my dear young friend. I am twenty-five years older than you, I have a weak heart, a ridiculous muscle, and the stamina of a rabbit. My fighting days are over. I can shoot straight, but shooting would only serve us here until our cartridges were gone--when the rush came a child could knock me over. You, on the contrary, have the constitution of an ox, the muscles of a bull, and the wind of an ostrich. You are, if you will pardon my saying so, a magnificent specimen of the animal man. In the event of trouble you would not hesitate to admit that your chances of escape would be at least double mine. Trent lit a match under pretence of lighting his pipe--in reality because only a few feet away he had seen a pair of bright eyes gleaming at them through a low shrub. A little native boy scuttled away--as black as night, woolly-headed, and shiny; he had crept up unknown to look with fearful eyes upon the wonderful white strangers. Trent threw a lump of earth at him and laughed as he dodged it.

"Well, go ahead, Monty," he said. "Let's hear what you're driving at. What a gab you've got to be sure!"

Monty waved his hand--a magnificent and silencing gesture.

"I have alluded to these matters," he continued, "merely in order to show you that the greater share of danger and discomfort in this expedition falls to my lot. Having reminded you of this, Trent, I refer to the concluding sentence of your last speech. The words indicated, as I understood them, some doubt of our ability to see this thing through."

He paused, peering over to where Trent was sitting with grim, immovable face, listening with little show of interest. He drew a long, deep breath and moved over nearer to the doorway. His manner was suddenly changed.

"Scarlett Trent," he cried, "Scarlett Trent, listen to me! You are young and I am old! To you this may be one adventure amongst many--it is my last. I've craved for such a chance as this ever since I set foot in this cursed land. It's come late enough, too late almost for me, but I'm going through with it while there's breath in my body. Swear to me now that you will not back out! Do you hear, Trent? Swear!"

Trent looked curiously at his companion, vastly interested in this sudden out-burst, in the firmness of his tone and the tightening of the weak mouth. After all, then, the old chap had some grit in him. To Trent, who had known him for years as a broken-down hanger-on of the settlement at Buckomari, a drunkard, gambler, a creature to all appearance hopelessly gone under, this look and this almost passionate appeal were like a revelation. He stretched out his great hand and patted his companion on the back--a proceeding which obviously caused him much discomfort.

"Bravo, old cockie!" he said. "Didn't imagine you'd got the grit. You know I'm not the chap to be let down easy. We'll go through with it, then, and take all chances! It's my game right along. Every copper I've got went to pay the bearers here and to buy the kickshaws and rum for old What's-his-name, and I'm not anxious to start again as a pauper. We'll stay here till we get our concessions, or till they bury us, then! It's a go!"

Monty--no one at Buckomari had ever known of any other name for him--stretched out a long hand, with delicate tapering fingers, and let it rest for a moment gingerly in the thick, brown palm of his companion. Then he glanced stealthily over his shoulder and his eyes gleamed.

"I think, if you will allow me, Trent, I will just moisten my lips--no more--with some of that excellent brandy."

Trent caught his arm and held it firmly.

"No, you don't," he said, shaking his head. "That's the last bottle, and we've got the journey back. We'll keep that, in case of fever."

A struggle went on in the face of the man whose hot breath fell upon Trent's cheek. It was the usual thing--the disappointment of the baffled drunkard--a little more terrible in his case perhaps because of the remnants of refinement still to be traced in his well-shaped features. His weak eyes for once were eloquent, but with the eloquence of cupidity and unwholesome craving, his lean cheeks twitched and his hands shook.

"Just a drop, Trent!" he pleaded. "I'm not feeling well, indeed I'm not! The odours here are so foul. A liqueur-glassful will do me all the good in the world."

"You won't get it, Monty, so it's no use whining," Trent said bluntly. "I've given way to you too much already. Buck up, man! We're on the threshold of fortune and we need all our wits about us."

"Of fortune--fortune!" Monty's head dropped upon his chest, his nostrils dilated, he seemed to fall into a state of stupor. Trent watched him half curiously, half contemptuously.

"You're terribly keen on money-making for an old 'un," he remarked, after a somewhat lengthy pause. "What do you want to do with it?"

"To do with it!" The old man raised his head. "To do with it!" The gleam of reawakened desire lit up his face. He sat for a moment thinking. Then he laughed softly.

"I will tell you, Master Scarlett Trent," he said, "I will tell you why I crave for wealth. You are a young and an ignorant man. Amongst other things you do not know what money will buy. You have your coarse pleasures I do not doubt, which seem sweet to you! Beyond them--what? A tasteless and barbaric display, a vulgar generosity, an ignorant and purposeless prodigality. Bah! How different it is with those who know! There are many things, my young friend, which I learned in my younger days, and amongst them was the knowledge of how to spend money. How to spend it, you understand! It is an art, believe me! I mastered it, and, until the end came, it was magnificent. In London and Paris to-day to have wealth and to know how to spend it is to be the equal of princes! The salons of the beautiful fly open before you, great men will clamour for your friendship, all the sweetest triumphs which love and sport can offer are yours. You stalk amongst a world of pygmies a veritable giant, the adored of women, the envied of men! You may be old--it matters not; ugly--you will be fooled into reckoning yourself an Adonis. Nobility is great, art is great, genius is great, but the key to the pleasure storehouse of the world is a key of gold--of gold!"

He broke off with a little gasp. He held his throat and looked imploringly towards the bottle. Trent shook his head stonily. There was something pitiful in the man's talk, in that odd mixture of bitter cynicism and passionate earnestness, but there was also something fascinating. As regards the brandy, however, Trent was adamant.

"Not a drop," he declared. "What a fool you are to want it, Monty! You're a wreck already. You want to pull through, don't you? Leave the filthy stuff alone. You'll not live a month to enjoy your coin if we get it!"

"Live!" Monty straightened himself out. A tremor went through all his frame.

"Live!" he repeated, with fierce contempt; "you are making the common mistake of the whole ignorant herd. You are measuring life by its length, when its depth alone is of any import. I want no more than a year or two at the most, and I promise you, Mr. Scarlett Trent, my most estimable young companion, that, during that year, I will live more than you in your whole lifetime. I will drink deep of pleasures which you know nothing of, I will be steeped in joys which you will never reach more nearly than the man who watches a change in the skies or a sunset across the ocean! To you, with boundless wealth, there will be depths of happiness which you will never probe, joys which, if you have the wit to see them at all, will be no more than a mirage to you."

Trent laughed outright, easily and with real mirth. Yet in his heart were sown already the seeds of a secret dread. There was a ring of passionate truth in Monty's words. He believed what he was saying. Perhaps he was right. The man's inborn hatred of a second or inferior place in anything stung him. Were there to be any niches after all in the temple of happiness to which he could never climb? He looked back rapidly, looked down the avenue of a squalid and unlovely life, saw himself the child of drink-sodden and brutal parents, remembered the Board School with its unlovely surroundings, his struggles at a dreary trade, his running away and the fierce draughts of delight which the joy and freedom of the sea had brought to him on the morning when he had crept on deck, a stowaway, to be lashed with every rope-end and to do the dirty work of every one. Then the slavery at a Belgian settlement, the job on a steamer trading along the Congo, the life at Buckomari, and lastly this bold enterprise in which the savings of years were invested. It was a life which called aloud for fortune some day or other to make a little atonement. The old man was dreaming. Wealth would bring him, uneducated though he was, happiness enough and to spare.

A footstep fell softly upon the turf outside. Trent sprang at once into an attitude of rigid attention. His revolver, which for four days had been at full cock by his side, stole out and covered the approaching shadow stealing gradually nearer and nearer. The old man saw nothing, for he slept, worn out with excitement and exhaustion.

CHAPTER II

A fat, unwholesome--looking creature, half native, half Belgian, waddled across the open space towards the hut in which the two strangers had been housed. He was followed at a little distance by two sturdy natives bearing a steaming pot which they carried on a pole between them. Trent set down his revolver and rose to his feet.

"What news, Oom Sam?" he asked. "Has the English officer been heard of? He must be close up now."

"No news," the little man grunted. "The King, he send some of his own supper to the white men. 'They got what they want,' he say. 'They start work mine soon as like, but they go away from here.' He not like them about the place! See!"

"Oh, that be blowed!" Trent muttered. "What's this in the pot? It don't smell bad."

"Rabbit," the interpreter answered tersely. "Very good. Part King's own supper. White men very favoured."

Trent bent over the pot which the two men had set upon the ground. He took a fork from his belt and dug it in.

"Very big bones for a rabbit, Sam," he remarked doubtfully.

Sam looked away. "Very big rabbits round here," he remarked. "Best keep pot. Send men away."

Trent nodded, and the men withdrew.

"Stew all right," Sam whispered confidentially. "You eat him. No fear. But you got to go. King beginning get angry. He say white men not to stay. They got what he promised, now they go. I know King--know this people well! You get away quick. He think you want be King here! You got the papers--all you want, eh?"

"Not quite, Sam," Trent answered. "There's an Englishman, Captain Francis, on his way here up the Coast, going on to Walgetta Fort. He must be here to-morrow. I want him to see the King's signature. If he's a witness these niggers can never back out of the concession. They're slippery devils. Another chap may come on with more rum and they'll forget us and give him the right to work the mines too. See!"

"I see," Sam answered; "but him not safe to wait. You believe me. I know these tam niggers. They take two days get drunk, then get devils, four--raving mad. They drunk now. Kill any one to-morrow--perhaps you. Kill you certain to-morrow night. You listen now!"

Trent stood up in the shadow of the overhanging roof. Every now and then came a wild, shrill cry from the lower end of the village. Some one was beating a frightful, cracked drum which they had got from a trader. The tumult was certainly increasing. Trent swore softly, and then looked irresolutely over his shoulder to where Monty was sleeping.

"If the worst comes we shall never get away quickly," he muttered. "That old carcase can scarcely drag himself along."

Sam looked at him with cunning eyes.

"He not fit only die," he said softly. "He very old, very sick man, you leave him here! I see to him."

Trent turned away in sick disgust.

"We'll be off to-morrow, Sam," he said shortly. "I say! I'm beastly hungry. What's in that pot?"

Sam spread out the palms of his hands.

"He all right, I see him cooked," he declared. "He two rabbits and one monkey."

Trent took out a plate and helped himself.

"All right," he said. "Be off now. We'll go to-morrow before these towsly-headed beauties are awake."

Sam nodded and waddled off. Trent threw a biscuit and hit his companion on the cheek.

"Here, wake up, Monty!" he exclaimed. "Supper's come from the royal kitchen. Bring your plate and tuck in!"

Monty struggled to his feet and came meekly towards where the pot stood simmering upon the ground.

"I'm not hungry, Trent," he said, "but I am very thirsty, very thirsty indeed. My throat is all parched. I am most uncomfortable. Really I think your behaviour with regard to the brandy is most unkind and ungenerous; I shall be ill, I know I shall. Won't you--"

"No, I won't," Trent interrupted. "Now shut up all that rot and eat something."

"I have no appetite, thank you," Monty answered, with sulky dignity.

"Eat something, and don't be a silly ass!" Trent insisted. "We've a hard journey before us, and you'll need all the strength in your carcase to land in Buckomari again. Here, you've dropped some of your precious rubbish."

Trent stooped forward and picked up what seemed to him at first to be a piece of cardboard from the ground. He was about to fling it to its owner, when he saw that it was a photograph. It was the likeness of a girl, a very young girl apparently, for her hair was still down her back and her dress was scarcely of the orthodox length. It was not particularly well taken, but Trent had never seen anything like it before. The lips were slightly parted, the deep eyes were brimming with laughter, the pose was full of grace, even though the girl's figure was angular. Trent had seen as much as this, when he felt the smart of a sudden blow upon the cheek, the picture was snatched from his hand, and Monty--his face convulsed with anger--glowered fiercely upon him.

"You infernal young blackguard! You impertinent meddling blockhead! How dare you presume to look at that photograph! How dare you, sir! How dare you!"

Trent was too thoroughly astonished to resent either the blow or the fierce words. He looked up into his aggressor's face in blank surprise.

"I only looked at it," he muttered. "It was lying on the floor."

"Looked at it! You looked at it! Like your confounded impertinence, sir! Who are you to look at her! If ever I catch you prying into my concerns again, I'll shoot you--by Heaven I will!"

Trent laughed sullenly, and, having finished eating, lit his pipe.

"Your concerns are of no interest to me," he said shortly; "keep 'em to yourself--and look here, old 'un, keep your hands off me! I ain't a safe man to hit let me tell you. Now sit down and cool off! I don't want any more of your tantrums."

Then there was a long silence between the two men. Monty sat where Trent had been earlier in the night at the front of the open hut, his eyes fixed upon the ever-rising moon, his face devoid of intelligence, his eyes dim. The fire of the last few minutes had speedily burnt out. His half-soddened brain refused to answer to the sudden spasm of memory which had awakened a spark of the former man. If he had thoughts at all, they hung around that brandy bottle. The calm beauty of the African night could weave no spell upon him. A few feet behind, Trent, by the light of the moon, was practising tricks with a pack of greasy cards. By and by a spark of intelligence found its way into Monty's brain. He turned round furtively.

"Trent," he said, "this is slow! Let us have a friendly game--you and I."

Trent yawned.

"Come on, then," he said. "Single Poker or Euchre, eh?"

"I do not mind," Monty replied affably. "Just which you prefer."

"Single Poker, then," Trent said.

"And the stakes?"

"We've nothing left to play for," Trent answered gloomily, "except cartridges."

Monty made a wry face. "Poker for love, my dear Trent," he said, "between you and me, would lack all the charm of excitement. It would be, in fact, monotonous! Let us exercise our ingenuity. There must be something still of value in our possession."

He relapsed into an affectation of thoughtfulness. Trent watched him curiously. He knew quite well that his partner was dissembling, but he scarcely saw to what end. Monty's eyes, moving round the grass-bound hut, stopped at Trent's knapsack which hung from the central pole. He uttered a little exclamation.

"I have it," he declared. "The very thing."

"Well!"

"You are pleased to set an altogether fictitious value upon half bottle of brandy we have left," he said. "Now I tell you what I will do. In a few months we shall both be rich men. I will play you for my I O U, for fifty pounds, fifty sovereigns, Trent, against half the contents of that bottle. Come, that is a fair offer, is it not? How we shall laugh at this in a year or two! Fifty pounds against a tumblerful--positively there is no more--a tumblerful of brandy."

He was watching Trent's face all the time, but the younger man gave no sign.

When he had finished, Trent took up the cards, which he had shuffled for Poker, and dealt them out for Patience. Monty's eyes were dim with disappointment.

"What!" he cried. "You don't agree! Did you understand me? Fifty pounds, Trent! Why, you must be mad!"

"Oh, shut up!" Trent growled. "I don't want your money, and the brandy's poison to you! Go to sleep!"

Monty crept a little nearer to his partner and laid his hand upon his arm. His shirt fell open, showing the cords of his throat swollen and twitching. His voice was half a sob.

"Trent, you are a young man--not old like me. You don't understand my constitution. Brandy is a necessity to me! I've lived on it so long that I shall die if you keep it from me. Remember, it's a whole day since I tasted a drop! Now I'll make it a hundred. What do you say to that? One hundred!"

Trent paused in his game, and looked steadfastly into the eager face thrust close to his. Then he shrugged his shoulders and gathered up the cards.

"You're the silliest fool I ever knew," he said bluntly, "but I suppose you'll worry me into a fever if you don't have your own way."

"You agree?" Monty shrieked. Trent nodded and dealt the cards.

"It must be a show after the draw," he said. "We can't bet, for we've nothing to raise the stakes with!"

Monty was breathing hard and his fingers trembled, as though the ague of the swamps was already upon him. He took up his cards one by one, and as he snatched up the last he groaned. Not a pair!

"Four cards," he whispered hoarsely. Trent dealt them out, looked at his own hand, and, keeping a pair of queens, took three more cards. He failed to improve, and threw them upon the floor. With frantic eagerness Monty grovelled down to see them--then with a shriek of triumph he threw down a pair of aces.

"Mine!" he said. "I kept an ace and drew another. Give me the brandy!"

Trent rose up, measured the contents of the bottle with his forefinger, and poured out half the contents into a horn mug. Monty stood trembling by.

"Mind," Trent said, "you are a fool to drink it and I am a fool to let you! You risk your life and mine. Sam has been up and swears we must clear out to-morrow. What sort of form do you think you'll be in to walk sixty miles through the swamps and bush, with perhaps a score of these devils at our heels? Come now, old 'un, be reasonable."

The veins on the old man's forehead stood out like whipcord.

"I won it," he cried. "Give it me! Give it me, I say."

Trent made no further protest. He walked back to where he had been lying and recommenced his Patience. Monty drank off the contents of the tumbler in two long, delicious gulps! Then he flung the horn upon the floor and laughed aloud.

"That's better," he cried, "that's better! What an ass you are, Trent! To imagine that a drain like that would have any effect at all, save to put life into a man! Bah! what do you know about it?"

Trent did not raise his head. He went on with his solitary game and, to all appearance, paid no heed to his companion's words. Monty was not in the humour to be ignored. He flung himself on the ground opposite to his companion.

"What a slow-blooded sort of creature you are, Trent!" he said. "Don't you ever drink, don't you ever take life a little more gaily?"

"Not when I am carrying my life in my hands," Trent answered grimly. "I get drunk sometimes--when there's nothing on and the blues come--never at a time like this though."

"It is pleasant to hear," the old man remarked, stretching out his limbs, "that you do occasionally relax. In your present frame of mind--you will not be offended I trust--you are just a little heavy as a companion. Never mind. In a year's time I will be teaching you how to dine--to drink champagne, to--by the way, Trent, have you ever tasted champagne?"

"Never," Trent answered gruffly "Don't know that I want to either."

Monty was compassionate. "My young friend," he said, "I would give my soul to have our future before us, to have your youth and never to have tasted champagne. Phew! the memory of it is delicious!"

"Why don't you go to bed?" Trent said. "You'll need all your strength to-morrow!"

Monty waved his hand with serene contempt.

"I am a man of humours, my dear friend," he said, "and to-night my humour is to talk and to be merry. What is it the philosophers tell us?--that the sweetest joys of life are the joys of anticipation. Here we are, then, on the eve of our triumph--let us talk, plan, be happy. Bah! how thirsty it makes one! Come, Trent, what stake will you have me set up against that other tumblerful of brandy."

"No stake that you can offer," Trent answered shortly. "That drop of brandy may stand between us and death. Pluck up your courage, man, and forget for a bit that there is such a thing as drink."

Monty frowned and looked stealthily across towards the bottle.

"That's all very well, my friend," he said, "but kindly remember that you are young, and well, and strong. I am old, and an invalid. I need support. Don't be hard on me, Trent. Say fifty again.

"No, nor fifty hundred," Trent answered shortly. "I don't want your money. Don't be such a fool, or you'll never live to enjoy it."

Monty shuffled on to his feet, and walked aimlessly about the hut. Once or twice as he passed the place where the bottle rested, he hesitated; at last he paused, his eyes lit up, he stretched out his hand stealthily. But before he could possess himself of it Trent's hand was upon his collar.

"You poor fool!" he said; "leave it alone can't you? You want to poison yourself I know. Well, you can do as you jolly well like when you are out of this--not before."

Monty's eyes flashed evil fires, but his tone remained persuasive. "Trent," he said, "be reasonable. Look at me! I ask you now whether I am not better for that last drop. I tell you that it is food and wine to me. I need it to brace me up for tomorrow. Now listen! Name your own stake! Set it up against that single glass! I am not a mean man, Trent. Shall we say one hundred and fifty?"

Trent looked at him half scornfully, half deprecatingly.

"You are only wasting your breath, Monty," he said. "I couldn't touch money won in such a way, and I want to get you out of this alive. There's fever in the air all around us, and if either of us got a touch of it that drop of brandy might stand between us and death. Don't worry me like a spoilt child. Roll yourself up and get to sleep! I'll keep watch."

"I will be reasonable," Monty whined. "I will go to sleep, my friend, and worry you no more when I have had just one sip of that brandy! It is the finest medicine in the world for me! It will keep the fever off. You do not want money you say! Come, is there anything in this world which I possess, or may possess, which you will set against that three inches of brown liquid?"

Trent was on the point of an angry negative. Suddenly he stopped--hesitated--and said nothing Monty's face lit up with sudden hope.

"Come," he cried, "there is something I see! You're the right sort, Trent. Don't be afraid to speak out. It's yours, man, if you win it. Speak up!"

"I will stake that brandy," Trent answered, "against the picture you let fall from your pocket an hour ago."

CHAPTER III

For a moment Monty stood as though dazed. Then the excitement which had shone in his face slowly subsided. He stood quite silent, muttering softly to himself, his eyes fixed upon Trent.

"Her picture! My little girl's picture! Trent, you're joking, you're mad!"

"Am I?" Trent answered nonchalantly. "Perhaps so! Anyhow those are my terms! You can play or not as you like! I don't care."

A red spot burned in Monty's cheeks, and a sudden passion shook him. He threw himself upon Trent and would have struck him but that he was as a child in the younger man's grasp. Trent held him at a distance easily and without effort.

"There's nothing for you to make a fuss about," he said gruffly. "I answered a plain question, that's all. I don't want to play at all. I should most likely lose, and you're much better without the brandy."

Monty was foaming with passion and baffled desire. "You beast!" he cried, "you low, ill-bred cur! How dared you look at her picture! How dare you make me such an offer! Let me go, I say! Let me go!"

But Trent did not immediately relax his grasp. It was evidently not safe to let him go. His fit of anger bordered upon hysterics. Presently he grew calmer but more maudlin. Trent at last released him, and, thrusting the bottle of brandy into his coat-pocket, returned to his game of Patience. Monty lay on the ground watching him with red, shifty eyes.

"Trent," he whimpered. But Trent did not answer him.

"Trent, you needn't have been so beastly rough. My arm is black and blue and I am sore all over."

But Trent remained silent. Monty crept a little nearer. He was beginning to feel a very injured person.

"Trent," he said, "I'm sorry we've had words. Perhaps I said more than I ought to have done. I did not mean to call you names. I apologise."

"Granted," Trent said tersely, bending over his game.

"You see, Trent," he went on, "you're not a family man, are you? If you were, you would understand. I've been down in the mire for years, an utter scoundrel, a poor, weak, broken-down creature. But I've always kept that picture! It's my little girl! She doesn't know I'm alive, never will know, but it's all I have to remind me of her, and I couldn't part with it, could I?"

"You'd be a blackguard if you did," Trent answered curtly.

Monty's face brightened.

"I was sure," he declared, "that upon reflection you would think so. I was sure of it. I have always found you very fair, Trent, and very reasonable. Now shall we say two hundred?"

"You seem very anxious for a game," Trent remarked. "Listen, I will play you for any amount you like, my I O U against your I O U. Are you agreeable?"

Monty shook his head. "I don't want your money, Trent," he said. "You know that I want that brandy. I will leave it to you to name the stake I am to set up against it."

"As regards that," Trent answered shortly, "I've named the stake; I'll not consider any other."

Monty's face once more grew black with anger.

"You are a beast, Trent--a bully!" he exclaimed passionately; "I'll not part with it!"

"I hope you won't," Trent answered. "I've told you what I should think of you if you did."

Monty moved a little nearer to the opening of the hut. He drew the photograph hesitatingly from his pocket, and looked at it by the moonlight. His eyes filled with maudlin tears. He raised it to his lips and kissed it.

"My little girl," he whispered. "My little daughter." Trent had re-lit his pipe and started a fresh game of Patience. Monty, standing in the opening, began to mutter to himself.

"I am sure to win--Trent is always unlucky at cards--such a little risk, and the brandy--ah!"

He sucked in his lips for a moment with a slight gurgling sound. He looked over his shoulder, and his face grew haggard with longing. His eyes sought Trent's, but Trent was smoking stolidly and looking at the cards spread out before him, as a chess-player at his pieces.

"Such a very small risk," Monty whispered softly to himself. "I need the brandy too. I cannot sleep without it! Trent!"

Trent made no answer. He did not wish to hear. Already he had repented. He was not a man of keen susceptibility, but he was a trifle ashamed of himself. At that moment he was tempted to draw the cork, and empty the brandy out upon the ground.

"Trent! Do you hear, Trent?"

He could no longer ignore the hoarse, plaintive cry. He looked unwillingly up. Monty was standing over him with white, twitching face and bloodshot eyes.

"Deal the cards," he muttered simply, and sat down.

Trent hesitated. Monty misunderstood him and slowly drew the photograph from his pocket and laid it face downwards upon the table. Trent bit his lip and frowned.

"Rather a foolish game this," he said. "Let's call it off, eh? You shall have--well, a thimbleful of the brandy and go to bed. I'll sit up, I'm not tired."

But Monty swore a very profane and a very ugly oath.

"I'll have the lot," he muttered. "Every drop; every d--d drop! Ay, and I'll keep the picture. You see, my friend, you see; deal the cards."

Then Trent, who had more faults than most men, but who hated bad language, looked at the back of the photograph, and, shuddering, hesitated no longer. He shuffled the cards and handed them to Monty.

"Your deal," he said laconically. "Same as before I suppose?"

Monty nodded, for his tongue was hot and his mouth dry, and speech was not an easy thing. But he dealt the cards, one by one with jealous care, and when he had finished he snatched upon his own, and looked at each with sickly disappointment.

"How many?" Trent asked, holding out the pack. Monty hesitated, half made up his mind to throw away three cards, then put one upon the table. Finally, with a little whine, he laid three down with trembling fingers and snatched at the three which Trent handed him. His face lit up, a scarlet flush burned in his cheek. It was evident that the draw had improved his hand.

Trent took his own cards up, looked at them nonchalantly, and helped himself to one card. Monty could restrain himself no longer. He threw his hand upon the ground.

"Three's," he cried in fierce triumph, "three of a kind--nines!"

Trent laid his own cards calmly down.

"A full hand," he said, "kings up."

Monty gave a little gasp and then a moan. His eyes were fixed with a fascinating glare upon those five cards which Trent had so calmly laid down. Trent took up the photograph, thrust it carefully into his pocket without looking at it, and rose to his feet.

"Look here, Monty," he said, "you shall have the brandy; you've no right to it, and you're best without it by long chalks. But there, you shall have your own way."

Monty rose to his feet and balanced himself against the post.

"Never mind--about the brandy," he faltered. "Give me back the photograph."

Trent shrugged his shoulders. "Why?" he asked coolly. "Full hand beats three, don't it? It was my win and my stake."

"Then--then take that!" But the blow never touched Trent. He thrust out his hand and held his assailant away at arm's length.

Monty burst into tears.

"You don't want it," he moaned; "what's my little girl to you? You never saw her, and you never will see her in your life."

"She is nothing to me of course," Trent answered. "A moment or so ago her picture was worth less to you than a quarter of a bottle of brandy."

"I was mad," Monty moaned. "She was my own little daughter, God help her!"

"I never heard you speak of her before," Trent remarked.

There was a moment's silence. Then Monty crept out between the posts into the soft darkness, and his voice seemed to come from a great distance.

"I have never told you about her," he said, "because she is not the sort of woman who is spoken of at all to such men as you. I am no more worthy to be her father than you are to touch the hem of her skirt. There was a time, Trent, many, many years ago, when I was proud to think that she was my daughter, my own flesh and blood. When I began to go down--it was different. Down and down and lower still! Then she ceased to be my daughter! After all it is best. I am not fit to carry her picture. You keep it. Trent--you keep it--and give me the brandy."

He staggered up on to his feet and crept back into the hut. His hands were outstretched, claw-like and bony, his eyes were fierce as a wild cat's. But Trent stood between him and the brandy bottle.

"Look here," he said, "you shall have the picture back--curse you! But listen. If I were you and had wife, or daughter, or sweetheart like this "--he touched the photograph almost reverently--"why, I'd go through fire and water but I'd keep myself decent; ain't you a silly old fool, now? We've made our piles, you can go back and take her a fortune, give her jewels and pretty dresses, and all the fal-de-lals that women love. You'll never do it if you muddle yourself up with that stuff. Pull yourself together, old 'un. Chuck the drink till we've seen this thing through at any rate!"

"You don't know my little girl," Monty muttered. "How should you? She'd care little for money or gewgaws, but she'd break her heart to see her old father--come to this--broken down--worthless--a hopeless, miserable wretch. It's too late. Trent, I'll have just a glass I think. It will do me good. I have been fretting, Trent, you see how pale I am."

He staggered towards the bottle. Trent watched him, interfering no longer. With a little chuckle of content he seized upon it and, too fearful of interference from Trent to wait for a glass, raised it to his lips. There was a gurgling in his throat--a little spasm as he choked, and released his lips for a moment. Then the bottle slid from his nerveless fingers to the floor, and the liquor oozed away in a little brown stream; even Trent dropped his pack of cards and sprang up startled. For bending down under the sloping roof was a European, to all appearance an Englishman, in linen clothes and white hat. It was the man for whom they had waited.

CHAPTER IV

Trent moved forward and greeted the newcomer awkwardly. "You're Captain Francis," he said. "We've been waiting for you."

The statement appeared to annoy the Explorer. He looked nervously at the two men and about the hut.

"I don't know how the devil you got to hear of my coming, or what you want with me," he answered brusquely. "Are you both English?"

Trent assented, waving his hand towards his companion in introductory fashion.

"That's my pal, Monty," he said. "We're both English right enough."

Monty raised a flushed face and gazed with bloodshot eyes at the man who was surveying him so calmly. Then he gave a little gurgling cry and turned away. Captain Francis started and moved a step towards him. There was a puzzled look in his face--as though he were making an effort to recall something familiar.

"What is the matter with him?" he asked Trent.

"Drink!"

"Then why the devil don't you see that he doesn't get too much?" the newcomer said sharply. "Don't you know what it means in this climate? Why, he's on the high-road to a fever now. Who on this earth is it he reminds me of?"

Trent laughed shortly.

"There's never a man in Buckomari--no, nor in all Africa--could keep Monty from the drink," he said. "Live with him for a month and try it. It wouldn't suit you--I don't think."

He glanced disdainfully at the smooth face and careful dress of their visitor, who bore the inspection with a kindly return of contempt.

"I've no desire to try," he said; "but he reminds me very strongly of some one I knew in England. What do you call him--Monty?"

Trent nodded.

"Never heard any other name," he said.

"Have you ever heard him speak of England?" Francis asked.

Trent hesitated. What was this newcomer to him that he should give away his pal? Less than nothing! He hated the fellow already, with a rough, sensitive man's contempt of a bearing and manners far above his own.

"Never. He don't talk."

Captain Francis moved a step towards the huddled-up figure breathing heavily upon the floor, but Trent, leaning over, stopped him.

"Let him be," he said gruffly. "I know enough of him to be sure that he needs no one prying and ferreting into his affairs. Besides, it isn't safe for us to be dawdling about here. How many soldiers have you brought with you?"

"Two hundred," Captain Francis answered shortly.

Trent whistled.

"We're all right for a bit, then," he said; "but it's a pretty sort of a picnic you're on, eh?"

"Never mind my business," Captain Francis answered curtly; "what about yours? Why have you been hanging about here for me?"

"I'll show you," Trent answered, taking a paper from his knapsack. "You see, it's like this. There are two places near this show where I've found gold. No use blowing about it down at Buckomari--the fellows there haven't the nerve of a kitten. This cursed climate has sapped it all out of them, I reckon. Monty and I clubbed together and bought presents for his Majesty, the boss here, and Monty wrote out this little document--sort of concession to us to sink mines and work them, you see. The old buffer signed it like winking, directly he spotted the rum, but we ain't quite happy about it; you see, it ain't to be supposed that he's got a conscience, and there's only us saw him put his mark there. We'll have to raise money to work the thing upon this, and maybe there'll be difficulties. So what we thought was this. Here's an English officer coming; let's get him to witness it, and then if the King don't go on the square, why, it's a Government matter."

Captain Francis lit a cigarette and smoked thoughtfully for a moment or two.

"I don't quite see," he said, "why we should risk a row for the sake of you two."

Trent snorted.

"Look here," he said; "I suppose you know your business. You don't want me to tell you that a decent excuse for having a row with this old Johnny is about the best thing that could happen to you. He's a bit too near the borders of civilisation to be a decent savage. Sooner or later some one will have to take him under their protection. If you don't do it, the French will. They're hanging round now looking out for an opportunity. Listen!"

Both men moved instinctively towards the open part of the hut and looked across towards the village. Up from the little open space in front of the King's dwelling-house leaped a hissing bright flame; they had kindled a fire, and black forms of men, stark naked and wounding themselves with spears, danced around it and made the air hideous with discordant cries. The King himself, too drunk to stand, squatted upon the ground with an empty bottle by his side. A breath of wind brought a strong, noxious odour to the two men who stood watching. Captain Francis puffed hard at his cigarette.

"Ugh!" he muttered; "beastly!"

"You may take my word for it," Trent said gruffly, "that if your two hundred soldiers weren't camped in the bush yonder, you and I and poor Monty would be making sport for them to-night. Now come. Do you think a quarrel with that crew is a serious thing to risk?"

"In the interests of civilisation," Captain Francis answered, with a smile, "I think not."

"I don't care how you put it," Trent answered shortly. "You soldiers all prate of the interests of civilisation. Of course it's all rot. You want the land--you want to rule, to plant a flag, and be called a patriot."

Captain Francis laughed. "And you, my superior friend," he said, glancing at Trent, gaunt, ragged, not too clean, and back at Monty--"you want gold--honestly if you can get it, if not--well, it is not too wise to ask. Your partnership is a little mysterious, isn't it--with a man like that? Out of your magnificent morality I trust that he may get his share."

Trent flushed a brick--red. An angry answer trembled upon his lips, but Oom Sam, white and with his little fat body quivering with fear, came hurrying up to them in the broad track of the moonlight.

"King he angry," he called out to them breathlessly. "Him mad drunk angry. He say white men all go away, or he fire bush and use the poisoned arrow. Me off! Got bearers waiting."

"If you go before we've finished," Trent said, "I'll not pay you a penny. Please yourself."

The little fat man trembled--partly with rage, partly with fear.

"You stay any longer," he said, "and King him send after you and kill on way home. White English soldiers go Buckomari with you?"

Trent shook his head.

"Going the other way," he said, "down to Wana Hill."

Oom Sam shook his head vigorously.

"Now you mind," he said; "I tell you, King send after you. Him blind mad."

Oom Sam scuttled away. Captain Francis looked thoughtful. "That little fat chap may be right," he remarked. "If I were you I'd get out of this sharp. You see, I'm going the other way. I can't help you."

Trent set his teeth.

"I've spent a good few years trying to put a bit together, and this is the first chance I've had," he said; "I'm going to have you back me as a British subject on that concession. We'll go down into the village now if you're ready."

"I'll get an escort," Francis said. "Best to impress 'em a bit, I think. Half a minute."

He stepped back into the hut and looked steadfastly at the man who was still lying doubled up upon the floor. Was it his fancy, or had those eyes closed swiftly at his turning--was it by accident, too, that Monty, with a little groan, changed his position at that moment, so that his face was in the shadow? Captain Francis was puzzled.

"It's like him," he said to himself softly; "but after all the thing's too improbable!"

He turned away with a shade upon his face and followed Trent out into the moonlight. The screeching from the village below grew louder and more hideous every minute.

CHAPTER V

The howls became a roar, blind passion was changed into purposeful fury. Who were these white men to march so boldly into the presence of the King without even the formality of sending an envoy ahead? For the King of Bekwando, drunk or sober, was a stickler for etiquette. It pleased him to keep white men waiting. For days sometimes a visitor was kept waiting his pleasure, not altogether certain either as to his ultimate fate, for there were ugly stories as to those who had journeyed to Bekwando and never been seen or heard of since. Those were the sort of visitors with whom his ebon Majesty loved to dally until they became pale with fright or furious with anger and impatience; but men like this white captain, who had brought him no presents, who came in overwhelming force and demanded a passage through his country as a matter of right were his special detestation. On his arrival he had simply marched into the place at the head of his columns of Hausas without ceremony, almost as a master, into the very presence of the King. Now he had come again with one of those other miscreants who at least had knelt before him and brought rum and many other presents. A slow, burning, sullen wrath was kindled in the King's heart as the three men drew near. His people, half-mad with excitement and debauch, needed only a cry from him to have closed like magic round these insolent intruders. His thick lips were parted, his breath came hot and fierce whilst he hesitated. But away outside the clearing was that little army of Hausas, clean-limbed, faithful, well drilled and armed. He choked down his wrath. There were grim stories about those who had yielded to the luxury of slaying these white men--stories of villages razed to the ground and destroyed, of a King himself who had been shot, of vengeance very swift and very merciless. He closed his mouth with a snap and sat up with drunken dignity. Oom Sam, in fear and trembling, moved to his side.

"What they want?" the King asked.

Oom Sam spread out the document which Trent had handed him upon a tree-stump, and explained. His Majesty nodded more affably. The document reminded him of the pleasant fact that there were three casks of rum to come to him every year. Besides, he rather liked scratching his royal mark upon the smooth, white paper. He was quite willing to repeat the performance, and took up the pen which Sam handed him readily.

"Him white man just come," Oom Sam explained; "want see you do this."

His Majesty was flattered, and, with the air of one to whom the signing of treaties and concessions is an everyday affair, affixed a thick, black cross upon the spot indicated.

"That all right?" he asked Oom Sam.

Oom Sam bowed to the ground.

"Him want to know," he said, jerking his head towards Captain Francis, "whether you know what means?"

His forefinger wandered aimlessly down the document. His Majesty's reply was prompt and cheerful.

"Three barrels of rum a year."

Sam explained further. "There will be white men come digging," he said; "white men with engines that blow, making holes under the ground and cutting trees."

The King was interested. "Where?" he asked.

Oom Sam pointed westward through the bush.

"Down by creek-side."

The King was thoughtful "Rum come all right?" he asked.

Oom Sam pointed to the papers.

"Say so there," he declared. "All quite plain."

The King grinned. It was not regal, but he certainly did it. If white men come too near they must be shot--carefully and from ambush. He leaned back with the air of desiring the conference to cease. Oom Sam turned to Captain Francis.

"King him quite satisfied," he declared. "Him all explained before--he agree."

The King suddenly woke up again. He clutched Sam by the arm, and whispered in his ear. This time it was Sam who grinned.

"King, him say him signed paper twice," he explained. "Him want four barrels of rum now."

Trent laughed harshly.

"He shall swim in it, Sam," he said; "he shall float down to hell upon it."

Oom Sam explained to the King that, owing to the sentiments of affection and admiration with which the white men regarded him, the three barrels should be made into four, whereupon his Majesty bluntly pronounced the audience at an end and waddled off into his Imperial abode.

The two Englishmen walked slowly back to the hut. Between them there had sprung up from the first moment a strong and mutual antipathy. The blunt savagery of Trent, his apparently heartless treatment of his weaker partner, and his avowed unscrupulousness, offended the newcomer much in the same manner as in many ways he himself was obnoxious to Trent. His immaculate fatigue-uniform, his calm superciliousness, his obvious air of belonging to a superior class, were galling to Trent beyond measure. He himself felt the difference--he realised his ignorance, his unkempt and uncared-for appearance. Perhaps, as the two men walked side by side, some faint foreshadowing of the future showed to Trent another and a larger world where they two would once more walk side by side, the outward differences between them lessened, the smouldering irritation of the present leaping up into the red-hot flame of hatred. Perhaps it was just as well for John Francis that the man who walked so sullenly by his side had not the eyes of a seer, for it was a wild country and Trent himself had drunk deep of its lawlessness. A little accident with a knife, a carelessly handled revolver, and the man who was destined to stand more than once in his way would pass out of his life for ever. But in those days Trent knew nothing of what was to come--which was just as well for John Francis.

*   *   *   *   *

Monty was sitting up when they reached the hut, but at the sight of Trent's companion he cowered back and affected sleepiness. This time, however, Francis was not to be denied. He walked to Monty's side, and stood looking down upon him.

"I think," he said gently, "that we have met before."

"A mistake," Monty declared. "Never saw you in my life. Just off to sleep."

But Francis had seen the trembling of the man's lips, and his nervously shaking hands.

"There is nothing to fear," he said; "I wanted to speak to you as a friend."

"Don't know you; don't want to speak to you," Monty declared.

Francis stooped down and whispered a name in the ear of the sullen man. Trent leaned forward, but he could not hear it--only he too saw the shudder and caught the little cry which broke from the white lips of his partner.

Monty sat up, white, despairing, with strained, set face and bloodshot eyes.

"Look here," he said, "I may be what you say, and I may not. It's no business of yours. Do you hear? Now be off and leave me alone! Such as I am, I am. I won't be interfered with. But--" Monty's voice became a shriek.

"Leave me alone!" he cried. "I have no name I tell you, no past, no future. Let me alone, or by Heaven I'll shoot you!"

Francis shrugged his shoulders, and turned away with a sigh.

"A word with you outside," he said to Trent--and Trent followed him out into the night. The moon was paling--in the east there was a faint shimmer of dawn. A breeze was rustling in the trees. The two men stood face to face.

"Look here, sir," Francis said, "I notice that this concession of yours is granted to you and your partner jointly whilst alive and to the survivor, in case of the death of either of you."

"What then?" Trent asked fiercely.

"This! It's a beastly unfair arrangement, but I suppose it's too late to upset it. Your partner is half sodden with drink now. You know what that means in this climate. You've the wit to keep sober enough yourself. You're a strong man, and he is weak. You must take care of him. You can if you will."

"Anything else?" Trent asked roughly.

The officer looked his man up and down.

"We're in a pretty rough country," he said, "and a man gets into the habit of having his own way here. But listen to me! If anything happens to your partner here or in Buckomari, you'll have me to reckon with. I shall not forget. We are bound to meet! Remember that!"

Trent turned his back upon him in a fit of passion which choked down all speech. Captain Francis lit a cigarette and walked across towards his camp.

CHAPTER VI

A sky like flame, and an atmosphere of sulphur. No breath of air, not a single ruffle in the great, drooping leaves of the African trees and dense, prickly shrubs. All around the dank, nauseous odour of poison flowers, the ceaseless dripping of poisonous moisture. From the face of the man who stood erect, unvanquished as yet in the struggle for life, the fierce sweat poured like rain--his older companion had sunk to the ground and the spasms of an ugly death were twitching at his whitening lips.

"I'm done, Trent," he gasped faintly. "Fight your way on alone. You've a chance yet. The way's getting a bit easier--I fancy we're on the right track and we've given those black devils the slip! Nurse your strength! You've a chance! Let me be. It's no use carrying a dead man." Gaunt and wild, with the cold fear of death before him also, the younger man broke out into a fit of cursing.

"May they rot in the blackest corner of hell, Oom Sam and those miserable vermin!" he shouted. "A path all the way, the fever season over, the swamps dry! Oh! when I think of Sam's smooth jargon I would give my chance of life, such as it is, to have him here for one moment. To think that beast must live and we die!"

"Prop me up against this tree, Trent--and listen," Monty whispered. "Don't fritter away the little strength you have left."

Trent did as he was told. He had no particular affection for his partner and the prospect of his death scarcely troubled him. Yet for twenty miles and more, through fetid swamps and poisoned jungles, he had carried him over his shoulder, fighting fiercely for the lives of both of them, while there remained any chance whatever of escape. Now he knew that it was in vain, he regretted only his wasted efforts--he had no sentimental regrets in leaving him. It was his own life he wanted--his own life he meant to fight for.

"I wouldn't swear at Oom Sam too hard," Monty continued. "Remember for the last two days he was doing all he could to get us out of the place. It was those fetish fellows who worked the mischief and he--certainly--warned us all he could. He took us safely to Bekwando and he worked the oracle with the King!"

"Yes, and afterwards sneaked off with Francis," Trent broke in bitterly, "and took every bearer with him--after we'd paid them for the return journey too. Sent us out here to be trapped and butchered like rats. If we'd only had a guide we should have been at Buckomari by now."

"He was right about the gold," Monty faltered. "It's there for the picking up. If only we could have got back we were rich for life. If you escape--you need never do another stroke of work as long as you live."

Trent stood upright, wiped the dank sweat from his forehead and gazed around him fiercely, and upwards at that lurid little patch of blue sky.

"If I escape!" he muttered. "I'll get out of this if I die walking. I'm sorry you're done, Monty," he continued slowly. "Say the word and I'll have one more spell at carrying you! You're not a heavy weight and I'm rested now!"

But Monty, in whose veins was the chill of death and who sought only for rest, shook his head.

"It shakes me too much," he said, "and it's only a waste of strength. You get on, Trent, and don't you bother about me. You've done your duty by your partner and a bit more. You might leave me the small revolver in case those howling savages come up--and Trent!"

"Yes--"

"The picture--just for a moment. I'd like to have one look at her!"

Trent drew it out from his pocket--awkwardly--and with a little shame at the care which had prompted him to wrap it so tenderly in the oilskin sheet. Monty shaded his face with his hands, and the picture stole up to his lips. Trent stood a little apart and hated himself for this last piece of inhumanity. He pretended to be listening for the stealthy approach of their enemies. In reality he was struggling with the feeling which prompted him to leave this picture with the dying man.

"I suppose you'd best have it," he said sullenly at last.

But Monty shook his head feebly and held out the picture.

Trent took it with an odd sense of shame which puzzled him. He was not often subject to anything of the sort.

"It belongs to you, Trent. I lost it on the square, and it's the only social law I've never broken--to pay my gambling debts. There's one word more!"

"Yes."

"It's about that clause in our agreement. I never thought it was quite fair, you know, Trent!"

"Which clause?"

"The clause which--at my death--makes you sole owner of the whole concession. You see--the odds were scarcely even, were they? It wasn't likely anything would happen to you!"

"I planned the thing," Trent said, "and I saw it through! You did nothing but find a bit of brass. It was only square that the odds should be in my favour. Besides, you agreed. You signed the thing."

"But I wasn't quite well at the time," Monty faltered. "I didn't quite understand. No, Trent, it's not quite fair. I did a bit of the work at least, and I'm paying for it with my life!"

"What's it matter to you now?" Trent said, with unintentional brutality. "You can't take it with you."

Monty raised himself a little. His eyes, lit with feverish fire, were fastened upon the other man.

"There's my little girl!" he said hoarsely. "I'd like to leave her something. If the thing turns out big, Trent, you can spare a small share. There's a letter here! It's to my lawyers. They'll tell you all about her."

Trent held out his hands for the letter.

"All right," he said, with sullen ungraciousness. "I'll promise something. I won't say how much! We'll see."

"Trent, you'll keep your word," Monty begged. "I'd like her to know that I thought of her."

"Oh, very well," Trent declared, thrusting the letter into his pocket. "It's a bit outside our agreement, you know, but I'll see to it anyhow. Anything else?"

Monty fell back speechless. There was a sudden change in his face. Trent, who had seen men die before, let go his hand and turned away without any visible emotion. Then he drew himself straight, and set his teeth hard together.

"I'm going to get out of this," he said to himself slowly and with fierce emphasis. "I'm not for dying and I won't die!"

He stumbled on a few steps, a little black snake crept out of its bed of mud, and looked at him with yellow eyes protruding from its upraised head. He kicked it savagely away--a crumpled, shapeless mass. It was a piece of brutality typical of the man. Ahead he fancied that the air was clearer--the fetid mists less choking--in the deep night-silence a few hours back he had fancied that he had heard the faint thunder of the sea. If this were indeed so, it would be but a short distance now to the end of his journey. With dull, glazed eyes and clenched hands, he reeled on. A sort of stupor had laid hold of him, but through it all his brain was working, and he kept steadily to a fixed course. Was it the sea in his ears, he wondered, that long, monotonous rolling of sound, and there were lights before his eyes--the lights of Buckomari, or the lights of death!

They found him an hour or two later unconscious, but alive, on the outskirts of the village.

Three days later two men were seated face to face in a long wooden house, the largest and most important in Buckomari village.

Smoking a corn-cob pipe and showing in his face but few marks of the terrible days through which he had passed was Scarlett Trent--opposite to him was Hiram Da Souza, the capitalist of the region. The Jew--of Da Souza's nationality it was impossible to have any doubt--was coarse and large of his type, he wore soiled linen clothes and was smoking a black cigar. On the little finger of each hand, thickly encrusted with dirt, was a diamond ring, on his thick, protruding lips a complacent smile. The concession, already soiled and dog-eared, was spread out before them.

It was Da Souza who did most of the talking. Trent indeed had the appearance of a man only indirectly interested in the proceedings.

"You see, my dear sir," Da Souza was saying, "this little concession of yours is, after all, a very risky business. These niggers have absolutely no sense honour. Do I not know it--alas--to my cost?"

Trent listened in contemptuous silence. Da Souza had made a fortune trading fiery rum on the Congo and had probably done more to debauch the niggers he spoke of so bitterly than any man in Africa.

"The Bekwando people have a bad name--very bad name. As for any sense of commercial honour--my dear Trent, one might as well expect diamonds to spring up like mushrooms under our feet."

"The document," Trent said, "is signed by the King and witnessed by Captain Francis, who is Agent-General out here, or something of the sort, for the English Government. It was no gift and don't you think it, but a piece of hard bartering. Forty bearers carried our presents to Bekwando and it took us three months to get through. There is enough in it to make us both millionaires.

"Then why," Da Souza asked, looking up with twinkling eyes, "do you want to sell me a share in it?"

"Because I haven't a darned cent to bless myself with," Trent answered curtly. "I've got to have ready money. I've never had my fist on five thousand pounds before--no, nor five thousand pence, but, as I'm a living man, let me have my start and I'll hold my own with you all."

Da Souza threw himself back in his chair with uplifted hands.

"But my dear friend," he cried, "my dear young friend, you were not thinking--do not say that you were thinking of asking such a sum as five thousand pounds for this little piece of paper!"

The amazement, half sorrowful, half reproachful, on the man's face was perfectly done. But Trent only snorted.

"That piece of paper, as you call it, cost us the hard savings of years, it cost us weeks and months in the bush and amongst the swamps--it cost a man's life, not to mention the niggers we lost. Come, I'm not here to play skittles. Are you on for a deal or not? If you're doubtful about it I've another market. Say the word and we'll drink and part, but if you want to do business, here are my terms. Five thousand for a sixth share!"

"Sixth share," the Jew screamed, "sixth share?"

Trent nodded.

"The thing's worth a million at least," he said. "A sixth share is a great fortune. Don't waste any time turning up the whites of your eyes at me. I've named my terms and I shan't budge from them. You can lay your bottom dollar on that."

Da Souza took up the document and glanced it through once more.

"The concession," he remarked, "is granted to Scarlett Trent and to one Monty jointly. Who is this Monty, and what has he to say to it?"

Trent set his teeth hard, and he never blenched.

"He was my partner, but he died in the swamps, poor chap. We had horrible weather coming back. It pretty near finished me."

Trent did not mention the fact that for four days and nights they were hiding in holes and up trees from the natives whom the King of Bekwando had sent after them, that their bearers had fled away, and that they had been compelled to leave the track and make their way through an unknown part of the bush.

"But your partner's share," the Jew asked. "What of that?"

"It belongs to me," Trent answered shortly. "We fixed it so before we started. We neither of us took much stock in our relations. If I had died, Monty would have taken the lot. It was a fair deal. You'll find it there!"

The Jew nodded.

"And your partner?" he said. "You saw him die! There is no doubt about that?"

Trent nodded.

"He is as dead," he said, "as Julius Caesar."

"If I offered you--" Da Souza began.

"If you offered me four thousand, nine hundred and ninety-nine pounds," Trent interrupted roughly, "I would tell you to go to glory."

Da Souza sighed. It was a hard man to deal with--this.

"Very well," he said, "if I give way, if I agree to your terms, you will be willing to make over this sixth share to me, both on your own account and on account of your late partner?"

"You're right, mate," Trent assented. "Plank down the brass, and it's a deal."

"I will give you four thousand pounds for a quarter share," Da Souza said.

Trent knocked the ashes from his pipe and stood up.

"Here, don't waste any more of my time," he said. "Stand out of the way, I'm off."

Da Souza kept his hands upon the concession.

"My dear friend," he said, "you are so violent. You are so abrupt. Now listen. I will give you five thousand for a quarter share. It is half my fortune."

"Give me the concession," Trent said. "I'm off."

"For a fifth," Da Souza cried.

Trent moved to the door without speech. Da Souza groaned.

"You will ruin me," he said, "I know it. Come then, five thousand for a sixth share. It is throwing money away."

"If you think so, you'd better not part," Trent said, still lingering in the doorway. "Just as you say. I don't care."

For a full minute Da Souza hesitated. He had an immense belief in the richness of the country set out in the concession; he knew probably more about it than Trent himself. But five thousand pounds was a great deal of money and there was always the chance that the Government might not back the concession holders in case of trouble. He hesitated so long that Trent was actually disappearing before he had made up his mind.

"Come back, Mr. Trent," he called out. "I have decided. I accept. I join with you."

Trent slowly returned. His manner showed no exultation.

"You have the money here?" he asked.

Da Souza laid down a heap of notes and gold upon the table. Trent counted them carefully and thrust them into his pocket. Then he took up a pen and wrote his name at the foot of the assignment which the Jew had prepared.

"Have a drink?" he asked.

Da Souza shook his head.

"The less we drink in this country," he said, "the better. I guess out here, spirits come next to poison. I'll smoke with you, if you have a cigar handy."

Trent drew a handful of cigars from his pocket. "They're beastly," he said, "but it's a beastly country. I'll be glad to turn my back on it."

"There is a good deal," Da Souza said, "which we must now talk about."

"To-morrow," Trent said curtly. "No more now! I haven't got over my miserable journey yet. I'm going to try and get some sleep."

He swung out into the heavy darkness. The air was thick with unwholesome odours rising from the lake-like swamp beyond the drooping circle of trees. He walked a little way towards the sea, and sat down upon a log. A faint land-breeze was blowing, a melancholy soughing came from the edge of the forest only a few hundred yards back, sullen, black, impenetrable. He turned his face inland unwillingly, with a superstitious little thrill of fear. Was it a coyote calling, or had he indeed heard the moan of a dying man, somewhere back amongst that dark, gloomy jungle? He scoffed at himself! Was he becoming as a girl, weak and timid? Yet a moment later he closed his eyes, and pressed his hands tightly over his hot eyeballs. He was a man of little imaginative force, yet the white face of a dying man seemed suddenly to have floated up out of the darkness, to have come to him like a will-o'-the-wisp from the swamp, and the hollow, lifeless eyes seemed ever to be seeking his, mournful and eloquent with dull reproach. Trent rose to his feet with an oath and wiped the sweat from his forehead. He was trembling, and he cursed himself heartily.

"Another fool's hour like this," he muttered, "and the fever will have me. Come out of the shadows, you white-faced, skulking reptile, you--bah! what a blithering fool I am! There is no one there! How could there be any one?"

He listened intently. From afar off came the faint moaning of the wind in the forest and the night sounds of restless animals. Nearer there was no one--nothing stirred. He laughed out loud and moved away to spend his last night in his little wooden home. On the threshold he paused, and faced once more that black, mysterious line of forest.

"Well, I've done with you now," he cried, a note of coarse exultation in his tone. "I've gambled for my life and I've won. To-morrow I'll begin to spend the stakes."

CHAPTER VII

In a handsomely appointed room of one of the largest hotels in London a man was sitting at the head of a table strewn with blotting-paper and writing materials of every description. Half a dozen chairs had been carelessly pushed back, there were empty champagne bottles upon the sideboard, the air was faintly odorous of tobacco smoke--blue wreaths were still curling upwards towards the frescoed ceiling. Yet the gathering had not been altogether a festive one. There were sheets of paper still lying about covered with figures, a brass-bound ledger lay open at the further end of the table, In the background a young man, slim, pale, ill-dressed in sober black, was filling a large tin box with documents and letters.

It had been a meeting of giants. Men whose names were great in the world of finance had occupied those elaborately decorated leather chairs. There had been cynicism, criticism, and finally enthusiasm. For the man who remained it had been a triumph. He had appeared to do but little in the way of persuasion. His manners had been brusque, and his words had been few. Yet he remained the master of the situation. He had gained a victory not only financial but moral, over men whose experience and knowledge were far greater than his. He was no City magnate, nor had he ever received any training in those arts and practices which go to the making of one. For his earlier life had been spent in a wilder country where the gambling was for life and not merely for gold. It was Scarlett Trent who sat there in thoughtful and absorbed silence. He was leaning a little back in a comfortably upholstered chair, with his eyes fixed on a certain empty spot upon the table. The few inches of polished mahogany seemed to him--empty of all significance in themselves--to be reflecting in some mysterious manner certain scenes in his life which were now very rarely brought back to him. The event of to-day he knew to be the culmination of a success as rapid as it had been surprising. He was a millionaire. This deal to-day, in which he had held his own against the shrewdest and most astute men of the great city, had more than doubled his already large fortune. A few years ago he had landed in England friendless and unknown, to-day he had stepped out from even amongst the chosen few and had planted his feet in the higher lands whither the faces of all men are turned. With a grim smile upon his lips, he recalled one by one the various enterprises into which he had entered, the courage with which he had forced them through, the solid strength with which he had thrust weaker men to the wall and had risen a little higher towards his goal upon the wreck of their fortunes. Where other men had failed he had succeeded. To-day the triumph was his alone. He was a millionaire--one of the princes of the world!

The young man, who had filled his box and also a black bag, was ready to go. He ventured most respectfully to break in upon the reflections of his employer.

"Is there anything more for me to do, sir?"

Trent woke from his day-dream into the present. He looked around the room and saw that no papers had been omitted. Then he glanced keenly into his clerk's face.

"Nothing more," he said. "You can go."

It was significant of the man that, notwithstanding his hour of triumph, he did not depart in the slightest degree from the cold gruffness of his tone. The little speech which his clerk had prepared seemed to stick in his throat.

"I trust, sir, that you will forgive--that you will pardon the liberty, if I presume to congratulate you upon such a magnificent stroke of business!"

Scarlett Trent faced him coldly. "What do you know about it?" he asked. "What concern is it of yours, young man, eh?"

The clerk sighed, and became a little confused. He had indulged in some wistful hopes that for once his master might have relaxed, that an opportune word of congratulation might awaken some spark of generosity in the man who had just added a fortune to his great store. He had a girl-wife from whose cheeks the roses were slowly fading, and very soon would come a time when a bank-note, even the smallest, would be a priceless gift. It was for her sake he had spoken. He saw now that he had made a mistake.

"I am very sorry, sir," he said humbly. "Of course I know that these men have paid an immense sum for their shares in the Bekwando Syndicate. At the same time it is not my business, and I am sorry that I spoke."

"It is not your business at any time to remember what I receive for properties," Scarlett Trent said roughly. "Haven't I told you that before? What did I say when you came to me? You were to hear nothing and see nothing outside your duties! Speak up, man! Don't stand there like a jay!"

The clerk was pale, and there was an odd sensation in his throat. But he thought of his girl-wife and he pulled himself together.

"You are quite right, sir," he said. "To any one else I should never have mentioned it. But we were alone, and I thought that the circumstances might make it excusable."

His employer grunted in an ominous manner.

"When I say forget, I mean forget," he declared. "I don't want to be reminded by you of my own business. D'ye think I don't know it?"

"I am very sure that you do, sir," the clerk answered humbly. "I quite see that my allusion was an error."

Scarlett Trent had turned round in his chair, and was eying the pale, nervous figure with a certain hard disapproval.

"That's a beastly coat you've got on, Dickenson," he said. "Why don't you get a new one?"

"I am standing in a strong light, sir," the young man answered, with a new fear at his heart. "It wants brushing, too. I will endeavour to get a new one--very shortly."

His employer grunted again.

"What's your salary?" he asked.

"Two pounds fifteen shillings a week, sir."

"And you mean to say that you can't dress respectably on that? What do you do with your money, eh? How do you spend it? Drink and music-halls, I suppose!"

The young man was able at last to find some spark of dignity. A pink spot burned upon his cheeks.

"I do not attend music-halls, sir, nor have I touched wine or spirits for years. I--I have a wife to keep, and perhaps--I am expecting--"

He stopped abruptly. How could he mention that other matter which, for all its anxieties, still possessed for him a sort of quickening joy in the face of that brutal stare. He did not conclude his sentence, the momentary light died out of his pale commonplace features. He hung his head and was silent.

"A wife," Scarlett Trent repeated with contempt, "and all the rest of it of course. Oh, what poor donkeys you young men are! Here are you, with your way to make in the world, with your foot scarcely upon the bottom rung of the ladder, grubbing along on a few bob a week, and you choose to go and chuck away every chance you ever might have for a moment's folly. A poor, pretty face I suppose. A moonlight walk on a Bank Holiday, a little maudlin sentiment, and over you throw all your chances in life. No wonder the herd is so great, and the leaders so few," he added, with a sneer.

The young man raised his head. Once more the pink spot was burning. Yet how hard to be dignified with the man from whom comes one's daily bread.

"You are mistaken, sir," he said. "I am quite happy and quite satisfied."

Scarlett Trent laughed scornfully.

"Then you don't look it," he exclaimed.

"I may not, sir," the young man continued, with a desperate courage, "but I am. After all happiness is spelt with different letters for all of us. You have denied yourself--worked hard, carried many burdens and run great risks to become a millionaire. I too have denied myself, have worked and struggled to make a home for the girl I cared for. You have succeeded and you are happy. I can hold Edith's--I beg your pardon, my wife's hand in mine and I am happy. I have no ambition to be a millionaire. I was very ambitious to win my wife."

Scarlett Trent looked at him for a moment open mouthed and open-eyed. Then he laughed outright and a chill load fell from the heart of the man who for a moment had forgotten himself. The laugh was scornful perhaps, but it was not angry.

"Well, you've shut me up," he declared. "You seem a poor sort of a creature to me, but if you're content, it's no business of mine. Here buy yourself an overcoat, and drink a glass of wine. I'm off!"

He rose from his seat and threw a bank-note over the table. The clerk opened it and handed it back with a little start.

"I am much obliged to you, sir," he said humbly, "but you have made a mistake. This note is for fifty pounds."

Trent glanced at it and held out his hand. Then he paused.

"Never mind," he said, with a short laugh, "I meant to give you a fiver, but it don't make much odds. Only see that you buy some new clothes."

The clerk half closed his eyes and steadied himself by grasping the back of a chair. There was a lump in his throat in earnest now.

"You--you mean it, sir?" he gasped. "I--I'm afraid I can't thank you!"

"Don't try, unless you want me to take it back," Trent said, strolling to the sideboard. "Lord, how those City chaps can guzzle! Not a drop of champagne left. Two unopened bottles though! Here, stick 'em in your bag and take 'em to the missis, young man. I paid for the lot, so there's no use leaving any. Now clear out as quick as you can. I'm off!"

"You will allow me, sir--"

Scarlett Trent closed the door with a slam and disappeared. The young man passed him a few moments later as he stood on the steps of the hotel lighting a cigar. He paused again, intent on stammering out some words of thanks. Trent turned his back upon him coldly.

CHAPTER VIII

Trent, on leaving the hotel, turned for almost the first time in his life west-wards. For years the narrow alleys, the thronged streets, the great build-ings of the City had known him day by day, almost hour by hour. Its roar and clamour, the strife of tongues and keen measuring of wits had been the salt of his life. Steadily, sturdily, almost insolently, he had thrust his way through to the front ranks. In many respects those were singular and unusual elements which had gone to the making of his success. His had not been the victory of honied false-hoods, of suave deceit, of gentle but legalised robbery. He had been a hard worker, a daring speculator with nerves of iron, and courage which would have glorified a nobler cause. Nor had his been the methods of good fellowship, the sharing of "good turns," the camaraderie of finance. The men with whom he had had large dealings he had treated as enemies rather than friends, ever watching them covertly with close but unslackening vigilance. And now, for the present at any rate it was all over. There had come a pause in his life. His back was to the City and his face was set towards an unknown world. Half unconsciously he had undertaken a little voy-age of exploration.

From the Strand he crossed Trafalgar Square into Pall Mall, and up the Hay-market into Piccadilly. He was very soon aware that he had wandered into a world whose ways were not his ways and with whom he had no kinship. Yet he set him-self sedulously to observe them, conscious that what he saw represented a very large side of life. From the first he was aware of a certain difference in himself and his ways. The careless glance of a lounger on the pavement of Pall Mall filled him with a sudden anger. The man was wearing gloves, an article of dress which Trent ignored, and smoking a cigarette, which he loathed. Trent was carelessly dressed in a tweed suit and red tie, his critic wore a silk hat and frock coat, patent-leather boots, and a dark tie of invisible pattern. Yet Trent knew that he was a type of that class which would look upon him as an outsider, and a black sheep, until he had bought his standing. They would expect him to conform to their type, to learn to speak their jargon, to think with their puny brains and to see with their short-sighted eyes. At the "Criterion" he turned in and had a drink, and, bolder for the wine which he had swallowed at a gulp, he told himself that he would do nothing of the sort. He would not alter a jot. They must take him as he was, or leave him. He suffered his thoughts to dwell for a moment upon his wealth, on the years which had gone to the winning of it, on a certain nameless day, the memory of which even now sent sometimes the blood running colder through his veins, on the weaker men who had gone under that he might prosper. Now that it was his, he wanted the best possible value for it; it was the natural desire of the man to be uppermost in the bargain. The delights of the world behind, it seemed to him that he had already drained. The crushing of his rivals, the homage of his less successful competitors, the grosser pleasures of wine, the music-halls, and the unlimited spending of money amongst people whom he despised had long since palled upon him. He had a keen, strong desire to escape once and for ever from his surroundings. He lounged along, smoking a large cigar, keen-eyed and observant, laying up for himself a store of impressions, unconsciously irritated at every step by a sense of ostracism, of being in some indefinable manner without kinship and wholly apart from this world, in which it seemed natural now that he should find some place. He gazed at the great houses without respect or envy, at the men with a fierce contempt, at the women with a sore feeling that if by chance he should be brought into contact with any of them they would regard him as a sort of wild animal, to be humoured or avoided purely as a matter of self-interest. The very brightness and brilliancy of their toilettes, the rustling of their dresses, the trim elegance and daintiness which he was able to appreciate without being able to understand, only served to deepen his consciousness of the gulf which lay between him and them. They were of a world to which, even if he were permitted to enter it, he could not possibly belong. He returned such glances as fell upon him with fierce insolence; he was indeed somewhat of a strange figure in his ill-fitting and inappropriate clothes amongst a gathering of smart people. A lady looking at him through raised lorgnettes turned and whispered something with a smile to her companion--once before he had heard an audible titter from a little group of loiterers. He returned the glance with a lightning-like look of diabolical fierceness, and, turning round, stood upon the curbstone and called a hansom.

A sense of depression swept over him as he was driven through the crowded streets towards Waterloo. The half-scornful, half-earnest prophecy, to which he had listened years ago in a squalid African hut, flashed into his mind. For the first time he began to have dim apprehensions as to his future. All his life he had been a toiler, and joy had been with him in the fierce combat which he had waged day by day. He had fought his battle and he had won--where were the fruits of his victory? A puny, miserable little creature like Dickenson could prate of happiness and turn a shining face to the future--Dickenson who lived upon a pittance, who depended upon the whim of his employer, and who confessed to ambitions which were surely pitiable. Trent lit a fresh cigar and smiled; things would surely come right with him--they must. What Dickenson could gain was surely his by right a thousand times over.

He took the train for Walton, travelling first class, and treated with much deference by the officials on the line. As he alighted and passed through the booking-hall into the station-yard a voice hailed him. He looked up sharply. A carriage and pair of horses was waiting, and inside a young woman with a very smart hat and a profusion of yellow hair.

"Come on, General," she cried. "I've done a skip and driven down to meet you. Such jokes when they miss me. The old lady will be as sick as they make 'em. Can't we have a drive round for an hour, eh?"

Her voice was high-pitched and penetrating. Listening to it Trent unconsciously compared it with the voices of the women of that other world into which he had wandered earlier in the afternoon. He turned a frowning face towards her.

"You might have spared yourself the trouble," he said shortly. "I didn't order a carriage to meet me and I don't want one. I am going to walk home."

She tossed her head.

"What a beastly temper you're in!" she remarked. "I'm not particular about driving. Do you want to walk alone?"

"Exactly!" he answered. "I do!"

She leaned back in the carriage with heightened colour.

"Well, there's one thing about me," she said acidly. "I never go where I ain't wanted."

Trent shrugged his shoulders and turned to the coachman.

"Drive home, Gregg," he said. "I'm walking."

The man touched his hat, the carriage drove off, and Trent, with a grim smile upon his lips, walked along the dusty road. Soon he paused before a little white gate marked private, and, unlocking it with a key which he took from his pocket, passed through a little plantation into a large park-like field. He took off his hat and fanned himself thoughtfully as he walked. The one taste which his long and absorbing struggle with the giants of Capel Court had never weakened was his love for the country. He lifted his head to taste the breeze which came sweeping across from the Surrey Downs, keenly relishing the fragrance of the new-mown hay and the faint odour of pines from the distant dark-crested hill. As he came up the field towards the house he looked with pleasure upon the great bed of gorgeous-coloured rhododendrons which bordered his lawn, the dark cedars which drooped over the smooth shaven grass, and the faint flush of colour from the rose-gardens beyond. The house itself was small, but picturesque. It was a grey stone building of two stories only, and from where he was seemed completely embowered in flowers and creepers. In a way, he thought, he would be sorry to leave it. It had been a pleasant summer-house for him, although of course it was no fit dwelling-house for a millionaire. He must look out for something at once now--a country house and estate. All these things would come as a matter of course.

He opened another gate and passed into an inner plantation of pines and shrubs which bordered the grounds. A winding path led through it, and, coming round a bend, he stopped short with a little exclamation. A girl was standing with her back to him rapidly sketching upon a little block which she had in her left hand.

"Hullo!" he remarked, "another guest! and who brought you down, young lady, eh?"

She turned slowly round and looked at him in cold surprise. Trent knew at once that he had made a mistake. She was plainly dressed in white linen and a cool muslin blouse, but there was something about her, unmistakable even to Trent, which placed her very far apart indeed from any woman likely to have become his unbidden guest. He knew at once that she was one of that class with whom he had never had any association. She was the first lady whom he had ever addressed, and he could have bitten out his tongues when he remembered the form of his doing so.

"I beg your pardon, miss," he said confusedly, "my mistake! You see, your back was turned to me."

She nodded and smiled graciously.

"If you are Mr. Scarlett Trent," she said, "it is I who should apologise, for I am a flagrant trespasser. You must let me explain."

CHAPTER IX

The girl had moved a step towards him as she spoke, and a gleam of sunlight which had found its way into the grove flashed for a moment on the stray little curls of her brown-gold hair and across her face. Her lips were parted in a delightful smile; she was very pretty, and inclined to be apologetic. But Scarlett Trent had seen nothing save that first glance when the sun had touched her face with fire. A strong man at all times, and more than commonly self-masterful, he felt himself now as helpless as a child. A sudden pallor had whitened his face to the lips, there were strange singings in his ears, and a mist before his eyes. It was she! There was no possibility of any mistake. It was the girl for whose picture he had gambled in the hut at Bekwando--Monty's baby-girl, of whom he had babbled even in death. He leaned against a tree, stricken dumb, and she was frightened. "You are ill," she cried. "I'm so sorry. Let me run to the house and fetch some one!"

He had strength enough to stop her. A few deep breaths and he was himself again, shaken and with a heart beating like a steam-engine, but able at least to talk intelligently.

"I'm sorry--didn't mean to frighten you," he said. "It's the heat. I get an attack like this sometimes. Yes, I'm Mr. Trent. I don't know what you're doing here, but you're welcome."

"How nice of you to say so!" she answered brightly. "But then perhaps you'll change your mind when you know what I have been doing."

He laughed shortly.

"Nothing terrible, I should say. Looks as though you've been making a picture of my house; I don't mind that."

She dived in her pocket and produced a card-case.

"I'll make full confession," she said frankly. "I'm a journalist."

"A what!" he repeated feebly.

"A journalist. I'm on the Hour. This isn't my work as a rule; but the man who should have come is ill, and his junior can't sketch, so they sent me! Don't look as though I were a ghost, please. Haven't you ever heard of a girl journalist before?"

"Never," he answered emphatically. "I didn't know that ladies did such things!"

She laughed gaily but softly; and Trent understood then what was meant by the music of a woman's voice.

"Oh, it's not at all an uncommon thing," she answered him. "You won't mind my interviewing you, will you?"

"Doing what?" he asked blankly.

"Interviewing you! That's what I've come for, you know; and we want a little sketch of your house for the paper. I know you don't like it. I hear you've been awfully rude to poor little Morrison of the Post; but I'll be very careful what I say, and very quick."

He stood looking at her, a dazed and bewildered man. From the trim little hat, with its white band and jaunty bunch of cornflowers, to the well-shaped patent shoes, she was neatly and daintily dressed. A journalist! He gazed once more into her face, at the brown eyes watching him now a little anxiously, the mouth with the humorous twitch at the corner of her lips. The little wisps of hair flashed again in the sunlight. It was she! He had found her.

She took his silence for hesitation, and continued a little anxiously.

"I really won't ask you many questions, and it would do me quite a lot of good to get an interview with you. Of course I oughtn't to have begun this sketch without permission. If you mind that, I'll give it up."

He found his tongue awkwardly, but vigorously.

"You can sketch just as long as ever you please, and make what use of it you like," he said. "It's only a bit of a place though!"

"How nice of you! And the interview?"

"I'll tell you whatever you want to know," he said quietly.

She could scarcely believe in her good fortune, especially when she remembered the description of the man which one of the staff had given. He was gruff, vulgar, ill-tempered; the chief ought to be kicked for letting her go near him! This was what she had been told. She laughed softly to herself.

"It is very good indeed of you, Mr. Trent," she said earnestly. "I was quite nervous about coming, for I had no idea that you would be so kind. Shall I finish my sketch first, and then perhaps you will be able to spare me a few minutes for the interview?"

"Just as you like," he answered. "May I look at it?"

"Certainly," she answered, holding out the block; "but it isn't half finished yet."

"Will it take long?"

"About an hour, I think."

"You are very clever," he said, with a little sigh.

She laughed outright.

"People are calling you the cleverest man in London to-day," she said.

"Pshaw! It isn't the cleverness that counts for anything that makes money."

Then he set his teeth hard together and swore vigorously but silently. She had become suddenly interested in her work. A shrill burst of laughter from the lawn in front had rung sharply out, startling them both. A young woman with fluffy hair and in a pale blue dinner-dress was dancing to an unseen audience. Trent's eyes flashed with anger, and his cheeks burned. The dance was a music-hall one, and the gestures were not refined. Before he could stop himself an oath had broken from his lips. After that he dared not even glance at the girl by his side.

"I'm very sorry," he muttered. "I'll stop that right away."

"You mustn't disturb your friends on my account," she said quietly. She did not look up, but Trent felt keenly the alteration in her manner.

"They're not my friends," he exclaimed passionately "I'll clear them out neck and crop."

She looked up for a moment, surprised at his sudden vehemence. There was no doubt about his being in earnest. She continued her work without looking at him, but her tone when she spoke was more friendly.

"This will take me a little longer than I thought to finish properly," she said. "I wonder might I come down early to-morrow morning? What time do you leave for the City?"

"Not until afternoon, at any rate," he said. "Come to-morrow, certainly--whenever you like. You needn't be afraid of that rabble. I'll see you don't have to go near them."

"You must please not make any difference or alter your arrangements on my account," she said. "I am quite used to meeting all sorts of people in my profession, and I don't object to it in the least. Won't you go now? I think that that was your dinner-bell."

He hesitated, obviously embarrassed but determined. "There is one question," he said, "which I should very much like to ask you. It will sound impertinent. I don't mean it so. I can't explain exactly why I want to know, but I have a reason."

"Ask it by all means," she said. "I'll promise that I'll answer it if I can."

"You say that you are--a journalist. Have you taken it up for a pastime, or--to earn money?"

"To earn money by all means," she answered, laughing. "I like the work, but I shouldn't care for it half so much if I didn't make my living at it. Did you think that I was an amateur?"

"I didn't know," he answered slowly. "Thank you. You will come to-morrow?"

"Of course! Good evening."

"Good evening."

Trent lifted his hat, and turned away unwillingly towards the house, full of a sense that something wonderful had happened to him. He was absent-minded, but he stopped to pat a little dog whose attentions he usually ignored, and he picked a creamy-white rose as he crossed the lawn and wondered why it should remind him of her.

CHAPTER X

Trent's appearance upon the lawn was greeted with a shout of enthusiasm. The young lady in blue executed a pas seut, and came across to him on her toes, and the girl with the yellow hair, although sulky, gave him to understand by a sidelong glance that her favour was not permanently withdrawn. They neither of the noticed the somewhat ominous air of civility with which he received their greetings, or the contempt in his eyes as he looked them silently over.

"Where are the lost tribe?" he inquired, as the girls, one on either side, escorted him to the house.

They received his witticism with a piercing shriek of laughter.

"Mamma and her rag of a daughter are in the drawing room," explained Miss Montressor--the young lady with fluffy hair who dressed in blue and could dance. "Such a joke, General! They don't approve of us! Mamma says that she shall have to take her Julie away if we remain. We are not fit associates for her. Rich, isn't it! The old chap's screwing up his courage now with brandy and soda to tell you so!"

Trent laughed heartily. The situation began to appeal to him. There was humour in it which he alone could appreciate.

"Does he expect me to send you away?" he asked.

"That's a cert!" Miss Montressor affirmed. "The old woman's been playing the respectable all day, turning up the whites of her eyes at me because I did a high kick in the hall, and groaning at Flossie because she had a few brandies; ain't that so, Flossie?"

The young lady with yellow hair confirmed the statement with much dignity.

"I had a toothache," she said, "and Mrs. Da Souza, or whatever the old cat calls herself, was most rude. I reckon myself as respectable as she is any day, dragging that yellow-faced daughter of hers about with her and throwing her at men's heads."

Miss Montressor, who had stopped to pick a flower, rejoined them.

"I say, General," she remarked, "fair's fair, and a promise is a promise. We didn't come down here to be made fools of by a fat old Jewess. You won't send us away because of the old wretch?"

"I promise," said Trent, "that when she goes you go, and not before. Is that sufficient?"

"Right oh!" the young lady declared cheerfully. "Now you go and prink up for dinner. We're ready, Flossie and I. The little Jew girl's got a new dress--black covered with sequins. It makes her look yellower than ever. There goes the bell, and we're both as hungry as hunters. Look sharp!"

Trent entered the house. Da Souza met him in the hall, sleek, curly, and resplendent in a black dinner-suit. The years had dealt lightly with him, or else the climate of England was kinder to his yellow skin than the moist heat of the Gold Coast. He greeted Trent with a heartiness which was partly tentative, partly boisterous.

"Back from the coining of the shekels, my dear friend," he exclaimed. "Back from the spoiling of the Egyptians, eh? How was money to-day?"

"An eighth easier," Trent answered, ascending the stairs.

Da Souza fidgeted about with the banisters, and finally followed him.

"There was just a word," he remarked, "a little word I wanted with you."

"Come and talk while I wash," Trent said shortly. "Dinner's on, and I'm hungry."

"Certainly, certainly," Da Souza murmured, closing the door behind them as they entered the lavatory. "It is concerning these young ladies."

"What! Miss Montressor and her friend?" Trent remarked thrusting his head into the cold water. "Phew!"

"Exactly! Two very charming young ladies, my dear friend, very charming indeed, but a little--don't you fancy just a little fast!"

"Hadn't noticed it," Trent answered, drying himself. "What about it?"

Da Souza tugged at his little black imperial, and moved uneasily about.

"We--er--men of the world, my dear Trent, we need not be so particular, eh?-

-but the ladies--the ladies are so observant."

"What ladies?" Trent asked coolly.

"It is my wife who has been talking to me," Da Souza continued. "You see, Julie is so young--our dear daughter she is but a child; and, as my wife says, we cannot be too particular, too careful, eh; you understand!"

"You want them to go? Is that it?"

Da Souza spread out his hands--an old trick, only now the palms were white and the diamonds real.

"For myself," he declared, "I find them charming. It is my wife who says to me, 'Hiram, those young persons, they are not fit company for our dear, innocent Julie! You shall speak to Mr. Trent. He will understand!' Eh?"

Trent had finished his toilet and stood, the hairbrushes still in his hands, looking at Da Souza's anxious face with a queer smile upon his lips.

"Yes, I understand, Da Souza," he said. "No doubt you are right, you cannot be too careful. You do well to be particular."

Da Souza winced. He was about to speak, but Trent interrupted him.

"Well, I'll tell you this, and you can let the missis know, my fond father. They leave to-morrow. Is that good enough?"

Da Souza caught at his host's hand, but Trent snatched it away.

"My dear--my noble--"

"Here, shut up and don't paw me," Trent interrupted. "Mind, not a word of this to any one but your wife; the girls don't know they're going themselves yet."

They entered the dining-room, where every one else was already assembled. Mrs. Da Souza, a Jewess portly and typical, resplendent in black satin and many gold chains and bangles, occupied the seat of honour, and by her side was a little brown girl, with dark, timid eyes and dusky complexion, pitiably over-dressed but with a certain elf-like beauty, which it was hard to believe that she could ever have inherited. Miss Montressor and her friend sat on either side of their host--an arrangement which Mrs. Da Souza lamented, but found herself powerless to prevent, and her husband took the vacant place. Dinner was served, and with the opening of the champagne, which was not long delayed, tongues were loosened.

"It was very hot in the City to-day," Mrs. Da Souza remarked to her host. "Dear Julie was saying what a shame it seemed that you should be there and we should be enjoying your beautiful gardens. She is so thoughtful, so sympathetic! Dear girl!"

"Very kind of your daughter," Trent answered, looking directly at her and rather inclined to pity her obvious shyness. "Come, drink up, Da Souza, drink up, girls! I've had a hard day and I want to forget for a bit that there's any such thing as work."

Miss Montressor raised her glass and winked at her host.

"It don't take much drinking, this, General," she remarked, cheerily draining her glass! "Different to the 'pop' they give us down at the 'Star,' eh, Flossie? Good old gooseberry I call that!"

"Da Souza, look after Miss Flossie," Trent said. "Why don't you fill her glass? That's right!"

"Hiram!"

Da Souza removed his hand from the back of his neighbour's chair and endeavoured to look unconscious. The girl tittered--Mrs. Da Souza was severely dignified. Trent watched them all, half in amusement, half in disgust. What a pandemonium! It was time indeed for him to get rid of them all. From where he sat he could see across the lawn into the little pine plantation. It was still light-if she could look in at the open window what would she think? His cheeks burned, and he thrust the hand which was seeking his under the table savagely away. And then an idea flashed in upon him--a magnificent, irresistible idea. He drank off a glass of champagne and laughed loud and long at one of his neighbour's silly sayings. It was a glorious joke! The more he thought of it, the more he liked it. He called for more champagne, and all, save the little brown girl, greeted the magnum which presently appeared with cheers. Even Mrs. Da Souza unbent a little towards the young women against whom she had declared war. Faces were flushed and voices grew a little thick. Da Souza's arm unchidden sought once more the back of his neighbour's chair, Miss Montressor's eyes did their utmost to win a tender glance from their lavish host. Suddenly Trent rose to his feet. He held a glass high over his head. His face was curiously unmoved, but his lips were parted in an enigmatic smile.

"A toast, my friends!" he cried. "Fill up, the lot of you! Come! To our next meeting! May fortune soon smile again, and may I have another home before long as worthy a resting-place for you as this!"

Bewilderment reigned. No one offered to drink the toast. It was Miss Montressor who asked the question which was on every one's lips.

"What's up?" she exclaimed. "What's the matter with our next meeting here to-morrow night, and what's all that rot about your next home and fortune?"

Trent looked at them all in well-simulated amazement.

"Lord!" he exclaimed, "you don't know--none of you! I thought Da Souza would have told you the news!"

"What news?" Da Souza cried, his beady eyes protuberant, and his glass arrested half-way to his mouth.

"What are you talking about, my friend?"

Trent set down his glass.

"My friends," he said unsteadily, "let me explain to you, as shortly as I can, what an uncertain position is that of a great financier."

Da Souza leaned across the table. His face was livid, and the corners of his eyes were bloodshot.

"I thought there was something up," he muttered. "You would not have me come into the City this morning. D--n it, you don't mean that you--"

"I'm bust!" Trent said roughly. "Is that plain enough? I've been bulling on West Australians, and they boomed and this afternoon the Government decided not to back us at Bekwando, and the mines are to be shut down. Tell you all about it if you like."

No one wanted to hear all about it. They shrunk from him as though he were a robber. Only the little brown girl was sorry, and she looked at him with dark, soft eyes.

"I've given a bill of sale here," Trent continued. "They'll be round to-morrow. Better pack to-night. These valuers are such robbers. Come, another bottle! It'll all have to be sold. We'll make a night of it."

Mrs. Da Souza rose and swept from the room--Da Souza had fallen forward with his head upon his hands. He was only half sober, but the shock was working like madness in his brain. The two girls, after whispering together for a moment, rose and followed Mrs. Da Souza. Trent stole from his place and out into the garden. With footsteps which were steady enough now he crossed the velvety lawns, and plunged into the shrubbery. Then he began to laugh softly as he walked. They were all duped! They had accepted his story without the slightest question. He leaned over the gate which led into the little plantation, and he was suddenly grave and silent. A night-wind was blowing fragrant and cool. The dark boughs of the trees waved to and fro against the background of deep blue sky. The lime leaves rustled softly, the perfume of roses came floating across from the flower-gardens. Trent stood quite still, listening and thinking.

"God! what a beast I am!" he muttered. "It was there she sat! I'm not fit to breathe the same air."

He looked back towards the house. The figures of the two girls, with Da Souza standing now between them, were silhouetted against the window. His face grew dark and fierce.

"Faugh!" he exclaimed, "what a kennel I have made of my house! What a low-down thing I have begun to make of life! Yet--I was a beggar--and I am a million-aire. Is it harder to change oneself? To-morrow"--he looked hard at the place where she had sat--"to-morrow I will ask her!"

On his way back to the house a little cloaked figure stepped out from behind a shrub. He looked at her in amazement. It was the little brown girl, and her eyes were wet with tears.

"Listen," she said quickly. "I have been waiting to speak to you! I want to say goodbye and to thank you. I am very, very sorry, and I hope that some day very soon you will make some more money and be happy again."

Her lips were quivering. A single glance into her face assured him of her honesty. He took the hand which she held out and pressed her fingers.

"Little Julie," he said, "you are a brick. Don't you bother about me. It isn't quite so bad as I made out--only don't tell your mother that."

"I'm very glad," she murmured. "I think that it is hateful of them all to rush away, and I made up my mind to say goodbye however angry it made them. Let me go now, please. I want to get back before mamma misses me."

He passed his arm around her tiny waist. She looked at him with frightened eyes.

"Please let me go," she murmured.

He kissed her lips, and a moment afterwards vaguely repented it. She buried her face in her hands and ran away sobbing. Trent lit a cigar and sat down upon a garden seat.

"It's a queer thing," he said reflectingly. "The girl's been thrown repeatedly at my head for a week and I might have kissed her at any moment, before her father and mother if I had liked, and they'd have thanked me. Now I've done it I'm sorry. She looked prettier than I've ever seen her too--and she's the only decent one of the lot. Lord! what a hubbub there'll be in the morning!"

The stars came out and the moon rose, and still Scarlett Trent lingered in the scented darkness. He was a man of limited imagination and little given to superstitions. Yet that night there came to him a presentiment. He felt that he was on the threshold of great events. Something new in life was looming up before him. He had cut himself adrift from the old--it was a very wonderful and a very beautiful figure which was beckoning him to follow in other paths. The triumph of the earlier part of the day seemed to lie far back in a misty and unimportant past. There was a new world and a greater, if fortune willed that he should enter it.

CHAPTER XI

Trent was awakened next morning by the sound of carriage wheels in the drive below. He rang his bell at once. After a few moments' delay it was answered by one of his two men-servants.

"Whose carriage is that in the drive?" he asked. "It is a fly for Mr. Da Souza, sir."

"What! has he gone?" Trent exclaimed.

"Yes, sir, he and Mrs. Da Souza and the young lady."

"And Miss Montressor and her friend?"

"They shared the fly, sir. The luggage all went down in one of the carts."

Trent laughed outright, half scornfully, half in amusement.

"Listen, Mason," he said, as the sound of wheels died away. "If any of those people come back again they are not to be admitted--do you hear? if they bring their luggage you are not to take it in. If they come themselves you are not to allow them to enter the house. You understand that?"

"Yes, sir.

"Very good! Now prepare my bath at once, and tell the cook, breakfast in half an hour. Let her know that I am hungry. Breakfast for one, mind! Those fools who have just left will get a morning paper at the station and they may come back. Be on the look-out for them and let the other servants know. Better have the lodge gate locked."

"Very good, sir."

The man who had been lamenting the loss of an easy situation and possibly even a month's wages, hastened to spread more reassuring news in the lower regions. It was a practical joke of the governor's--very likely a ruse to get rid of guests who had certainly been behaving as though the Lodge was their permanent home.

There was a chorus of thanksgiving. Groves, the butler, who read the money articles in the Standard every morning with solemn interest and who was suspected of investments, announced that from what he could make out the governor must have landed a tidy little lump yesterday. Whereupon the cook set to work to prepare a breakfast worthy of the occasion.

Trent had awakened with a keen sense of anticipated pleasure. A new and delightful interest had entered into his life. It is true that, at times, it needed all his strength of mind to keep his thoughts from wandering back into that unprofitable and most distasteful past--in the middle of the night even, he had woke up suddenly with an old man's cry in his ears--or was it the whispering of the night-wind in the tall elms? But he was not of an imaginative nature. He felt himself strong enough to set his heel wholly upon all those memories. If he had not erred on the side of generosity, he had at least played the game fairly. Monty, if he had lived, could only have been a disappointment and a humiliation. The picture was hers-- of that he had no doubt! Even then he was not sure that Monty was her father. In any case she would never know. He recognised no obligation on his part to broach the subject. The man had done his best to cut himself altogether adrift from his former life. His reasons doubtless had been sufficient. It was not necessary to pry into them--it might even be unkindness. The picture, which no man save himself had ever seen, was the only possible link between the past and the present--between Scarlett Trent and his drunken old partner, starved and fever-stricken, making their desperate effort for wealth in unknown Africa, and the millionaire of to-day. The picture remained his dearest possession--but, save his own, no other eyes had ever beheld it.

He dressed with more care than usual, and much less satisfaction. He was a man who rather prided himself upon neglecting his appearance, and, so far as the cut and pattern of his clothes went, he usually suggested the artisan out for a holiday. To-day for the first time he regarded his toilet with critical and disparaging eyes. He found the pattern of his tweed suit too large, and the colour too pronounced, his collars were old-fashioned and his ties hideous. It was altogether a new experience with him, this self-dissatisfaction and sensitiveness to criticism, which at any other time he would have regarded with a sort of insolent indifference. He remembered his walk westward yesterday with a shudder, as though indeed it had been a sort of nightmare, and wondered whether she too had regarded him with the eyes of those loungers on the pavement--whether she too was one of those who looked for a man to conform to the one arbitrary and universal type. Finally he tied his necktie with a curse, and went down to breakfast with little of his good-humour left.

The fresh air sweeping in through the long, open windows, the glancing sunlight and the sense of freedom, for which the absence of his guests was certainly responsible, soon restored his spirits. Blest with an excellent morning appetite--the delightful heritage of a clean life--he enjoyed his breakfast and thoroughly appreciated his cook's efforts. If he needed a sauce, Fate bestowed one upon him, for he was scarcely midway through his meal before a loud ringing at the lodge gates proved the accuracy of his conjectures. Mr. Da Souza had purchased a morning paper at the junction, and their host's perfidy had become apparent. Obviously they had decided to treat the whole matter as a practical joke and to brave it out, for outside the gates in an open fly were the whole party. They had returned, only to find that according to Trent's orders the gates were closed upon them.

Trent moved his seat to where he could have a better view, and continued his breakfast. The party in the cab looked hot, and tumbled, and cross. Da Souza was on his feet arguing with the lodge-keeper--the women seemed to be listening anxiously. Trent turned to the servant who was waiting upon him.

"Send word down," he directed, "that I will see Mr. Da Souza alone. No one else is to be allowed to enter. Pass me the toast before you go."

Da Souza entered presently, apologetic and abject, prepared at the same time to extenuate and deny. Trent continued his breakfast coolly.

"My dear friend!" Da Souza exclaimed, depositing his silk hat upon the table, "it is a very excellent joke of yours. You see, we have entered into the spirit of it-- oh yes, we have done so indeed! We have taken a little drive before breakfast, but we have returned. You knew, of course, that we would not dream of leaving you in such a manner. Do you not think, my dear friend, that the joke was carried now far enough? The ladies are hungry; will you send word to the lodge-keeper that he may open the gate?"

Trent helped himself to coffee, and leaned back in his chair, stirring it thoughtfully.

"You are right, Da Souza," he said. "It is an excellent joke. The cream of it is too that I am in earnest; neither you nor any of those ladies whom I see out there will sit at my table again."

"You are not in earnest! You do not mean it!"

"I can assure you," Trent replied grinning, "that I do!"

"But do you mean," Da Souza spluttered, "that we are to go like this--to be turned out--the laughing-stock of your servants, after we have come back too, all the way?--oh, it is nonsense! It's not to be endured!"

"You can go to the devil!" Trent answered coolly. "There is not one of you whom I care a fig to see again. You thought that I was ruined, and you scudded like rats from a sinking ship. Well, I found you out, and a jolly good thing too. All I have to say is now, be off, and the quicker the better!"

Then Da Souza cringed no longer, and there shot from his black eyes the venomous twinkle of the serpent whose fangs are out. He leaned over the table, and dropped his voice.

"I speak," he said, "for my wife, my daughter, and myself, and I assure you that we decline to go!"

CHAPTER XII

Trent rose up with flashing eyes. Da Souza shrank back from his outstretched hands. The two men stood facing one another. Da Souza was afraid, but the ugly look of determination remained upon his white face. Trent felt dimly that there was something which must be explained between them. There had been hints of this sort before from Da Souza. It was time the whole thing was cleared up. The lion was ready to throw aside the jackal.

"I give you thirty seconds," he said, "to clear out. If you haven't come to your senses then, you'll be sorry for it."

"Thirty seconds is not long enough," Da Souza answered, "for me to tell you why I decline to go. Better listen to me quietly, my friend. It will be best for you. Afterwards you will admit it."

"Go ahead," Trent said, "I'm anxious to hear what you've got to say. Only look here! I'm a bit short-tempered this morning, and I shouldn't advise you to play with your words!"

"This is no play at all," Da Souza remarked, with a sneer. "I ask you to remember, my friend, our first meeting."

Trent nodded.

"Never likely to forget it," he answered.

"I came down from Elmina to deal with you," Da Souza continued. "I had made money trading in Ashanti for palm-oil and mahogany. I had money to invest--and you needed it. You had land, a concession to work gold-mines, and build a road to the coast. It was speculative, but we did business. I came with you to England. I found more money."

"You made your fortune," Trent said drily. "I had to have the money, and you ground a share out of me which is worth a quarter of a million to you!"

"Perhaps it is," Da Souza answered, "perhaps it is not. Perhaps it is worth nothing at all. Perhaps, instead of being a millionaire, you yourself are a swindler and an adventurer!"

"If you don't speak out in half a moment," Trent said in a low tone, "I'll twist the tongue out of your head."

"I am speaking out," Da Souza answered. "It is an ugly thing I have to say, but you must control yourself."

The little black eyes were like the eyes of a snake. He was showing his teeth. He forgot to be afraid.

"You had a partner," he said. "The concession was made out to him together with yourself."

"He died," Trent answered shortly. "I took over the lot by arrangement."

"A very nice arrangement," Da Souza drawled with a devilish smile. "He is old and weak. You were with him up at Bekwando where there are no white men--no one to watch you. You gave him brandy to drink--you watch the fever come, and you write on the concession if one should die all goes to the survivor. And you gave him brandy in the bush where the fever is, and--behold you return alone! When people know this they will say, 'Oh yes, it is the way millionaires are made.'"

He stopped, out of breath, for the veins were standing out upon his forehead, and he remembered what the English doctor at Cape Coast Castle had told him. So he was silent for a moment, wiping the perspiration away and struggling against the fear which was turning the blood to ice in his veins. For Trent's face was not pleasant to look upon.

"Anything else?"

Da Souza pulled himself together. "Yes," he said; "what I have said is as nothing. It is scandalous, and it would make talk, but it is nothing. There is something else."

"Well?"

"You had a partner whom you deserted."

"It is a lie! I carried him on my back for twenty hours with a pack of yelling niggers behind. We were lost, and I myself was nigh upon a dead man. Who would have cumbered himself with a corpse? Curse you and your vile hints, you mongrel, you hanger-on, you scurrilous beast! Out, and spread your stories, before my fingers get on your throat! Out!" Da Souza slunk away before the fire in Trent's eyes, but he had no idea of going. He stood in safety near the door, and as he leaned forward, speaking now in a hoarse whisper, he reminded Trent momentarily of one of those hideous fetish gods in the sacred grove at Bekwando.

"Your partner was no corpse when you left him," he hissed out. "You were a fool and a bungler not to make sure of it. The natives from Bekwando found him and carried him bound to the King, and your English explorer, Captain Francis, rescued him. He's alive now!"

Trent stood for a moment like a man turned to stone. Alive! Monty alive! The impossibility of the thing came like a flash of relief to him. The man was surely on the threshold of death when he had left him, and the age of miracles was past.

"You're talking like a fool, Da Souza. Do you mean to take me in with an old woman's story like that?"

"There's no old woman's story about what I've told you," Da Souza snarled. "The man's alive and I can prove it a dozen times over. You were a fool and a bungler."

Trent thought of the night when he had crept back into the bush and had found no trace of Monty, and gradually there rose up before him a lurid possibility Da Souza's story was true. The very thought of it worked like madness in his brains. When he spoke he strove hard to steady his voice, and even to himself it sounded like the voice of one speaking a long way off.

"Supposing that this were true," he said, "what is he doing all this time? Why does he not come and claim his share?"

Da Souza hesitated. He would have liked to have invented another reason, but it was not safe. The truth was best.

"He is half-witted and has lost his memory. He is working now at one of the Basle mission-places near Attra."

"And why have you not told me this before?"

Da Souza shrugged his shoulders. "It was not necessary," he said. "Our interests were the same, it was better for you not to know."

"He remembers nothing, then?"

Da Souza hesitated. "Oom Sam," he said, "my half-brother, keeps an eye on him. Sometimes he gets restless, he talks, but what matter? He has no money. Soon he must die. He is getting an old man!"

"I shall send for him," Trent said slowly. "He shall have his share!"

It was the one fear which had kept Da Souza silent. The muscles of his face twitched, and his finger-nails were buried in the flesh of his fat, white hands. Side by side he had worked with Trent for years without being able to form any certain estimate of the man or his character. Many a time he had asked himself what Trent would do if he knew--only the fear of his complete ignorance of the man had kept him silent all these years. Now the crisis had come! He had spoken! It might mean ruin.

"Send for him?" Da Souza said. "Why? His memory has gone--save for occasional fits of passion in which he raves at you. What would people say?--that you tried to kill him with brandy, that the clause in the concession was a direct incentive for you to get rid of him, and you left him in the bush only a few miles from Buckomari to be seized by the natives. Besides, how can you pay him half? I know pretty well how you stand. On paper, beyond doubt you are a millionaire; but what if all claims were suddenly presented against you to be paid in sovereigns? I tell you this, my friend, Mr. Scarlett Trent, and I am a man of experience and I know. To-day in the City it is true that you could raise a million pounds in cash, but let me whisper a word, one little word, and you would be hard pressed to raise a thousand. It is true there is the Syndicate, that great scheme of yours yesterday from which you were so careful to exclude me--you are to get great monies from them in cash. Bah! don't you see that Monty's existence breaks up that Syndicate--smashes it into tiny atoms, for you have sold what was not yours to sell, and they do not pay for that, eh? They call it fraud!"

He paused, out of breath, and Trent remained silent; he knew very well that he was face to face with a great crisis. Of all things this was the most fatal which could have happened to him. Monty alive! He remembered the old man's passionate cry for life, for pleasure, to taste once more, for however short a time, the joys of wealth. Monty alive, penniless, half-witted, the servant of a few ill-paid missionaries, toiling all day for a living, perhaps fishing with the natives or digging, a slave still, without hope or understanding, with the end of his days well in view! Surely it were better to risk all things, to have him back at any cost? Then a thought more terrible yet than any rose up before him like a spectre, there was a sudden catch at his heart-strings, he was cold with fear. What would she think of the man who deserted his partner, an old man, while life was yet in him, and safety close at hand? Was it possible that he could ever escape the everlasting stigma of cowardice--ay, and before him in great red letters he saw written in the air that fatal clause in the agreement, to which she and all others would point with bitter scorn, indubitable, overwhelming evidence against him. He gasped for breath and walked restlessly up and down the room. Other thoughts came crowding in upon him. He was conscious of a new element in himself. The last few years had left their mark upon him. With the handling of great sums of money and the acquisition of wealth had grown something of the financier's fever. He had become a power, solidly and steadfastly he had hewn his way into a little circle whose fascination had begun to tell in his blood. Was he to fall without a struggle from amongst the high places, to be stripped of his wealth, shunned as a man who was morally, if not in fact, a murderer, to be looked upon with never-ending scorn by the woman whose picture for years had been a religion to him, and whose appearance only a few hours ago had been the most inspiring thing which had entered into his life? He looked across the lawn into the pine grove with steadfast eyes and knitted brows, and Da Souza watched him, ghastly and nervous. At least he must have time to decide!

"If you send for him," Da Souza said slowly, "you will be absolutely ruined. It will be a triumph for those whom you have made jealous, who have measured their wits with yours and gone under. Oh! but the newspapers will enjoy it--that is very certain. Our latest millionaire, his rise and fall! Cannot you see it in the placards? And for what? To give wealth to an old man long past the enjoyment of it-ay, imbecile already! You will not be a madman, Trent?"

Trent winced perceptibly. Da Souza saw it and rejoiced. There was another awkward silence. Trent lit a cigar and puffed furiously at it.

"I will think it over, at least," he said in a low tone. "Bring back your wife and daughter, and leave me alone for a while."

"I knew," Da Souza murmured, "that my friend would be reasonable."

"And the young ladies?"

"Send them to--"

"I will send them back to where they came from," Da Souza interrupted blandly.

CHAPTER XIII

It is probable that Mrs. Da Souza, excellent wife and mother though she had proved herself to be, had never admired her husband more than when, followed by the malevolent glances of Miss Montressor and her friend, she, with her daughter and Da Souza, re-entered the gates of the Lodge. The young ladies had announced their intention of sitting in the fly until they were allowed speech with their late host; to which he had replied that they were welcome to sit there until doomsday so long as they remained outside his gates. Mr. Da Souza lingered for a moment behind and laid his finger upon his nose.

"It ain't no use, my dears," he whispered confidentially. "He's fairly got the hump. Between you and me he'd give a bit not to have us, but me and him being old friends--you see, we know a bit about one another."

"Oh, that's it, is it?" Miss Montressor remarked, with a toss of her head. "Well, you and your wife and your little chit of a daughter are welcome to him so far as we are concerned, aren't they, Flossie?"

"Well, I should say so," agreed the young lady, who rather affected Americanisms.

Da Souza stroked his little imperial, and winked solemnly.

"You are young ladies of spirit," he declared. "Now--"

"Hiram!"

"I am coming, my dear," he called over his shoulder. "One word more, my charming young friends! No. 7, Racket's Court, City, is my address. Look in sometime when you're that way, and we'll have a bit of lunch together, and just at present take my advice. Get back to London and write him from there. He is not in a good humour at present."

"We are much obliged, Mr. Da Souza," the young lady answered loftily. "As we have engagements in London this afternoon, we may as well go now--eh, Flossie?"

"Right along," answered the young lady, "I'm with you, but as to writing Mr. Trent, you can tell him from me, Mr. Da Souza, that we want to have nothing more to do with him. A fellow that can treat ladies as he has treated us is no gentleman. You can tell him that. He's an ignorant, common fellow, and for my part I despise him."

"Same here," echoed Miss Montressor, heartily. "We ain't used to associate with such as him!"

"Hiram!"

Mr. Da Souza raised his hat and bowed; the ladies were tolerably gracious and the fly drove off. Whereupon Mr. Da Souza followed his wife and daughter along the drive and caught them up upon the doorstep. With mingled feelings of apprehension and elation he ushered them into the morning-room where Trent was standing looking out of the window with his hands behind him. At their entrance he did not at once turn round. Mr. Da Souza coughed apologetically.

"Here we are, my friend," he remarked. "The ladies are anxious to wish you good morning."

Trent faced them with a sudden gesture of impatience. He seemed on the point of an angry exclamation, when his eyes met Julie Da Souza's. He held his breath for a moment and was silent. Her face was scarlet with shame, and her lips were trembling. For her sake Trent restrained himself.

"Glad to see you back again, Julie," he said, ignoring her mother's outstretched hand and beaming smile of welcome. "Going to be a hot day, I think. You must get out in the hay-field. Order what breakfast you please, Da Souza," he continued on his way to the door; "you must be hungry-after such an early start!"

Mrs. Da Souza sat down heavily and rang the bell.

"He was a little cool," she remarked, "but that was to be expected. Did you observe the notice he took of Julie? Dear child!"

Da Souza rubbed his hands and nodded meaningly. The girl, who, between the two, was miserable enough, sat down with a little sob. Her mother looked at her in amazement.

"My Julie," she exclaimed, "my dear child! You see, Hiram, she is faint! She is overcome!"

The child, she was very little more, broke out at last in speech, passionately, yet with a miserable fore-knowledge of the ineffectiveness of anything she might say.

"It is horrible," she cried, "it is maddening! Why do we do it? Are we paupers or adventurers? Oh! let me go away! I am ashamed to stay in this house!"

Her father, his thumbs in the armholes of his waistcoat and his legs far apart, looked at her in blank and speechless amazement; her mother, with more consideration but equal lack of sympathy, patted her gently on the back of her hand.

"Silly Julie," she murmured, "what is there that is horrible, little one?"

The dark eyes blazed with scorn, the delicately curved lips shook.

"Why, the way we thrust ourselves upon this man is horrible!" she cried. "Can you not see that we are not welcome, that he wishes us gone?"

Da Souza smiled in a superior manner; the smile of a man who, if only he would, could explain all things. He patted his daughter on the head with a touch which was meant to be playful.

"My little one," he said, "you are mistaken! Leave these matters to those who are older and wiser than you. It is but just now that my good friend said to me, 'Da Souza,' he say, 'I will not have you take your little daughter away!' Oh, we shall see! We shall see!"

Julie's tears crept through the fingers closely pressed over her eyes.

"I do not believe it," she sobbed. "He has scarcely looked at me all the time, and I do not want him to. He despises us all--and I don't blame him. It is horrid!"

Mrs. Da Souza, with a smile which was meant to be arch, had something to say, but the arrival of breakfast broke up for a while the conversation. Her husband, whom Nature had blessed with a hearty appetite at all times, was this morning after his triumph almost disposed to be boisterous. He praised the cooking, chaffed the servants to their infinite disgust, and continually urged his wife and daughter to keep pace with him in his onslaught upon the various dishes which were placed before him. Before the meal was over Julie had escaped from the table crying softly. Mr. Da Souza's face darkened as he looked up at the sound of her movement, only to see her skirt vanishing through the door.

"Shall you have trouble with her, my dear?" he asked his wife anxiously.

That estimable lady shook her head with a placid smile. "Julie is so sensitive," she muttered, "but she is not disobedient. When the time comes I can make her mind."

"But the time has come!" Da Souza exclaimed. "It is here now, and Julie is sulky. She will have red eyes and she is not gay! She will not attract him. You must speak with her, my dear."

"I will go now--this instant," she answered, rising. "But, Hiram, there is one thing I would much like to know."

"Ugh! You women! You are always like that! There is so much that you want to know!"

"Most women, Hiram--not me! Do I ever seek to know your secrets? But this time--yes, it would be wiser to tell me a little!"

"Well?"

"This Mr. Trent, he asked us here, but it is plain that our company is not pleasant to him. He does his best to get rid of us--he succeeds--he plans that we shall not return. You see him alone and all that is altered. His little scheme has been in vain. We remain! He does not look at our Julie. He speaks of marriage with contempt. Yet you say he will marry her--he, a millionaire! What does it mean, Hiram?"

"The man, he is in my power," Da Souza says in a ponderous and stealthy whisper. "I know something."

She rose and imprinted a solemn kiss upon his forehead. There was something sacramental about the deliberate caress.

"Hiram," she said, "you are a wonderful man!"

CHAPTER XIV

Scarlett Trent spent the first part of the morning, to which he had been looking forward so eagerly, alone in his study with locked door to keep out all intruders. He had come face to face with the first serious check in his career, and it had been dealt him too by the one man whom, of all his associates, he disliked and despised. In the half-open drawer by his side was the barrel of a loaded revolver. He drew it out, laid it on the table before him, and regarded it with moody, fascinated eyes. If only it could be safely done, if only for one moment he could find himself face to face with Da Souza in Bekwando village, where human life was cheap and the slaying of a man an incident scarcely worth noting in the day's events! The thing was easy enough there--here it was too risky. He thrust the weapon back into the drawer with a sigh of regret, just as Da Souza himself appeared upon the scene.

"You sent for me, Trent," the latter remarked timidly. "I am quite ready to answer any more questions."

"Answer this one, then," was the gruff reply. "In Buckomari village before we left for England I was robbed of a letter. I don't think I need ask you who was the thief."

"Really, Trent--I--"

"Don't irritate me; I'm in an ill humour for anything of that sort. You stole it! I can see why now! Have you got it still?"

The Jew shrugged his shoulders.

"Yes."

"Hand it over."

Da Souza drew a large folding case from his pocket and after searching through it for several moments produced an envelope. The handwriting was shaky and irregular, and so faint that even in the strong, sweet light of the morning sunshine Trent had difficulty in reading it. He tore it open and drew out a half-sheet of coarse paper. It was a message from the man who for long he had counted dead.

"BEKWANDO.

"MY DEAR TRENT,-I have been drinking as usual! Some men see snakes, but I have seen death leering at me from the dark corners of this vile hut, and death is an evil thing to look at when one's life has been evil as mine has been. Never mind! I have sown and I must reap! But, my friend, a last word with you. I have a notion, and more than a notion, that I shall never pass back alive through these pestilential swamps. If you should arrive, as you doubtless will, here is a charge which I lay upon you. That agreement of ours is scarcely a fair one, is it, Trent? When I signed it, I wasn't quite myself. Never mind! I'll trust to you to do what's fair. If the thing turns out a great success, put some sort of a share at any rate to my credit and let my daughter have it. You will find her address from Messrs. Harris and Culsom, Solicitors, Lincoln's Inn Fields. You need only ask them for Monty's daughter and show them this letter. They will understand. I believe you to be a just man, Scarlett Trent, although I know you to be a hard one. Do then as I ask.

"MONTY."

Da Souza had left the room quietly. Trent read the letter through twice and locked it up in his desk. Then he rose and lit a pipe, knocking out the ashes carefully and filling the bowl with dark but fragrant tobacco. Presently he rang the bell.

"Tell Mr. Da Souza I wish to see him here at once," he told the servant, and, though the message was a trifle peremptory from a host to his guest, Da Souza promptly appeared, suave and cheerful.

"Shut the door," Trent said shortly.

Da Souza obeyed with unabashed amiability. Trent watched him with something like disgust. Da Souza returning caught the look, and felt compelled to protest.

"My dear Trent," he said, "I do not like the way you address me, or your manners towards me. You speak as though I were a servant. I do not like it all, and it is not fair. I am your guest, am I not?"

"You are my guest by your own invitation," Trent answered roughly, "and if you don't like my manners you can turn out. I may have to endure you in the house till I have made up my mind how to get rid of you, but I want as little of your company as possible. Do you hear?"

Da Souza did hear it, and the worm turned. He sat down in the most comfortable easy-chair, and addressed Trent directly.

"My friend," he said, "you are out of temper, and that is a bad thing. Now listen to me! You are in my power. I have only to go into the City to-morrow and breathe here and there a word about a certain old gentleman who shall be nameless, and you would be a ruined man in something less than an hour; added to this, my friend, you would most certainly be arrested for conspiracy and fraud. That Syndicate of yours was a very smart stroke of business, no doubt, and it was clever of you to keep me in ignorance of it, but as things have turned out now, that will be your condemnation. They will say, why did you keep me in ignorance of this move, and the answer--why, it is very clear! I knew you were selling what was not yours to sell!"

"I kept you away," Trent said scornfully, "because I was dealing with men who would not have touched the thing if they had known that you were in it!"

"Who will believe it?" Da Souza asked, with a sneer. "They will say that it is but one more of the fairy tales of this wonderful Mr. Scarlett Trent."

The breath came through Trent's lips with a little hiss and his eyes were flashing with a dull fire. But Da Souza held his ground. He had nerved himself up to this and he meant going through with it.

"You think I dare not breathe a word for my own sake," he continued. "There is reason in that, but I have other monies. I am rich enough without my sixth share of that Bekwando Land and Mining Company which you and the Syndicate are going to bring out! But then, I am not a fool! I have no wish to throw away money. Now I propose to you therefore a friendly settlement. My daughter Julie is very charming. You admire her, I am sure. You shall marry her, and then we will all be one family. Our interests will be the same, and you may be sure that I shall look after them. Come! Is that not a friendly offer?"

For several minutes Trent smoked furiously, but he did not speak. At the end of that time he took the revolver once more from the drawer of his writing-table and fingered it.

"Da Souza," he said, "if I had you just for five minutes at Bekwando we would talk together of black-mail, you and I, we would talk of marrying your daughter. We would talk then to some purpose--you hound! Get out of the room as fast as your legs will carry you. This revolver is loaded, and I'm not quite master of myself."

Da Souza made off with amazing celerity. Trent drew a short, quick breath. There was a great deal of the wild beast left in him still. At that moment the desire to kill was hot in his blood. His eyes glared as he walked up and down the room. The years of civilisation seemed to have become as nothing. The veneer of the City speculator had fallen away. He was once more as he had been in those wilder days when men made their own laws, and a man's hold upon life was a slighter thing than his thirst for gold. As such, he found the atmosphere of the little room choking him, he drew open the French windows of his little study and strode out into the perfumed and sunlit morning. As such, he found himself face to face unexpectedly and without warning with the girl whom he had discovered sketching in the shrubbery the day before.

CHAPTER XV

Probably nothing else in the world could so soon have transformed Scarlett Trent from the Gold Coast buccaneer to the law-abiding tenant of a Surrey villa. Before her full, inquiring eyes and calm salute he found himself at once abashed and confused. He raised his hand to his head, only to find that he had come out without a hat, and he certainly appeared, as he stood there, to his worst possible advantage.

"Good morning, miss," he stammered; "I'm afraid I startled you!"

She winced a little at his address, but otherwise her manner was not ungracious.

"You did a little," she admitted. "Do you usually stride out of your windows like that, bareheaded and muttering to yourself?"

"I was in a beastly temper," he admitted. "If I had known who was outside--it would have been different."

She looked into his face with some interest. "What an odd thing!" she remarked. "Why, I should have thought that to-day you would have been amiability itself. I read at breakfast-time that you had accomplished something more than ordinarily wonderful in the City and had made--I forget how many hundreds of thousands of pounds. When I showed the sketch of your house to my chief, and told him that you were going to let me interview you to-day, I really thought that he would have raised my salary at once."

"It's more luck than anything," he said. "I've stood next door to ruin twice. I may again, although I'm a millionaire to-day."

She looked at him curiously--at his ugly tweed suit, his yellow boots, and up into the strong, forceful face with eyes set in deep hollows under his protruding brows, at the heavy jaws giving a certain coarseness to his expression, which his mouth and forehead, well-shaped though they were, could not altogether dispel. And at he same time he looked at her, slim, tall, and elegant, daintily clothed from her shapely shoes to her sailor hat, her brown hair, parted in the middle, escaping a little from its confinement to ripple about her forehead, and show more clearly the delicacy of her complexion. Trent was an ignorant man on many subjects, on others his taste seemed almost intuitively correct. He knew that this girl belonged to a class from which his descent and education had left him far apart, a class of which he knew nothing, and with whom he could claim no kinship. She too was realising it--her interest in him was, however, none the less deep. He was a type of those powers which to-day hold the world in their hands, make kingdoms tremble, and change the fate of nations. Perhaps he was all the more interesting to her because, by all the ordinary standards of criticism, he would fail to be ranked, in the jargon of her class, as a gentleman. He represented something in flesh and blood which had never seemed more than half real to her--power without education. She liked to consider herself--being a writer with ambitions who took herself seriously--a student of human nature. Here was a specimen worth impaling, an original being, a creature of a new type such as never had come within the region of her experience. It was worth while ignoring small idiosyncrasies which might offend, in order to annex him. Besides, from a journalistic point of view, the man was more than interesting--he was a veritable treasure.

"You are going to talk to me about Africa, are you not?" she reminded him. "Couldn't we sit in the shade somewhere. I got quite hot walking from the station."

He led the way across the lawn, and they sat under a cedar-tree. He was awkward and ill at ease, but she had tact enough for both.

"I can't understand," he began, "how people are interested in the stuff which gets into papers nowadays. If you want horrors though, I can supply you. For one man who succeeds over there, there are a dozen who find it a short cut down into hell. I can tell you if you like of my days of starvation."

"Go on!"

Like many men who talk but seldom, he had the gift when he chose to speak of reproducing his experiences in vivid though unpolished language. He told her of the days when he had worked on the banks of the Congo with the coolies, a slave in everything but name, when the sun had burned the brains of men to madness, and the palm wine had turned them into howling devils. He told her of the natives of Bekwando, of the days they had spent amongst them in that squalid hut when their fate hung in the balance day by day, and every shout that went up from the warriors gathered round the house of the King was a cry of death. He spoke of their ultimate success, of the granting of the concession which had laid the foundation of his fortunes, and then of that terrible journey back through the bush, followed by the natives who had already repented of their action, and who dogged their footsteps hour after hour, waiting for them only to sleep or rest to seize upon them and haul them back to Bekwando, prisoners for the sacrifice.

"It was only our revolvers which kept them away," he went on. "I shot eight or nine of them at different times when they came too close, and to hear them wailing over the bodies was one of the most hideous things you can imagine. Why, for months and months afterwards I couldn't sleep. I'd wake up in the night and fancy that I heard that cursed yelling outside my window--ay, even on the steamer at night-time if I was on deck before moonlight, I'd seem to hear it rising up out of the water. Ugh!"

She shuddered.

"But you both escaped?" she said.

There was a moment's silence. The shade of the cedar-tree was deep and cool, but it brought little relief to Trent. The perspiration stood out on his forehead in great beads, he breathed for a moment in little gasps as though stifled.

"No," he answered; "my partner died within a mile or two of the Coast. He was very ill when we started, and I pretty well had to carry him the whole of the last day. I did my best for him. I did, indeed, but it was no good. I had to leave him. There was no use sacrificing oneself for a dead man."

She inclined her head sympathetically.

"Was he an Englishman?" she asked.

He faced the question just as he had faced death years before leering at him, a few feet from the muzzle of his revolver.

"He was an Englishman. The only name we had ever heard him called by was 'Monty.' Some said he was a broken-down gentleman. I believe he was."

She was unconscious of his passionate, breathless scrutiny, unconscious utterly of the great wave of relief which swept into his face as he realised that his words were without any special meaning to her.

"It was very sad indeed," she said. "If he had lived, he would have shared with you, I suppose, in the concession?"

Trent nodded.

"Yes, we were equal partners. We had an arrangement by which, if one died, the survivor took the lot. I didn't want it though, I'd rather he had pulled through. I would indeed," he repeated with nervous force.

"I am quite sure of that," she answered. "And now tell me something about your career in the City after you came to England. Do you know, I have scarcely ever been in what you financiers call the City. In a way it must be interesting."

"You wouldn't find it so," he said. "It is not a place for such as you. It is a life of lies and gambling and deceit. There are times when I have hated it. I hate it now!"

She was unaffectedly surprised. What a speech for a millionaire of yesterday!

"I thought," she said, "that for those who took part in it, it possessed a fascination stronger than anything else in the world."

He shook his head.

"It is an ugly fascination," he said. "You are in the swim, and you must hold your own. You gamble with other men, and when you win you chuckle. All the time you're whittling your conscience away--if ever you had any. You're never quite dishonest, and you're never quite honest. You come out on top, and afterwards you hate yourself. It's a dirty little life!"

"Well," she remarked after a moment's pause, "you have surprised me very much. At any rate you are rich enough now to have no more to do with it."

He kicked a fir cone savagely away.

"If I could," he said, "I would shut up my office to-morrow, sell out, and live upon a farm. But I've got to keep what I've made. The more you succeed the more involved you become. It's a sort of slavery."

"Have you no friends?" she asked.

"I have never," he answered, "had a friend in my life."

"You have guests at any rate!"

"I sent 'em away last night!"

"What, the young lady in blue?" she asked demurely.

"Yes, and the other one too. Packed them clean off, and they're not coming back either!"

"I am very pleased to hear it," she remarked.

"There's a man and his wife and daughter here I can't get rid of quite so easily," he went on gloomily, "but they've got to go!"

"They would be less objectionable to the people round here who might like to come and see you," she remarked, "than two unattached young ladies."

"May be," he answered. "Yet I'd give a lot to be rid of them."

He had risen to his feet and was standing with his back to the cedar-tree, looking away with fixed eyes to where the sunlight fell upon a distant hillside gorgeous with patches and streaks of yellow gorse and purple heather. Presently she noticed his abstraction and looked also through the gap in the trees.

"You have a beautiful view here," she said. "You are fond of the country, are you not?"

"Very," he answered.

"It is not every one," she remarked, "who is able to appreciate it, especially when their lives have been spent as yours must have been."

He looked at her curiously. "I wonder," he said, "if you have any idea how my life has been spent."

"You have given me," she said, "a very fair idea about some part of it at any rate."

He drew a long breath and looked down at her.

"I have given you no idea at all," he said firmly. "I have told you a few incidents, that is all. You have talked to me as though I were an equal. Listen! you are probably the first lady with whom I have ever spoken. I do not want to deceive you. I never had a scrap of education. My father was a carpenter who drank himself to death, and my mother was a factory girl. I was in the workhouse when I was a boy. I have never been to school. I don't know how to talk properly, but I should be worse even than I am, if I had not had to mix up with a lot of men in the City who had been properly educated. I am utterly and miserably ignorant. I've got low tastes and lots of 'em. I was drunk a few nights ago--I've done most of the things men who are beasts do. There! Now, don't you want to run away?"

She shook her head and smiled up at him. She was immensely interested.

"If that is the worst," she said gently, "I am not at all frightened. You know that it is my profession to write about men and women. I belong to a world of worn-out types, and to meet any one different is quite a luxury."

"The worst!" A sudden fear sent an icy coldness shivering through his veins. His heart seemed to stop beating, his cheeks were blanched. The worst of him. He had not told her that he was a robber, that the foundation of his fortunes was a lie; that there lived a man who might bring all this great triumph of his shattered and crumbling about his ears. A passionate fear lest she might ever knew of these things was born in his heart at that moment, never altogether to leave him.

The sound of a footstep close at hand made them both turn their heads. Along the winding path came Da Souza, with an ugly smirk upon his white face, smoking a cigar whose odour seemed to poison the air. Trent turned upon him with a look of thunder.

"What do you want here, Da Souza?" he asked fiercely.

Da Souza held up the palms of his hands.

"I was strolling about," he said, "and I saw you through the trees. I did not know that you were so pleasantly engaged," he added, with a wave of his hat to the girl, "or I would not have intruded."

Trent kicked open the little iron gate which led into the garden beyond.

"Well, get out, and don't come here again," he said shortly. "There's plenty of room for you to wander about and poison the air with those abominable cigars of yours without coming here."

Da Souza replaced his hat upon his head. "The cigars, my friend, are excellent. We cannot all smoke the tobacco of a millionaire, can we, miss?"

The girl, who was making some notes in her book, continued her work without the slightest appearance of having heard him.

Da Souza snorted, but at that moment he felt a grip like iron upon his shoulder, and deemed retreat expedient.

"If you don't go without another word," came a hot whisper in his ear, "I'll throw you into the horse-pond."

He went swiftly, ungracious, scowling. Trent returned to the girl. She looked up at him and closed her book.

"You must change your friends," she said gravely. "What a horrible man!"

"He is a beast," Trent answered, "and go he shall. I would to Heaven that I had never seen him."

She rose, slipped her note-book into her pocket, and drew on her gloves.

"I have taken up quite enough of your time," she said. "I am so much obliged to you, Mr. Trent, for all you have told me. It has been most interesting."

She held out her hand, and the touch of it sent his heart beating with a most unusual emotion. He was aghast at the idea of her imminent departure. He realised that, when she passed out of his gate, she passed into a world where she would be hopelessly lost to him, so he took his courage into his hands, and was very bold indeed.

"You have not told me your name," he reminded her.

She laughed lightly.

"How very unprofessional of me! I ought to have given you a card! For all you know I may be an impostor, indulging an unpardonable curiosity. My name is Wendermott--Ernestine Wendermott."

He repeated it after her. "Thank you," he said. "I am beginning to think of some more things which I might have told you."

"Why, I should have to write a novel then to get them all in," she said. "I am sure you have given me all the material I need here."

"I am going," he said abruptly, "to ask you something very strange and very presumptuous!"

She looked at him in surprise, scarcely understanding what he could mean.

"May I come and see you some time?"

The earnestness of his gaze and the intense anxiety of his tone almost disconcerted her. He was obviously very much in earnest, and she had found him far from uninteresting.

"By all means," she answered pleasantly, "if you care to. I have a little flat in Culpole Street--No. 81. You must come and have tea with me one afternoon."

"Thank you," he said simply, with a sigh of immense relief.

He walked with her to the gate, and they talked about rhododendrons.

Then he watched her till she became a speck in the dusty road--she had refused a carriage, and he had had tact enough not to press any hospitality upon her.

"His little girl!" he murmured. "Monty's little girl!"

CHAPTER XVI

Ernestine Wendermott travelled back to London in much discomfort, being the eleventh occupant of a third-class carriage in a particularly unpunctual and dilatory train. Arrived at Waterloo, she shook out her skirts with a little gesture of relief and started off to walk to the Strand. Half-way across the bridge she came face to face with a tall, good-looking young man who was hurrying in the opposite direction. He stopped short as he recognised her, dropped his eyeglass, and uttered a little exclamation of pleasure.

"Ernestine, by all that's delightful! I am in luck to-day!"

She smiled slightly and gave him her hand, but it was evident that this meeting was not wholly agreeable to her.

"I don't quite see where the luck comes in," she answered. "I have no time to waste talking to you now. I am in a hurry."

"You will allow me," he said hopefully, "to walk a little way with you?"

"I am not able to prevent it--if you think it worth while," she answered.

He looked down--he was by her side now--in good-humoured protest.

"Come, Ernestine," he said, "you mustn't bear malice against me. Perhaps I was a little hasty when I spoke so strongly about your work. I don't like your doing it and never shall like it, but I've said all I want to. You won't let it divide us altogether, will you?"

"For the present," she answered, "it occupies the whole of my time, and the whole of my thoughts."

"To the utter exclusion, I suppose," he remarked, "of me?"

She laughed gaily.

"My dear Cecil! when have I ever led you to suppose for a moment that I have ever wasted any time thinking of you?"

He was determined not to be annoyed, and he ignored both the speech and the laugh.

"May I inquire how you are getting on?"

"I am getting on," she answered, "very well indeed. The Editor is beginning to say very nice things to me, and already the men treat me just as though I were a comrade! It is so nice of them!"

"Is it?" he muttered doubtfully.

"I have just finished," she continued, "the most important piece of work they have trusted me with yet, and I have been awfully lucky. I have been to interview a millionaire!"

"A man?"

She nodded. "Of course!"

"It isn't fit work for you," he exclaimed hastily.

"You will forgive me if I consider myself the best judge of that," she answered coldly. "I am a journalist, and so long as it is honest work my sex doesn't count. If every one whom I have to see is as courteous to me as Mr. Trent has been, I shall consider myself very lucky indeed."

"As who?" he cried.

She looked up at him in surprise. They were at the corner of the Strand, but as though in utter forgetfulness of their whereabouts, he had suddenly stopped short and gripped her tightly by the arm. She shook herself free with a little gesture of annoyance.

"Whatever is the matter with you, Cecil? Don't gape at me like that, and come along at once, unless you want to be left behind. Yes, we are very short-handed and the chief let me go down to see Mr. Trent. He didn't expect for a moment that I should get him to talk to me, but I did, and he let me sketch the house. I am awfully pleased with myself I can tell you."

The young man walked by her side for a moment in silence. She looked up at him casually as they crossed the street, and something in his face surprised her.

"Why, Cecil, what on earth is the matter with you?" she exclaimed.

He looked down at her with a new seriousness.

"I was thinking," he said, "how oddly things turn out. So you have been down to interview Mr. Scarlett Trent for a newspaper, and he was civil to you!"

"Well, I don't see anything odd about that," she exclaimed impatiently. "Don't be so enigmatical. If you've anything to say, say it! Don't look at me like an owl!"

"I have a good deal to say to you," he answered gravely. "How long shall you be at the office?"

"About an hour--perhaps longer."

"I will wait for you!"

"I'd rather you didn't. I don't want them to think that I go trailing about with an escort."

"Then may I come down to your flat? I have something really important to say to you, Ernestine. It does not concern myself at all. It is wholly about you. It is something which you ought to know."

"You are trading upon my curiosity for the sake of a tea," she laughed. "Very well, about five o'clock."

He bowed and walked back westwards with a graver look than usual upon his boyish face, for he had a task before him which was very little to his liking. Ernestine swung open the entrance door to the "Hour", and passed down the rows of desks until she reached the door at the further end marked "Sub-Editor." She knocked and was admitted at once.

A thin, dark young man, wearing a pince-nez and smoking a cigarette, looked up from his writing as she entered. He waved her to a seat, but his pen never stopped for a second.

"Back, Miss Wendermott! Very good! What did you get?"

"Interview and sketch of the house," she responded briskly.

"Interview by Jove! That's good! Was he very difficult?"

"Ridiculously easy! Told me everything I asked and a lot more. If I could have got it all down in his own language it would have been positively thrilling."

The sub-editor scribbled in silence for a moment or two. He had reached an important point in his own work. His pen went slower, hesitated for a moment, and then dashed on with renewed vigour.

"Read the first few sentences of what you've got," he remarked.

Ernestine obeyed. To all appearance the man was engrossed in his own work, but when she paused he nodded his head appreciatively.

"It'll do!" he said. "Don't try to polish it. Give it down, and see that the proofs are submitted to me. Where's the sketch?"

She held it out to him. For a moment he looked away from his own work and took the opportunity to light a fresh cigarette. Then he nodded, hastily scrawled some dimensions on the margin of the little drawing and settled down again to work.

"It'll do," he said. "Give it to Smith. Come back at eight to look at your proofs after I've done with them. Good interview! Good sketch! You'll do, Miss Wendermott."

She went out laughing softly. This was quite the longest conversation she had ever had with the chief. She made her way to the side of the first disengaged typist, and sitting in an easy-chair gave down her copy, here and there adding a little but leaving it mainly in the rough. She knew whose hand, with a few vigorous touches would bring the whole thing into the form which the readers of the "Hour", delighted in, and she was quite content to have it so. The work was interesting and more than an hour had passed before she rose and put on her gloves.

"I am coming back at eight," she said, "but the proofs are to go in to Mr. Darrel! Nothing come in for me, I suppose?"

The girl shook her head, so Ernestine walked out into the street. Then she remembered Cecil Davenant and his strange manner--the story which he was even now waiting to tell her. She looked at her watch and after a moment's hesitation called a hansom.

81, Culpole Street, she told him. "This is a little extravagant," she said to herself as the man wheeled his horse round, "but to-day I think that I have earned it."

CHAPTER XVII

Ernestine," he said gravely, "I am going to speak to you about your father!"

She looked up at him in swift surprise.

"Is it necessary?"

"I think so," he answered. "You won't like what I'm going to tell you! You'll think you've been badly treated. So you have! I pledged my word, in a weak hour, with the others. To-day I'm going to break it. I think it best."

"Well?"

"You've been deceived! You were told always that your father had died in prison. He didn't."

"What!"

Her sharp cry rang out strangely into the little room. Already he could see signs of the coming storm, and the task which lay before him seemed more hateful than ever.

"Listen," he said. "I must tell you some things which you know in order to explain others which you do not know. Your father was a younger son born of extravagant parents, virtually penniless and without the least capacity for earning money. I don't blame him--who could? I couldn't earn money myself. If I hadn't got it I daresay that I should go to the bad as he did."

The girl's lips tightened, and she drew a little breath through her teeth. Davenant hesitated.

"You know all about that company affair. Of course they made your father the butt of the whole thing, although he was little more than a tool. He was sent to prison for seven years. You were only a child then and your mother was dead. Well, when the seven years were up, your relations and mine too, Ernestine, concocted what I have always considered an ill-begotten and a miserably selfish plot.

Your father, unfortunately, yielded to them, for your sake. You were told that he had died in prison. He did not. He lived through his seven years there, and when he came out did so in another name and went abroad on the morning of the day of his liberation."

"Good God!" she cried. "And now!"

"He is dead," Davenant answered hastily, "but only just lately. Wait a minute. You are going to be furiously angry. I know it, and I don't blame you. Only listen for a moment. The scheme was hatched up between my father and your two uncles. I have always hated it and always protested against it. Remember that and be fair to me. This is how they reasoned. Your father's health, they said, was ruined, and if he lives the seven years what is there left for him when he comes out? He was a man, as you know, of aristocratic and fastidious tastes. He would have the best of everything--society, clubs, sport. Now all these were barred against him. If he had reappeared he could not have shown his face in Pall Mall, or on the racecourses, and every moment of his life would be full of humiliations and bitterness. Virtually then, for such a man as he was, life in England was over. Then there was you. You were a pretty child and the Earl had no children. If your father was dead the story would be forgotten, you would marry brilliantly and an ugly page in the family history would be blotted out. That was how they looked at it--it was how they put it to your father."

"He consented?"

"Yes, he consented! He saw the wisdom of it for your sake, for the sake of the family, even for his own sake. The Earl settled an income upon him and he left England secretly on the morning of his release. We had the news of his death only a week or two ago."

She stood up, her eyes blazing, her hands clenched together.

"I thank God," she said "that I have found the courage to break away from those people and take a little of my life into my own hands. You can tell them this if you will, Cecil,--my uncle Lord Davenant, your mother, and whoever had a say in this miserable affair. Tell them from me that I know the truth and that they are a pack of cowardly, unnatural old women. Tell them that so long as I live It will never willingly speak to one of them again.

"I was afraid you'd take it like that," he remarked dolefully.

"Take it like that!" she repeated in fierce scorn. "How else could a woman hear such news? How else do you suppose she could feel to be told that she had been hoodwinked, and kept from her duty and a man's heart very likely broken, to save the respectability of a worn-out old family. Oh, how could they have dared to do it? How could they have dared to do it?"

"It was a beastly mistake," he admitted.

A whirlwind of scorn seemed to sweep over her. She could keep still no longer. She walked up and down the little room. Her hands were clenched, her eyes flashing.

"To tell me that he was dead--to let him live out the rest of his poor life in exile and alone! Did they think that I didn't care? Cecil," she exclaimed, suddenly turning and facing him, "I always loved my father! You may think that I was too young to remember him--I wasn't, I loved him always. When I grew up and they told me of his disgrace I was bitterly sorry, for I loved his memory--but it made no difference. And all the time it was a weak, silly lie! They let him come out, poor father, without a friend to speak to him and they hustled him out of the country. And I, whose place was there with him, never knew!"

"You were only a child, Ernestine. It was twelve years ago."

"Child! I may have been only a child, but I should have been old enough to know where my place was. Thank God I have done with these people and their disgusting shibboleth of respectability."

"You are a little violent," he remarked.

"Pshaw!" She flashed a look of scorn upon him. "You don't understand! How should you, you are of their kidney--you're only half a man. Thank God that my mother was of the people! I'd have died to have gone smirking through life with a brick for a heart and milk and water in my veins! Of all the stupid pieces of brutality I ever heard of, this is the most callous and the most heartbreaking."

"It was a great mistake," he said, "but I believe they did it for the best."

She sat down with a little gesture of despair.

"I really think you'd better go away, Cecil," she said. "You exasperate me too horribly. I shall strike you or throw something at you soon. Did it for the best! What a miserable whine! Poor dear old dad, to think that they should have done this thing."

She buried her face in her handkerchief and sobbed for the second time since her childhood. Davenant was wise enough to attempt no sort of consolation. He leaned a little forward and hid his own face with the palm of his hand. When at last she looked up her face had cleared and her tone was less bitter. It would have gone very hard with the Earl of Eastchester, however, if he had called to see his niece just then.

"Well," she said, "I want to know now why, after keeping silent all this time, you thought it best to tell me the truth this afternoon?"

"Because," he answered, "you told me that you had just been to see Scarlett Trent!"

"And what on earth had that to do with it?"

"Because Scarlett Trent was with your father when he died. They were on an excursion somewhere up in the bush--the very excursion that laid the foundation of Trent's fortune."

"Go on," she cried. "Tell me all that you know! this is wonderful!"

"Well, I am glad to tell you this at any rate," he said. "I always liked your father and I saw him off when he left England, and have written to him often since. I believe I was his only correspondent in this country, except his solicitors. He had a very adventurous and, I am afraid, not a very happy time. He never wrote cheerfully, and he mortgaged the greater part of his income. I don't blame him for anything he did. A man needs some responsibility, or some one dependent upon him to keep straight. To be frank with you, I don't think he did."

"Poor dad," she murmured, "of course he didn't! I know I'd have gone to the devil as fast as I could if I'd been treated like it!"

"Well, he drifted about from place to place and at last he got to the Gold Coast. Here I half lost sight of him, and his few letters were more bitter and despairing than ever. The last I had told me that he was just off on an expedition into the interior with another Englishman. They were to visit a native King and try to obtain from him certain concessions, including the right to work a wonderful gold-mine somewhere near the village of Bekwando."

"Why, the great Bekwando Land Company!" she cried. "It is the one Scarlett Trent has just formed a syndicate to work."

Davenant nodded.

"Yes. It was a terrible risk they were running," he said, "for the people were savage and the climate deadly. He wrote cheerfully for him, though. He had a partner, he said, who was strong and determined, and they had presents, to get which he had mortgaged the last penny of his income. It was a desperate enterprise perhaps, but it suited him, and he went on to tell me this, Ernestine. If he succeeded and he became wealthy, he was returning to England just for a sight of you. He was so changed, he said, that no one in the world would recognise him. Poor fellow! It was the last line I had from him."

"And you are sure," Ernestine said slowly, "that Scarlett Trent was his partner?"

"Absolutely. Trent's own story clinches the matter. The prospectus of the mine quotes the concession as having been granted to him by the King of Bekwando in the same month as your father wrote to me."

"And what news," she asked, "have you had since?"

"Only this letter--I will read it to you--from one of the missionaries of the Basle Society. I heard nothing for so long that I made inquiries, and this is the result."

Ernestine took it and read it out steadily.

"FORTNRENIG.

"DEAR Sir,-In reply to your letter and inquiry, respecting the whereabouts of a Mr. Richard Grey, the matter was placed in my hands by the agent of Messrs. Castle, and I have personally visited Buckoman, the village at which he was last heard of. It seems that in February, 18--he started on an expedition to Bekwando in the interior with an Englishman by the name of Trent, with a view to buying land from a native King, or obtaining the concession to work the valuable gold-mines of that country. The expedition seems to have been successful, but Trent returned alone and reported that his companion had been attacked by bush-fever on the way back and had died in a few hours.

"I regret very much having to send you such sad and scanty news in return for your handsome donation to our funds. I have made every inquiry, but cannot trace any personal effects or letter. Mr. Grey, I find, was known out here altogether by the nickname of Monty.

"I deeply regret the pain which this letter will doubtless cause you, and trusting that you may seek and receive consolation where alone it may be found,

"I am,

"Yours most sincerely,

"Chas. ADDISON."

Ernestine read the letter carefully through, and instead of handing it back to Davenant, put it into her pocket when she rose up. "Cecil," she said, "I want you to leave me at once! You may come back to-morrow at the same time. I am going to think this out quietly."

He took up his hat. "There is one thing more, Ernestine," he said slowly. "Enclosed in the letter from the missionary at Attra was another and a shorter note, which, in accordance with his request, I burnt as soon as I read it. I believe the man was honest when he told me that for hours he had hesitated whether to send me those few lines or not. Eventually he decided to do so, but he appealed to my honour to destroy the note as soon as I had read it."

"Well!"

"He thought it his duty to let me know that there had been rumours as to how your father met his death. Trent, it seems, had the reputation of being a reckless and daring man, and, according to some agreement which they had, he profited enormously by your father's death. There seems to have been no really definite ground for the rumour except that the body was not found where Trent said that he had died. Apart from that, life is held cheap out there, and although your father was in delicate health, his death under such conditions could not fail to be suspicious. I hope I haven't said too much. I've tried to put it to you exactly as it was put to me!"

"Thank you," Ernestine said, "I think I understand."

CHAPTER XVIII

Dinner at the Lodge that night was not a very lively affair. Trent had great matters in his brain and was not in the least disposed to make conversation for the sake of his unbidden guests. Da Souza's few remarks he treated with silent contempt, and Mrs. Da Souza he answered only in monosyllables. Julie, nervous and depressed, stole away before dessert, and Mrs. Da Souza soon followed her, very massive, and frowning with an air of offended dignity. Da Souza, who opened the door for them, returned to his seat, moodily flicking the crumbs from his trousers with his serviette.

"Hang it all, Trent," he remarked in an aggrieved tone, "you might be a bit more amiable! Nice lively dinner for the women I must say."

"One isn't usually amiable to guests who stay when they're not asked," Trent answered gruffly. "However, if I hadn't much to say to your wife and daughter, I have a word or two to say to you, so fill up your glass and listen."

Da Souza obeyed, but without heartiness. He stretched himself out in his chair and looked down thoughtfully at the large expanse of shirt-front, in the centre of which flashed an enormous diamond.

"I've been into the City to-day as you know," Trent continued, "and I found as I expected that you have been making efforts to dispose of your share in the Bekwando Syndicate."

"I can assure you--"

"Oh rot!" Trent interrupted. "I know what I'm talking about. I won't have you sell out. Do you hear? If you try it on I'll queer the market for you at any risk. I won't marry your daughter, I won't be blackmailed, and I won't be bullied. We're in this together, sink or swim. If you pull me down you've got to come too. I'll admit that if Monty were to present himself in London to-morrow and demand his full pound of flesh we should be ruined, but he isn't going to do it. By your own showing there is no immediate risk, and you've got to leave the thing in my hands to do what I think best. If you play any hanky-panky tricks--look here, Da Souza, I'll kill you, sure! Do you hear? I could do it, and no one would be the wiser so far as I was concerned. You take notice of what I say, Da Souza. You've made a fortune, and be satisfied. That's all!"

"You won't marry Julie, then?" Da Souza said gloomily.

"No, I'm shot if I will!" Trent answered. "And look here, Da Souza, I'm leaving here for town to-morrow--taken a furnished flat in Dover Street--you can stay here if you want, but there'll only be a caretaker in the place. That's all I've got to say. Make yourself at home with the port and cigars. Last night, you know! You'll excuse me! I want a breath of fresh air."

Trent strolled through the open window into the garden, and breathed a deep sigh of relief. He was a free man again now. He had created new dangers--a new enemy to face--but what did he care? All his life had been spent in facing dangers and conquering enemies. What he had done before he could do again! As he lit a pipe and walked to and fro, he felt that this new state of things lent a certain savour to life--took from it a certain sensation of finality not altogether agreeable, which his recent great achievements in the financial world seemed to have inspired. After all, what could Da Souza do? His prosperity was altogether bound up in the success of the Bekwando Syndicate--he was never the man to kill the goose which was laying such a magnificent stock of golden eggs. The affair, so far as he was concerned, troubled him scarcely at all on cool reflection. As he drew near the little plantation he even forgot all about it. Something else was filling his thoughts!

The change in him became physical as well as mental. The hard face of the man softened, what there was of coarseness in its rugged outline became altogether toned down. He pushed open the gate with fingers which were almost reverent; he came at last to a halt in the exact spot where he had seen her first. Perhaps it was at that moment he realised most completely and clearly the curious thing which had come to him--to him of all men, hard-hearted, material, an utter stranger in the world of feminine things. With a pleasant sense of self-abandonment he groped about, searching for its meaning. He was a man who liked to understand thoroughly everything he saw and felt, and this new atmosphere in which he found himself was a curious source of excitement to him. Only he knew that the central figure of it all was this girl, that he had come out here to think about her, and that henceforth she had become to him the standard of those things which were worth having in life. Everything about her had been a revelation to him. The women whom he had come across in his battle upwards, barmaids and their fellows, fifth-rate actresses, occasionally the suburban wife of a prosperous City man, had impressed him only with a sort of coarse contempt. It was marvellous how thoroughly and clearly he had recognised Ernestine at once as a type of that other world of womenkind, of which he admittedly knew nothing. Yet it was so short a time since she had wandered into his life, so short a time that he was even a little uneasy at the wonderful strength of this new passion, a thing which had leaped up like a forest tree in a world of magic, a live, fully-grown thing, mighty and immovable in a single night. He found himself thinking of all the other things in life from a changed standpoint. His sense of proportions was altered, his financial triumphs were no longer omnipotent. He was inclined even to brush them aside, to consider them more as an incident in his career. He associated her now with all those plans concerning the future which he had been dimly formulating since the climax of his successes had come. She was of the world which he sought to enter--at once the stimulus and the object of his desires. He forgot all about Da Souza and his threats, about the broken-down, half-witted old man who was gazing with wistful eyes across the ocean which kept him there, an exile--he remembered nothing save the wonderful, new thing which had come into his life. A month ago he would have scoffed at the idea of there being anything worth considering outside the courts and alleys of the money-changers' market. To-night he knew of other things. To-night he knew that all he had done so far was as nothing--that as yet his foot was planted only on the threshold of life, and in the path along which he must hew his way lay many fresh worlds to conquer. To-night he told himself that he was equal to them all. There was something out here in the dim moonlight, something suggested by the shadows, the rose-perfumed air, the delicate and languid stillness, which crept into his veins and coursed through his blood like magic.

*　　*　　*　　*　　*

Yet every now and then the same thought came; it lay like a small but threatening black shadow across all those brilliant hopes and dreams which were filling his brain. So far he had played the game of life as a hard man, perhaps, and a selfish one, but always honestly. Now, for the first time, he had stepped aside from the beaten track. He told himself that he was not bound to believe Da Souza's story, that he had left Monty with the honest conviction that he was past all human help. Yet he knew that such consolation was the merest sophistry. Through the twilight, as he passed to and fro, he fancied more than once that the wan face of an old man, with wistful, sorrowing eyes, was floating somewhere before him--and he stopped to listen with bated breath to the wind rustling in the elm-trees, fancying he could bear that same passionate cry ringing still in his ears--the cry of an old man parted from his kin and waiting for death in a lonely land.

CHAPTER XIX

Ernestine found a letter on her plate a few mornings afterwards which rather puzzled her. It was from a firm of solicitors in Lincoln's Inn--the Eastchester family solicitors--requesting her to call that morning to see them on important business. There was not a hint as to the nature of it, merely a formal line or two and a signature. Ernestine, who had written insulting letters to all her relatives during the last few days, smiled as she laid it down. Perhaps the family had called upon Mr. Cuthbert to undertake their defence and bring her round to a reasonable view of things. The idea was amusing enough, but her first impulse was not to go. Nothing but the combination of an idle morning and a certain measure of curiosity induced her to keep the appointment.

She was evidently expected, for she was shown at once into the private office of the senior partner. The clerk who ushered her in pronounced her name indistinctly, and the elderly man who rose from his chair at her entrance looked at her inquiringly.

"I am Miss Wendermott," she said, coming forward. "I had a letter from you this morning; you wished to see me, I believe."

Mr. Cuthbert dropped at once his eyeglass and his inquiring gaze, and held out his hand.

"My dear Miss Wendermott," he said, "you must pardon the failing eyesight of an old man. To be sure you are, to be sure. Sit down, Miss Wendermott, if you please. Dear me, what a likeness!"

"You mean to my father?" she asked quietly.

"To your father, certainly, poor, dear old boy! You must excuse me, Miss Wendermott. Your father and I were at Eton together, and I think I may say that we were always something more than lawyer and client--a good deal more, a good deal more! He was a fine fellow at heart--a fine, dear fellow. Bless me, to think that you are his daughter!"

"It's very nice to hear you speak of him so, Mr. Cuthbert," she said. "My father may have been very foolish--I suppose he was really worse than foolish--but I think that he was most abominably and shamefully treated, and so long as I live I shall never forgive those who were responsible for it. I don't mean you, Mr. Cuthbert, of course. I mean my grand-father and my uncle." Mr. Cuthbert shook his head slowly.

"The Earl," he said, "was a very proud man--a very proud man."

"You may call it pride," she exclaimed. "I call it rank and brutal selfishness! They had no right to force such a sacrifice upon him. He would have been content, I am sure, to have lived quietly in England--to have kept out of their way, to have conformed to their wishes in any reasonable manner. But to rob him of home and friends and family and name--well, may God call them to account for it, and judge them as they judged him!"

"I was against it," he said sadly, "always."

"So Mr. Davenant told me," she said. "I can't quite forgive you, Mr. Cuthbert, for letting me grow up and be so shamefully imposed upon, but of course I don't blame you as I do the others. I am only thankful that I have made myself independent of my relations. I think, after the letters which I wrote to them last night, they will be quite content to let me remain where they put my father--outside their lives."

"I had heard," Mr. Cuthbert said hesitatingly, "that you were following some occupation. Something literary, is it not?"

"I am a journalist," Ernestine answered promptly, "and I'm proud to say that I am earning my own living."

He looked at her with a fine and wonderful curiosity. In his way he was quite as much one of the old school as the Earl of Eastchester, and the idea of a lady--a Wendermott, too--calling herself a journalist and proud of making a few hundreds a year was amazing enough to him. He scarcely knew how to answer her.

"Yes, yes," he said, "you have some of your father's spirit, some of his pluck too. And that reminds me--we wrote to you to call."

"Yes."

"Mr. Davenant has told you that your father was engaged in some enterprise with this wonderful Mr. Scarlett Trent, when he died."

"Yes! He told me that!"

"Well, I have had a visit just recently from that gentleman. It seems that your father when he was dying spoke of his daughter in England, and Mr. Trent is very anxious now to find you out, and speaks of a large sum of money which he wishes to invest in your name."

"He has been a long time thinking about it," Ernestine remarked.

"He explained that," Mr. Cuthbert continued, "in this way. Your father gave him our address when he was dying, but the envelope on which it was written got mislaid, and he only came across it a day or two ago. He came to see me at once, and he seems prepared to act very handsomely. He pressed very hard indeed for your name and address, but I did not feel at liberty to disclose them before seeing you."

"You were quite right, Mr. Cuthbert," she answered. "I suppose this is the reason why Mr. Davenant has just told me the whole miserable story."

"It is one reason," he admitted, "but in any case I think that Mr. Davenant had made up his mind that you should know."

"Mr. Trent, I suppose, talks of this money as a present to me?"

"He did not speak of it in that way," Mr. Cuthbert answered, "but in a sense that is, of course, what it amounts to. At the same time I should like to say that under the peculiar circumstances of the case I should consider you altogether justified in accepting it."

Ernestine drew herself up. Once more in her finely flashing eyes and resolute air the lawyer was reminded of his old friend.

"I will tell you what I should call it, Mr. Cuthbert," she said, "I will tell you what I believe it is! It is blood-money."

Mr. Cuthbert dropped his eyeglass, and rose from his chair, startled.

"Blood-money! My dear young lady! Blood-money!"

"Yes! You have heard the whole story, I suppose! What did it sound like to you? A valuable concession granted to two men, one old, the other young! one strong, the other feeble! yet the concession read, if one should die the survivor should take the whole. Who put that in, do you suppose? Not my father! you may be sure of that. And one of them does die, and Scarlett Trent is left to take everything. Do you think that reasonable? I don't. Now, you say, after all this time he is fired with a sudden desire to behave handsomely to the daughter of his dead partner. Fiddlesticks! I know Scarlett Trent, although he little knows who I am, and he isn't that sort of man at all. He'd better have kept away from you altogether, for I fancy he's put his neck in the noose now! I do not want his money, but there is something I do want from Mr. Scarlett Trent, and that is the whole knowledge of my father's death."

Mr. Cuthbert sat down heavily in his chair.

"But, my dear young lady," he said, "you do not suspect Mr. Trent of--er--making away with your father!'

"And why not? According to his own showing they were alone together when he died. What was to prevent it? I want to know more about it, and I am going to, if I have to travel to the Gold Coast myself. I will tell you frankly, Mr. Cuthbert--I suspect Mr. Scarlett Trent. No, don't interrupt me. It may seem absurd to you now that he is Mr. Scarlett Trent, millionaire, with the odour of civilisation clinging to him, and the respectability of wealth. But I, too, have seen him, and I have heard him talk. He has helped me to see the other man--half-savage, splendidly masterful, forging his way through to success by sheer pluck and unswerving obstinacy. Listen, I admire your Mr. Trent! He is a man, and when he speaks to you you know that he was born with a destiny. But there is the other side. Do you think that he would let a man's life stand in his way? Not he! He'd commit a murder, or would have done in those days, as readily as you or I would sweep away a fly. And it is because he is that sort of man that I want to know more about my father's death."

"You are talking of serious things, Miss Wendermott," Mr. Cuthbert said gravely.

"Why not? Why shirk them? My father's death was a serious thing, wasn't it? I want an account of it from the only man who can render it."

"When you disclose yourself to Mr. Trent I should say that he would willingly give you--"

She interrupted him, coming over and standing before him, leaning against his table, and looking him in the face.

"You don't understand. I am not going to disclose myself! You will reply to Mr. Trent that the daughter of his old partner is not in need of charity, however magnificently tendered. You understand?"

"I understand, Miss Wendermott."

"As to her name or whereabouts you are not at liberty to disclose them. You can let him think, if you will, that she is tarred with the same brush as those infamous and hypocritical relatives of hers who sent her father out to die."

Mr. Cuthbert shook his head.

"I think, young lady, if you will allow me to say so that you are making a needless mystery of the matter, and further, that you are embarking upon what will certainly prove to be a wild-goose chase. We had news of your father not long before his sad death, and he was certainly in ill-health."

She set her lips firmly together, and there was a look in her face which alone was quite sufficient to deter Mr. Cuthbert from further argument.

"It may be a wild-goose chase," she said. "It may not. At any rate nothing will alter my purpose. Justice sleeps sometimes for very many years, but I have an idea that Mr. Scarlett Trent may yet have to face a day of settlement."

*   *   *   *   *

She walked through the crowded streets homewards, her nerves tingling and her pulses throbbing with excitement. She was conscious of having somehow ridded herself of a load of uncertainty and anxiety. She was committed now at any rate to a definite course. There had been moments of indecision--moments in which she had been inclined to revert to her first impressions of the man, which, before she had heard Davenant's story, had been favourable enough. That was all over now. That pitifully tragic figure--the man who died with a tardy fortune in his hands, an outcast in a far off country--had stirred in her heart a passionate sympathy--reason even gave way before it. She declared war against Mr. Scarlett Trent.

CHAPTER XX

Ernestine walked from Lincoln's Inn to the office of the Hour, where she stayed until nearly four. Then, having finished her day's work, she made her way homewards. Davenant was waiting for her in her rooms. She greeted him with some surprise.

"You told me that I might come to tea," he reminded her. "If you're expecting any one else, or I'm in the way at all, don't mind saying so, please!"

She shook her head.

"I'm certainly not expecting any one," she said. "To tell you the truth my visiting-list is a very small one; scarcely any one knows where I live. Sit down, and I will ring for tea."

He looked at her curiously. "What a colour you have, Ernestine!" he remarked. "Have you been walking fast?"

She laughed softly, and took off her hat, straightening the wavy brown hair, which had escaped bounds a little, in front of the mirror. She looked at herself long and thoughtfully at the delicately cut but strong features, the clear, grey eyes and finely arched eyebrows, the curving, humorous mouth and dainty chin. Davenant regarded her in amazement.

"Why, Ernestine," he exclaimed, "are you taking stock of your good looks?"

"Precisely what I am doing," she answered laughing. "At that moment I was wondering whether I possessed any."

"If you will allow me," he said, "to take the place of the mirror, I think that I could give you any assurances you required."

She shook her head.

"You might be more flattering," she said, "but you would be less faithful."

He remained standing upon the hearthrug. Ernestine returned to the mirror.

"May I know," he asked, "for whose sake is this sudden anxiety about your appearance?"

She turned away and sat in a low chair, her hands clasped behind her head, her eyes fixed upon vacancy.

"I have been wondering," she said, "whether if I set myself to it as to a task I could make a man for a moment forget himself--did I say forget?--I mean betray!"

"If I were that man," he remarked smiling, "I will answer for it that you could."

"You! But then you are only a boy, you have nothing to conceal, and you are partial to me, aren't you? No, the man whom I want to influence is a very different sort of person. It is Scarlett Trent."

He frowned heavily. "A boor," he said. "What have you to do with him? The less the better I should say."

"And from my point of view, the more the better," she answered. "I have come to believe that but for him my father would be alive to-day."

"I do not understand! If you believe that, surely you do not wish to see the man--to have him come near you!"

"I want him punished!"

He shook his head. "There is no proof. There never could be any proof!"

"There are many ways," she said softly, "in which a man can be made to suffer."

"And you would set yourself to do this?"

"Why not? Is not anything better than letting him go scot-free? Would you have me sit still and watch him blossom into a millionaire peer, a man of society, drinking deep draughts of all the joys of life, with never a thought for the man he left to rot in an African jungle? Oh, any way of punishing him is better than that. I have declared war against Scarlett Trent."

"How long," he asked, "will it last?"

"Until he is in my power," she answered slowly. "Until he has fallen back again to the ruck. Until he has tasted a little of the misery from which at least he might have saved my father!"

"I think," he said, "that you are taking a great deal too much for granted. I do not know Scarlett Trent, and I frankly admit that I am prejudiced against him and all his class. Yet I think that he deserves his chance, like any man. Go to him and ask him, face to face, how your father died, declare yourself, press for all particulars, seek even for corroboration of his word. Treat him if you will as an enemy, but as an honourable one!"

She shook her head.

"The man," she said, "has all the plausibility of his class. He has learned it in the money school, where these things become an art. He believes himself secure--he is even now seeking for me. He is all prepared with his story. No, my way is best."

"I do not like your way," he said. "It is not like you, Ernestine."

"For the sake of those whom one loves," she said, "one will do much that one hates. When I think that but for this man my father might still have been alive, might have lived to know how much I loathed those who sent him into exile--well, I feel then that there is nothing in the world I would not do to crush him!"

He rose to his feet--his fresh, rather boyish, face was wrinkled with care.

"I shall live to be sorry, Ernestine," he said, "that I ever told you the truth about your father."

"If I had discovered it for myself," she said, "and, sooner or later, I should have discovered it, and had learned that you too had been in the conspiracy, I should never have spoken to you again as long as I lived."

"Then I must not regret it," he said, "only I hate the part you are going to play. I hate to think that I must stand by and watch, and say nothing."

"There is no reason," she said, "why you should watch it; why do you not go away for a time?"

"I cannot," he answered sadly, "and you know why."

She was impatient, but she looked at him for a moment with a gleam of sadness in her eyes.

"It would be much better for you," she said, "if you would make up your mind to put that folly behind you."

"It may be folly, but it is not the sort of folly one forgets."

"You had better try then, Cecil," she said, "for it is quite hopeless. You know that. Be a man and leave off dwelling upon the impossible. I do not wish to marry, and I do not expect to, but if ever I did, it would not be you!"

He was silent for a few moments--looking gloomily across at the girl, loathing the thought that she, his ideal of all those things which most become a woman, graceful, handsome, perfectly bred, should ever be brought into contact at all with such a man as this one whose confidence she was planning to gain. No, he could not go away and leave her! He must be at hand, must remain her friend.

"I wonder," he said, "couldn't we have one of our old evenings again? Listen--"

"I would rather not," she interrupted softly. "If you will persist in talking of a forbidden subject you must go away. Be reasonable, Cecil."

He was silent for a moment. When he spoke again his tone was changed.

"Very well," he said. "I will try to let things be as you wish--for the present. Now do you want to hear some news?"

She nodded.

"Of course."

"It's about Dick--seems rather a coincidence too. He was at the Cape, you know, with a firm of surveyors, and he's been offered a post on the Gold Coast."

"The Gold Coast! How odd! Anywhere near--?"

"The offer came from the Bekwando Company!"

"Is he going?"

"Yes."

She was full of eager interest. "How extraordinary! He might be able to make some inquiries for me."

He nodded.

"What there is to be discovered about Mr. Scarlett Trent, he can find out! But, Ernestine, I want you to understand this! I have nothing against the man, and although I dislike him heartily, I think it is madness to associate him in any way with your father's death."

"You do not know him. I do!"

"I have only told you my opinion," he answered, "it is of no consequence. I will see with your eyes. He is your enemy and he shall be my enemy. If there is anything shady in his past out there, depend upon it Dick will hear of it."

She pushed the wavy hair back from her forehead--her eyes were bright, and there was a deep flush of colour in her cheeks. But the man was not to be deceived. He knew that these things were not for him. It was the accomplice she welcomed and not the man.

"It is a splendid stroke of fortune," she said. "You will write to Fred to-day, won't you? Don't prejudice him either way. Write as though your interest were merely curiosity. It is the truth I want to get at, that is all. If the man is innocent I wish him no harm--only I believe him guilty."

"There was a knock at the door--both turned round. Ernestine's trim little maidservant was announcing a visitor who followed close behind.

"Mr. Scarlett Trent."

CHAPTER XXI

Ernestine was a delightful hostess, she loved situations, and her social tact was illimitable. In a few minutes Trent was seated in a comfortable and solid chair with a little round table by his side, drinking tea and eating buttered scones, and if not altogether at his ease very nearly so. Opposite him was Davenant, dying to escape yet constrained to be agreeable, and animated too with a keen, distasteful curiosity to watch Ernestine's methods. And Ernestine herself chatted all the time, diffused good fellowship and tea--she made an atmosphere which had a nameless fascination for the man who had come to middle-age without knowing what a home meant. Davenant studied him and became thoughtful. He took note of the massive features, the iron jaw, the eyes as bright as steel, and his thoughtfulness became anxiety. Ernestine too was strong, but this man was a rock. What would happen if she carried out her purpose, fooled, betrayed him, led him perhaps to ruin? Some day her passion would leap up, she would tell him, they would be face to face, injured man and taunting woman. Davenant had an ugly vision as he sat there. He saw the man's eyes catch fire, the muscles of his face twitch, he saw Ernestine shrink back, white with terror and the man followed her.

"Cecil! Aren't you well? you're looking positively ghastly!"

He pulled himself together--it had been a very realistic little interlude.

"Bad headache!" he said, smiling. "By the by, I must go!"

"If you ever did such a thing as work," she remarked, "I should say that you, had been doing too much. As it is, I suppose you have been sitting up too late. Good-bye. I am so glad that you were here to meet Mr. Trent. Mr. Davenant is my cousin, you know," she continued, turning to her visitor, "and he is almost the only one of my family who has not cast me off utterly."

Davenant made his adieux with a heavy heart. He hated the hypocrisy with which he hoped for Scarlett Trent's better acquaintance and the latter's bluff acceptance of an invitation to look him up at his club. He walked out into the street cursing his mad offer to her and the whole business. But Ernestine was very well satisfied.

She led Trent to talk about Africa again, and he plunged into the subject without reserve. He told her stories and experiences with a certain graphic and picturesque force which stamped him as the possessor of an imaginative power and command of words for which she would scarcely have given him credit. She had the unusual gift of making the best of all those with whom she came in contact. Trent felt that he was interesting her, and gained confidence in himself.

All the time she was making a social estimate of him. He was not by any means impossible. On the contrary there was no reason why he should not become a success. That he was interested in her was already obvious, but that had become her intention. The task began to seem almost easy as she sat and listened to him.

Then he gave her a start. Quietly and without any warning he changed the subject into one which was fraught with embarrassment for her. At his first words the colour faded from her cheeks.

"I've been pretty lucky since I got back. Things have gone my way a bit and the only disappointment I've had worth speaking of has been in connection with a matter right outside money. I've been trying to find the daughter of that old partner of mine--I told you about her--and I can't."

She changed her seat a little. There was no need for her to affect any interest in what he was saying. She listened to every word intently.

"Monty," he said reflectingly, "was a good old sort in a way, and I had an idea, somehow, that his daughter would turn out something like the man himself, and at heart Monty was all right. I didn't know who she was or her name--Monty was always precious close, but I had the address of a firm of lawyers who knew all about her. I called there the other day and saw an old chap who questioned and cross-questioned me until I wasn't sure whether I was on my head or my heels, and, after all, he told me to call again this afternoon for her address. I told him of course that Monty died a pauper and he'd no share of our concession to will away, but I'd done so well that I thought I'd like to make over a trifle to her--in fact I'd put away 10,000 pounds worth of Bekwando shares for her. I called this afternoon, and do you know, Miss Wendermott, the young lady declined to have anything to say to me--wouldn't let me know who she was that I might have gone and talked this over in a friendly way with her. Didn't want money, didn't want to hear about her father!"

"You must have been disappointed."

"I'll admit it," he replied. "I was; I'd come to think pretty well of Monty although he was a loose fish and I'd a sort of fancy for seeing his daughter."

She took up a screen as though to shield the fire from her face. Would the man's eyes never cease questioning her--could it be that he suspected? Surely that was impossible!

"Why have you never tried to find her before?" she asked.

"That's a natural question enough," he admitted. "Well, first, I only came across a letter Monty wrote with the address of those lawyers a few days ago, and, secondly, the Bekwando Mine and Land Company has only just boomed, and you see that made me feel that I'd like to give a lift up to any one belonging to poor old Monty I could find. I've a mind to go on with the thing myself and find out somehow who this young lady is!"

"Who were the lawyers?"

"Cuthbert and Cuthbert."

"They are most respectable people," she said. "I know Mr. Cuthbert and their standing is very high. If Mr. Cuthbert told you that the young lady wished to remain unknown to you, I am quite sure that you may believe him."

"That's all right," Trent said, "but here's what puzzles me. The girl may be small enough and mean enough to decline to have anything to say to me because her father was a bad lot, and she doesn't want to be reminded of him, but for that very reason can you imagine her virtually refusing a large sum of money? I told old Cuthbert all about it. There was 10,000 pounds worth of shares waiting for her and no need for any fuss. Can you understand that?"

"It seems very odd," she said. "Perhaps the girl objects to being given money. It is a large sum to take as a present from a stranger."

"If she is that sort of girl," he said decidedly, "she would at least want to meet and talk with the man who saw the last of her father. No, there's something else in it, and I think that I ought to find her. Don't you?"

She hesitated.

"I'm afraid I can't advise you," she said; "only if she has taken so much pains to remain unknown, I am not sure--I think that if I were you I would assume that she has good reason for it."

"I can see no good reason," he said, "and there is a mystery behind it which I fancy would be better cleared up. Some day I will tell you more about it."

Evidently Ernestine was weary of the subject, for she suddenly changed it. She led him on to talk of other things. When at last he glanced at the clock he was horrified to see how long he had stayed.

"You'll remember, I hope, Miss Wendermott," he said, "that this is the first afternoon call I've ever paid. I've no idea how long I ought to have stayed, but certainly not two hours."

"The time has passed quickly," she said, smiling upon him, so that his momentary discomfort passed away. "I have been very interested in the stories of your past, Mr. Trent, but do you know I am quite as much interested, more so even, in your future."

"Tell me what you mean," he asked.

"You have so much before you, so many possibilities. There is so much that you may gain, so much that you may miss."

He looked puzzled.

"I have a lot of money," he said. "That's all! I haven't any friends nor any education worth speaking of. I don't see quite where the possibilities come in."

She crossed the room and came over close to his side, resting her arm upon the mantelpiece. She was still wearing her walking-dress, prim and straight in its folds about her tall, graceful figure, and her hair, save for the slight waviness about the forehead, was plainly dressed. There were none of the cheap arts about her to which Trent had become accustomed in women who sought to attract. Yet, as she stood looking down at him, a faint smile, half humorous, half satirical, playing about the corners of her shapely mouth, he felt his heart beat faster than ever it had done in any African jungle. It was the nervous and emotional side of the man to which she appealed. He felt unlike himself, undergoing a new phase of development. There was something stirring within him which he could not understand.

"You haven't any friends," she said softly, "nor any education, but you are a millionaire! That is quite sufficient. You are a veritable Caesar with undiscovered worlds before you."

"I wish I knew what you meant," he said, with some hesitation.

She laughed softly.

"Don't you understand," she said, "that you are the fashion? Last year it was Indian Potentates, the year before it was actors, this year it is millionaires. You have only to announce yourself and you may take any place you choose in society. You have arrived at the most auspicious moment. I can assure you that before many months are past you will know more people than ever you have spoken to in your life before--men whose names have been household words to you and nothing else will be calling you 'old chap' and wanting to sell you horses, and women, who last week would look at you through lorgnettes as though you were a denizen of some unknown world, will be lavishing upon you their choicest smiles and whispering in your ear their 'not at home' afternoon. Oh, it's lucky I'm able to prepare you a little for it, or you would be taken quite by storm."

He was unmoved. He looked at her with a grim tightening of the lips.

"I want to ask you this," he said. "What should I be the better for it all? What use have I for friends who only gather round me because I am rich? Shouldn't I be better off to have nothing to do with them, to live my own life, and make my own pleasures?"

She shrugged her shoulders.

"These people," she said, "of whom I have been speaking are masters of the situation. You can't enjoy money alone! You want to race, hunt, entertain, shoot, join in the revels of country houses! You must be one of them or you can enjoy nothing."

Monty's words were ringing back in his ears. After all, pleasures could be bought--but happiness!

"And you," he said, "you too think that these things you have mentioned are the things most to be desired in life?"

A certain restraint crept into her manner.

"Yes," she answered simply.

"I have been told," he said, "that you have given up these things to live your life differently. That you choose to be a worker. You have rich relations--you could be rich yourself!"

She looked him steadily in the face.

"You are wrong," she said, "I have no money. I have not chosen a profession willingly--only because I am poor!"

"Ah!"

The monosyllable was mysterious to her. But for the wild improbability of the thing she would have wondered whether indeed he knew her secret. She brushed the idea away. It was impossible.

"At least," he said, "you belong to these people."

"Yes," she answered, "I am one of the poor young women of society."

"And you would like," he continued, "to be one of the rich ones--to take your place amongst them on equal terms. That is what you are looking forward to in life!"

She laughed gaily.

"Of course I am! If there was the least little chance of it I should be delighted. You mustn't think that I'm different from other girls in that respect because I'm more independent. In this country there's only one way of enjoying life thoroughly, and that you will find out for yourself very soon."

He rose and held out his hand.

"Thank you very much," he said, "for letting me come. May I--"

"You may come," she said quietly, "as often as you like."

CHAPTER XXII

M r. Scarlett Trent, the Gold King, left for Africa on Thursday last on the Dunottar Castle, to pay a brief visit to his wonderful possessions there before the great Bekwando Mining and Exploration Company is offered to the public. Mr. Trent is already a millionaire, and should he succeed in floating the Company on the basis of the Prospectus, he will be a multi-millionaire, and certainly one of the richest of Englishmen. During his absence workmen are to be kept going night and day at his wonderful palace in Park Lane, which he hopes to find ready for occupation on his return. Mr. Trent's long list of financial successes are too well known to be given here, but who will grudge wealth to a man who is capable of spending it in such a lordly fashion? We wish Mr. Trent a safe voyage and a speedy return."

The paper slipped from his fingers and he looked thoughtfully out seaward. It was only one paragraph of many, and the tone of all was the same. Ernestine's words had come true--he was already a man of note. A few months had changed his life in the most amazing way--when he looked back upon it now it was with a sense of unreality--surely all these things which had happened were part of a chimerical dream. It was barely possible for him to believe that it was he, Scarlett Trent, who had developed day by day into what he was at that moment. For the man was changed in a hundred ways. His grey flannel clothes was cut by the Saville Row tailor of the moment, his hands and hair, his manner of speech and carriage were all altered. He recalled the men he had met, the clubs he had joined, his stud of horses at Newmarket, the country-houses at which he had visited. His most clear impression of the whole thing was how easy everything had been made for him. His oddness of speech, his gaucheries, his ignorances and nervousness had all been so lightly treated that they had been brushed away almost insensibly. He had been able to do so little that was wrong--his mistakes were ignored or admired as origi-nality, and yet in some delicate way the right thing had been made clear to him. Er-nestine had stood by his side, always laughing at this swift fulfilment of her proph-ecy, always encouraging him, always enigmatic. Yet at the thought of her a vague sense of trouble crept into his heart. He took a worn photograph from his pocket and looked at it long and searchingly, and when he put it away he sighed. It made no difference of course, but he would rather have found her like that, the child with sweet, trustful eyes and a laughing mouth. Was there no life at all, then, outside this little vortex into which at her bidding he had plunged? Would she never have been content with anything else? He looked across the placid, blue sea to where the sun gleamed like silver on a white sail, and sighed again. He must make himself what she would have him. There was no life for him without her.

The captain came up for his morning chat and some of the passengers, who eyed him with obvious respect, lingered for a moment about his chair on their prom-enade. Trent lit a cigar and presently began to stroll up and down himself. The salt sea-air was a wonderful tonic to him after the nervous life of the last few months. He found his spirits rapidly rising. This voyage had been undertaken in obedience to a sudden but overpowering impulse. It had come to him one night that he must know for himself how much truth there was in Da Souza's story. He could not live with the thought that a thunderbolt was ever in the skies, that at any moment his life might lie wrecked about him. He was going out by one steamer and back by the next, the impending issue of his great Company afforded all the excuse that was necessary. If Da Souza's story was true--well, there were many things which might be done, short of a complete disclosure. Monty might be satisfied, if plenty of money were forthcoming, to abandon his partnership and release the situation from its otherwise endless complications. Trent smoked his cigar placidly and, tak-ing off his cap bared his head to the sweeping sea-wind, which seemed laden with life and buoyancy. Suddenly as he swung round by the companion-way he found himself confronted by a newcomer who came staggering out from the gangway. There was a moment's recoil and a sharp exclamation. Trent stood quite still and a heavy frown darkened his face.

"Da Souza!" he exclaimed. "How on earth came you on board?"

Da Souza's face was yellower than ever and he wore an ulster buttoned up to his chin. Yet there was a flash of malice in his eyes as he answered--

"I came by late tender at Southampton," he said.

"It cost me a special from London and the agents told me I couldn't do it, but here I am, you see!"

"And a poor-looking object you are," Trent said contemptuously. "If you've life enough in you to talk, be so good as to tell me what the devil you mean by following me like this!"

"I came," Da Souza answered, "in both our interests--chiefly in my own!"

"I can believe that," Trent answered shortly, "now speak up. Tell me what you want."

Da Souza groaned and sank down upon a vacant deck-chair.

"I will sit down," he said, "I am not well! The sea disagrees with me horribly. Well, well, you want to know why I came here! I can answer that question by another. What are you doing here? Why are you going to Africa?"

"I am going," Trent said, "to see how much truth there was in that story you told me. I am going to see old Monty if he is alive."

Da Souza groaned.

"It is cruel madness," he said, "and you are such an obstinate man! Oh dear! oh dear!"

"I prefer," Trent said, "a crisis now, to ruin in the future. Besides, I have the remnants of a conscience."

"You will ruin yourself, and you will ruin me," Da Souza moaned. "How am I to have a quarter share if Monty is to come in for half, and how are you to repay him all that you would owe on a partnership account? You couldn't do it, Trent. I've heard of your four-in-hand, and your yacht, and your racers, and that beautiful house in Park Lane. I tell you that to part with half your fortune would ruin you, and the Bekwando Company could never be floated."

"I don't anticipate parting with half," Trent said coolly. "Monty hasn't long to live--and he ought not to be hard to make terms with."

Da Souza beat his hands upon the handles of his deck-chair.

"But why go near him at all? He thinks that you are dead. He has no idea that you are in England. Why should he know? Why do you risk ruin like this?"

"There are three reasons," Trent answered. "First, he may find his way to England and upset the applecart; secondly, I've only the shreds of a conscience, but I can't leave a man whom I'm robbing of a fortune in a state of semi-slavery, as I daresay he is, and the third reason is perhaps the strongest of all; but I'm not going to tell it you."

Da Souza blinked his little eyes and looked up with a cunning smile.

"Your first reason," he said, "is a poor sort of one. Do you suppose I don't have him looked after a bit?--no chance of his getting hack to England, I can tell you. As for the second, he's only half-witted, and if he was better off he wouldn't know it."

"Even if I gave way to you in this," Trent answered, "the third reason is strong enough."

Da Souza's face was gloomy. "I know it's no use trying to move you," he said, "but you're on a silly, dangerous, wild goose-chase."

"And what about yourself?" Trent asked. "I imagine you have some other purpose in taking this voyage than just to argue with me."

"I am going to see," Da Souza said, "that you do as little mischief as possible."

Trent walked the length of the deck and back. "Da Souza," he said, stopping in front of him, "you're a fool to take this voyage. You know me well enough to be perfectly assured that nothing you could say would ever influence me. There's more behind it. You've a game of your own to play over there. Now listen! If I catch you interfering with me in any way, we shall meet on more equal terms than when you laughed at my revolver at Walton Lodge! I never was over-scrupulous in those old days, Da Souza, you know that, and I have a fancy that when I find myself on African soil again I may find something of the old man in me yet. So look out, my friend, I've no mind to be trifled with, and, mark me--if harm comes to that old man, it will be your life for his, as I'm a living man. You were afraid of me once, Da Souza. I haven't changed so much as you may think, and the Gold Coast isn't exactly the centre of civilisation. There! I've said my say. The less I see of you now till we land, the better I shall be pleased."

He walked away and was challenged by the Doctor to a game of shuffleboard. Da Souza remained in his chair, his eyes blinking as though with the sun, and his hands gripping nervously the sides of his chair.

CHAPTER XXIII

After six weeks' incessant throbbing the great engines were still, and the Dunottar Castle lay at anchor a mile or two from the African coast and off the town of Attra. The heat, which in motion had been hard enough to bear, was positively stifling now. The sun burned down upon the glassy sea and the white deck till the varnish on the rails cracked and blistered, and the sweat streamed like water from the faces of the labouring seamen. Below at the ship's side half a dozen surf boats were waiting, manned by Kru boys, who alone seemed perfectly comfortable, and cheerful as usual. All around were preparations for landing--boxes were being hauled up from the hold, and people were going about in reach of small parcels and deck-chairs and missing acquaintances. Trent, in white linen clothes and puggaree, was leaning over the railing, gazing towards the town, when Da Souza came up to him--

"Last morning, Mr. Trent!"

Trent glanced round and nodded.

"Are you disembarking here?" he asked.

Da Souza admitted the fact. "My brother will meet me," he said. "He is very afraid of the surf-boats, or he would have come out to the steamer. You remember him?"

"Yes, I remember him," Trent answered. "He was not the sort of person one forgets."

"He is a very rough diamond," Da Souza said apologetically. "He has lived here so long that he has become almost half a native."

"And the other half a thief," Trent muttered.

Da Souza was not in the least offended.

"I am afraid," he admitted, "that his morals are not up to the Threadneedle

Street pitch, eh, Mr. Trent? But he has made quite a great deal of money. Oh, quite a sum I can assure you. He sends me some over to invest!"

"Well, if he's carrying on the same old game," Trent remarked, "he ought to be coining it! By the by, of course he knows exactly where Monty is?"

"It is what I was about to say," Da Souza assented, with a vigorous nod of the head. "Now, my dear Mr. Trent, I know that you will have your way. It is no use my trying to dissuade you, so listen. You shall waste no time in searching for Monty. My brother will tell you exactly where he is."

Trent hesitated. He would have preferred to have nothing at all to do with Da Souza, and the very thought of Oom Sam made him shudder. On the other hand, time was valuable to him and he might waste weeks looking for the man whom Oom Sam could tell him at once where to find. On the whole, it was better to accept Da Souza's offer.

"Very well, Da Souza," he said, "I have no time to spare in this country and the sooner I get back to England the better for all of us. If your brother knows where Monty is, so much the better for both of us. We will land together and meet him."

Already the disembarking had commenced. Da Souza and Trent took their places side by side on the broad, flat-bottomed boat, and soon they were off shorewards and the familiar song of the Kru boys as they bent over their oars greeted their ears. The excitement of the last few strokes was barely over before they sprang upon the beach and were surrounded by a little crowd, on the outskirts of whom was Oom Sam. Trent was seized upon by an Englishman who was representing the Bekwando Land and Mining Investment Company and, before he could regain Da Souza, a few rapid sentences had passed between the latter and his brother in Portuguese. Oom Sam advanced to Trent hat in hand--

"Welcome back to Attra, senor?"

Trent nodded curtly.

"Place isn't much changed," he remarked.

"It is very slowly here," Oom Sam said, "that progress is made! The climate is too horrible. It makes dead sheep of men."

"You seem to hang on pretty well," Trent remarked carelessly. "Been up country lately?"

"I was trading with the King of Bekwando a month ago," Oom Sam answered.

"Palm-oil and mahogany for vile rum I suppose," Trent said.

The man extended his hands and shrugged his shoulders. The old gesture.

"They will have it," he said. "Shall we go to the hotel, Senor Trent, and rest?"

Trent nodded, and the three men scrambled up the beach, across an open space, and gained the shelter of a broad balcony, shielded by a striped awning which surrounded the plain white stone hotel. A Kru boy welcomed them with beaming face and fetched them drinks upon a Brummagem tray. Trent turned to the Englishman who had followed them up.

"To-morrow," he said, "I shall see you about the contracts. My first business is a private matter with these gentlemen. Will you come up here and breakfast with me?"

The Englishman, a surveyor from a London office, assented with enthusiasm.

"I can't offer to put you up," he said gloomily. "Living out here's beastly. See you in the morning, then."

He strolled away, fanning himself. Trent lit a long cigar.

"I understand," he said turning to Oom Sam, "that old Monty is alive still. If so, it's little short of a miracle, for I left him with scarcely a gasp in his body, and I was nearly done myself.

"It was," Oom Sam said, "veree wonderful. The natives who were chasing you, they found him and then the Englishman whom you met in Bekwando on his way inland, he rescued him. You see that little white house with a flagstaff yonder?"

He pointed to a little one-storey building about a mile away along the coast. Trent nodded.

"That is," Oom Sam said, "a station of the Basle Mission and old Monty is there. You can go and see him any time you like, but he will not know you."

"Is he as far gone as that?" Trent asked slowly.

"His mind," Oom Sam said, "is gone. One little flickering spark of life goes on. A day! a week! who can tell how long?"

"Has he a doctor?" Trent asked.

"The missionary, he is a medical man," Oom Sam explained. "Yet he is long past the art of medicine."

It seemed to Trent, turning at that moment to relight his cigar, that a look of subtle intelligence was flashed from one to the other of the brothers. He paused with the match in his fingers, puzzled, suspicious, anxious. So there was some scheme hatched already between these precious pair! It was time indeed that he had come.

"There was something else I wanted to ask," he said a moment or two later. "What about the man Francis. Has he been heard of lately?"

Oom Sam shook his head.

"Ten months ago," he answered, "a trader from Lulabulu reported having passed him on his way to the interior. He spoke of visiting Sugbaroo, another country beyond. If he ventured there, he will surely never return."

Trent set down his glass without a word, and called to some Kru boys in the square who carried litters.

"I am going," he said, "to find Monty."

CHAPTER XXIV

An old man, with his face turned to the sea, was making a weary attempt at digging upon a small potato patch. The blaze of the tropical sun had become lost an hour or so before in a strange, grey mist, rising not from the sea, but from the swamps which lay here and there--brilliant, verdant patches of poison and pestilence. With the mist came a moist, sticky heat, the air was fetid. Trent wiped the perspiration from his forehead and breathed hard. This was an evil moment for him.

Monty turned round at the sound of his approaching footsteps. The two men stood face to face. Trent looked eagerly for some sign of recognition--none came.

"Don't you know me?" Trent said huskily. "I'm Scarlett Trent--we went up to Bekwando together, you know. I thought you were dead, Monty, or I wouldn't have left you."

"Eh! What!"

Monty mumbled for a moment or two and was silent. A look of dull disappointment struggled with the vacuity of his face. Trent noticed that his hands were shaking pitifully and his eyes were bloodshot.

"Try and think, Monty," he went on, drawing a step nearer to him. "Don't you remember what a beastly time we had up in the bush--how they kept us day after day in that villainous hut because it was a fetish week, and how after we had got the concessions those confounded niggers followed us! They meant our lives, Monty, and I don't know how you escaped! Come! make an effort and pull yourself together. We're rich men now, both of us. You must come back to England and help me spend a bit."

Monty had recovered a little his power of speech. He leaned over his spade and smiled benignly at his visitor.

"There was a Trentham in the Guards," he said slowly, "the Honourable George Trentham, you know, one of poor Abercrombie's sons, but I thought he was dead. You must dine with me one night at the Travellers'! I've given up eating myself, but I'm always thirsty."

He looked anxiously away towards the town and began to mumble. Trent was in despair. Presently he began again.

"I used to belong to the Guards,--always dined there till Jacques left. Afterwards the cooking was beastly, and--I can't quite remember where I went then. You see--I think I must be getting old. I don't remember things. Between you and me," he sidled a little closer to Trent, "I think I must have got into a bit of a scrape of some sort--I feel as though there was a blank somewhere...."

Again he became unintelligible. Trent was silent for several minutes. He could not understand that strained, anxious look which crept into Monty's face every time he faced the town. Then he made his last effort.

"Monty, do you remember this?"

Zealously guarded, yet a little worn at the edges and faded, he drew the picture from its case and held it before the old man's blinking eyes. There was a moment of suspense, then a sharp, breathless cry which ended in a wail.

"Take it away," Monty moaned. "I lost it long ago. I don't want to see it! I don't want to think."

"I have come," Trent said, with an unaccustomed gentleness in his tone, "to make you think. I want you to remember that that is a picture of your daughter. You are rich now and there is no reason why you should not come back to her. Don't you understand, Monty?"

It was a grey, white face, shrivelled and pinched, weak eyes without depth, a vapid smile in which there was no meaning. Trent, carried away for a moment by an impulse of pity, felt only disappointment at the hopelessness of his task. He would have been honestly glad to have taken the Monty whom he had known back to England, but not this man! For already that brief flash of awakened life seemed to have died away. Monty's head was wagging feebly and he was casting continually little, furtive glances towards the town.

"Please go away," he said. "I don't know you and you give me a pain in my head. Don't you know what it is to feel a buzz, buzz, buzzing inside? I can't remember things. It's no use trying."

"Monty, why do you look so often that way?" Trent said quietly. "Is some one coming out from the town to see you?"

Monty threw a quick glance at him and Trent sighed. For the glance was full of cunning, the low cunning of the lunatic criminal.

"No one, no one," he said hastily. "Who should come to see me? I'm only poor Monty. Poor old Monty's got no friends. Go away and let me dig."

Trent walked a few paces apart, and passed out of the garden to a low, shelving bank and looked downward where a sea of glass rippled on to the broad, firm sands. What a picture of desolation! The grey, hot mist, the whitewashed cabin, the long, ugly potato patch, the weird, pathetic figure of that old man from whose brain the light of life had surely passed for ever. And yet Trent was puzzled. Monty's furtive glance inland, his half-frightened, half-cunning denial of any anticipated visit suggested that there was some one else who was interested in his existence, and some one too with whom he shared a secret. Trent lit a cigar and sat down upon the sandy turf. Monty resumed his digging. Trent watched him through the leaves of a stunted tree, underneath which he had thrown himself.

For an hour or more nothing happened. Trent smoked, and Monty, who had apparently forgotten all about his visitor, plodded away amongst the potato furrows, with every now and then a long, searching look towards the town. Then there came a black speck stealing across the broad rice-field and up the steep hill, a speck which in time took to itself the semblance of a man, a Kru boy, naked as he was born save for a ragged loin-cloth, and clutching something in his hand. He was invisible to Trent until he was close at hand; it was Monty whose changed attitude and deportment indicated the approach of something interesting. He had relinquished his digging and, after a long, stealthy glance towards the house, had advanced to the extreme boundary of the potato patch. His behaviour here for the first time seemed to denote the hopeless lunatic. He swung his long arms backward and forwards, cracking his fingers, and talked unintelligibly to himself, hoarse, guttural murmurings without sense or import. Trent changed his place and for the first time saw the Kru boy. His face darkened and an angry exclamation broke from his lips. It was something like this which he had been expecting.

The Kru boy drew nearer and nearer. Finally he stood upright on the rank, coarse grass and grinned at Monty, whose lean hands were outstretched towards him. He fumbled for a moment in his loin-cloth. Then he drew out a long bottle and handed it up. Trent stepped out as Monty's nervous fingers were fumbling with the cork. He made a grab at the boy who glided off like an eel. Instantly he whipped out a revolver and covered him.

"Come here," he cried.

The boy shook his head. "No understand."

"Who sent you here with that filthy stuff?" he asked sternly. "You'd best answer me."

The Kru boy, shrinking away from the dark muzzle of that motionless revolver, was spellbound with fear. He shook his head.

"No understand."

There was a flash of light, a puff of smoke, a loud report. The Kru boy fell forward upon his face howling with fear. Monty ran off towards the house mumbling to himself.

"The next time," Trent said coolly, "I shall fire at you instead of at the tree. Remember I have lived out here and I know all about you and your kind. You can understand me very well if you choose, and you've just got to. Who sends you here with that vile stuff?"

"Massa, I tell! Massa Oom Sam, he send me!"

"And what is the stuff?"

"Hamburgh gin, massa! very good liquor! Please, massa, point him pistol the other way."

Trent took up the flask, smelt its contents and threw it away with a little exclamation of disgust.

"How often have you been coming here on this errand?" he asked sternly.

"Most every day, massa--when him Mr. Price away."

Trent nodded.

"Very good," he said. "Now listen to me. If ever I catch you round here again or anywhere else on such an errand, I'll shoot you like a dog. Now be off."

The boy bounded away with a broad grin of relief. Trent walked up to the house and asked for the missionary's wife. She came to him soon, in what was called the parlour. A frail, anaemic-looking woman with tired eyes and weary expression.

"I'm sorry to trouble you, Mrs. Price," Trent said, plunging at once into his subject, "but I want to speak to you about this old man, Monty. You've had him some time now, haven't you?"

"About four years," she answered. "Captain Francis left him with my husband; I believe he found him in one of the villages inland, a prisoner."

Trent nodded.

"He left you a little money with him, I believe."

The woman smiled faintly.

"It was very little," she said, "but such as it is, we have never touched it. He eats scarcely anything and we consider that the little work he has done has about paid us for keeping him."

"Did you know," Trent asked bluntly, "that he had been a drunkard?"

"Captain Francis hinted as much," the woman answered. "That was one reason why he wanted to leave him with us. He knew that we did not allow anything in the house."

"It was a pity," Trent said, "that you could not have watched him a little more out of it. Why, his brain is sodden with drink now!"

The woman was obviously honest in her amazement. "How can that be?" she exclaimed. "He has absolutely no money and he never goes off our land."

"He has no need," Trent answered bitterly. "There are men in Attra who want him dead, and they have been doing their best to hurry him off. I caught a Kru boy bringing him gin this afternoon. Evidently it has been a regular thing."

"I am very sorry indeed to hear this," the woman said, "and I am sure my husband will be too. He will feel that, in a certain measure, he has betrayed Captain Francis's trust. At the same time we neither of us had any idea that anything of this sort was to be feared, or we would have kept watch."

"You cannot be blamed," Trent said. "I am satisfied that you knew nothing about it. Now I am going to let you into a secret. Monty is a rich man if he had his rights, and I want to help him to them. I shall take him back to England with me, but I can't leave for a week or so. If you can keep him till then and have some one to watch him day and night, I'll give your husband a hundred pounds for your work here, and build you a church. It's all right! Don't look as though I were mad. I'm a very rich man, that's all, and I shan't miss the money, but I want to feel that Monty is safe till I can start back to England. Will you undertake this?"

"Yes," the woman answered promptly, "we will. We'll do our honest best."

Trent laid a bank-note upon the table.

"Just to show I'm in earnest," he remarked, rising. "I shall be up-country for about a month. Look after the old chap well and you'll never regret it."

Trent went thoughtfully back to the town. He had committed himself now to a definite course of action. He had made up his mind to take Monty back with him to England and face the consequences.

CHAPTER XXV

On the summit of a little knoll, with a pipe between his teeth and his back against a palm-tree, Trent was lounging away an hour of the breathless night. Usually a sound sleeper, the wakefulness, which had pursued him from the instant his head had touched his travelling pillow an hour or so back, was not only an uncommon occurrence, but one which seemed proof against any effort on his part to overcome it. So he had risen and stolen away from the little camp where his companions lay wrapped in heavy slumber. They had closed their eyes in a dense and tropical darkness--so thick indeed that they had lit a fire, notwithstanding the stifling heat, to remove that vague feeling of oppression which chaos so complete seemed to bring with it. Its embers burnt now with a faint and sickly glare in the full flood of yellow moonlight which had fallen upon the country. From this point of vantage Trent could trace backwards their day's march for many miles, the white posts left by the surveyor even were visible, and in the background rose the mountains of Bekwando. It had been a hard week's work for Trent. He had found chaos, discontent, despair. The English agent of the Bekwando Land Company was on the point of cancelling his contract, the surveyors were spending valuable money without making any real attempt to start upon their undoubtedly difficult task. Everywhere the feeling seemed to be that the prosecution of his schemes was an impossibility. The road was altogether in the clouds. Trent was flatly told that the labour they required was absolutely unprocurable. Fortunately Trent knew the country, and he was a man of resource. From the moment when he had appeared upon the spot, things had begun to right themselves. He had found Oom Sam established as a sort of task-master and contractor, and had promptly dismissed him, with the result that the supply of Kru boys was instantly doubled. He had found other sources of labour and started them at once on clearing work, scornfully indifferent to the often-expressed doubts of the English surveyor as to possibility of making the road at all. He had chosen overseers with that swift and intuitive insight into character which in his case amounted almost to genius. With a half-sheet of notepaper and a pencil, he had mapped out a road which had made one, at least, of the two surveyors thoughtful, and had largely increased his respect for the English capitalist. Now he was on his way back from a tour almost to Bekwando itself by the route of the proposed road. Already the work of preparation had begun. Hundreds of natives left in their track were sawing down palm-trees, cutting away the bush, digging and making ready everywhere for that straight, wide thoroughfare which was to lead from Bekwando village to the sea-coast. Cables as to his progress had already been sent back to London. Apart from any other result, Trent knew that he had saved the Syndicate a fortune by his journey here.

The light of the moon grew stronger--the country lay stretched out before him like a map. With folded arms and a freshly-lit pipe Trent leaned with his back against the tree and fixed eyes. At first he saw nothing but that road, broad and white, stretching to the horizon and thronged with oxen-drawn wagons. Then the fancy suddenly left him and a girl's face seemed to be laughing into his--a face which was ever changing, gay and brilliant one moment, calm and seductively beautiful the next. He smoked his pipe furiously, perplexed and uneasy. One moment the face was Ernestine's, the next it was Monty's little girl laughing up at him from the worn and yellow tin-type. The promise of the one--had it been fulfilled in the woman? At least he knew that here was the one great weakness of his life. The curious flood of sentiment, which had led him to gamble for the child's picture, had merged with equal suddenness into passion at the coming of her later present-ment. High above all his plans for the accumulation of power and wealth, he set before him now a desire which had become the moving impulse of his life--a desire primitive but overmastering--the desire of a strong man for the woman he loves. In London he had scarcely dared admit so much even to himself. Here, in this vast solitude, he was more master of himself--dreams which seemed to him the most beautiful and the most daring which he had ever conceived, filled his brain and stirred his senses till the blood in his veins seemed flowing to a new and wonderful music. Those were wonderful moments for him.

His pipe was nearly out, and a cooler breeze was stealing over the plain. After all, perhaps an hour or so's sleep would be possible now. He stretched himself and yawned, cast one more glance across the moonlit plain, and then stood suddenly still, stiffened into an attitude of breathless interest. Yonder, between two lines of shrubs, were moving bodies--men, footsore and weary, crawling along with slow, painful movements; one at least of them was a European, and even at that distance Trent could tell that they were in grievous straits. He felt for his revolver, and, finding that it was in his belt, descended the hill quickly towards them.

With every step which he took he could distinguish them more plainly. There were five Kru boys, a native of a tribe which he did not recognise, and a European who walked with reeling footsteps, and who, it was easy to see, was on the point of exhaustion. Soon they saw him, and a feeble shout greeted his approach. Trent was within hailing distance before he recognised the European. Then, with a little exclamation of surprise, he saw that it was Captain Francis.

They met face to face in a moment, but Francis never recognised him. His eyes were bloodshot, a coarse beard disguised his face, and his clothes hung about him in rags. Evidently he was in a terrible plight. When he spoke his voice sounded shrill and cracked.

"We are starving men," he said; "can you help us?"

"Of course we can," Trent answered quickly. "This way. We've plenty of stores."

The little party stumbled eagerly after him. In a few moments they were at the camp. Trent roused his companions, packages were hastily undone and a meal prepared. Scarcely a word was said or a question asked. One or two of the Kru boys seemed on the verge of insanity--Francis himself was hysterical and faint. Trent boiled a kettle and made some beef-tea himself. The first mouthful Francis was unable to swallow. His throat had swollen and his eyes were hideously bloodshot. Trent, who had seen men before in dire straits, fed him from a spoon and forced brandy between his lips. Certainly, at the time, he never stopped to consider that he was helping back to life the man who in all the world was most likely to do him ill.

"Better?" he asked presently.

"Much. What luck to find you. What are you after--gold?"

Trent shook his head.

"Not at present. We're planning out the new road from Attra to Bekwando."

Francis looked up with surprise.

"Never heard of it," he said; "but there's trouble ahead for you. They are danc-ing the war-dance at Bekwando, and the King has been shut up for three days with the priest and never opened his mouth. We were on our way from the interior, and relied upon them for food and drink. They've always been friendly, but this time we barely escaped with our lives."

Trent's face grew serious. This was bad news for him, and he was thankful that they had not carried out their first plan and commenced their prospecting at Bekwando village.

"We have a charter," he said, "and, if necessary, we must fight. I'm glad to be prepared though."

"A charter!" Francis pulled himself together and looked curiously at the man who was still bending over him.

"Great Heavens!" he exclaimed, "why, you are Scarlett Trent, the man whom I met with poor Villiers in Bekwando years ago."

Trent nodded.

"We waited for you," he said, "to witness our concession. I thought that you would remember."

"I thought," Francis said slowly, "that there was something familiar about you.... I remember it all now. You were gambling with poor old Monty for his daughter's picture against a bottle of brandy."

Trent winced a little.

"You have an excellent memory," he said drily.

Francis raised himself a little, and a fiercer note crept into his tone.

"It is coming back to me," he said. "I remember more about you now, Scarlett Trent. You are the man who left his partner to die in a jungle, that you might rob him of his share in the concession. Oh yes, you see my memory is coming back! I have an account against you, my man."

"It's a lie!" said Trent passionately. "When I left him, I honestly believed him to be a dead man."

"How many people will believe that?" Francis scoffed. "I shall take Monty with me to England. I have finished with this country for awhile--and then--and then--"

He was exhausted, and sank back speechless. Trent sat and watched him, smoking in thoughtful silence. They two were a little apart from the others, and Francis was fainting. A hand upon his throat--a drop from that phial in the medicine-chest--and his faint would carry him into eternity. And still Trent sat and smoked.

CHAPTER XXVI

It was Trent himself who kept watch through that last long hour of moonlit darkness till the wan morning broke. With its faint, grey streaks came the savages of Bekwando, crawling up in a semicircle through the long, rough grass, then suddenly, at a signal, bounding upright with spears poised in their hands--an ugly sight in the dim dawn for men chilled with the moist, damp air and only half-awake. But Trent had not been caught napping. His stealthy call to arms had aroused them in time at least to crawl behind some shelter and grip their rifles. The war-cry of the savages was met with a death-like quiet--there were no signs of confusion nor terror. A Kru boy, who called out with fright, was felled to the ground by Trent with a blow which would have staggered an ox. With their rifles in hand, and every man stretched flat upon the ground, Trent's little party lay waiting. Barely a hundred yards separated them, yet there was no sign of life from the camp. The long line of savages advanced a few steps more, their spears poised above their heads, their half-naked forms showing more distinctly as they peered forward through the grey gloom, savage and ferocious. The white men were surely sleeping still. They were as near now as they could get. There was a signal and then a wild chorus of yells. They threw aside all disguise and darted forward, the still morning air hideous with their cry of battle. Then, with an awful suddenness, their cry became the cry of death, for out from the bushes belched a yellow line of fire as the rifles of Trent and his men rang out their welcome. A dozen at least of the men of Bekwando looked never again upon the faces of their wives, the rest hesitated. Trent, in whom was the love of fighting, made then his first mistake. He called for a sally, and rushed out, revolver in hand, upon the broken line. Half the blacks ran away like rabbits; the remainder, greatly outnumbering Trent and his party, stood firm. In a moment it was hand-to-hand fighting, and Trent was cursing already the bravado which had brought him out to the open.

For a while it was a doubtful combat. Then, with a shout of triumph, the chief, a swarthy, thick-set man of herculean strength, recognised Francis and sprang upon him. The blow which he aimed would most surely have killed him, but that Trent, with the butt-end of a rifle, broke its force a little. Then, turning round, he blew out the man's brains as Francis sank backwards. A dismal yell from his followers was the chief's requiem; then they turned and fled, followed by a storm of bullets as Trent's men found time to reload. More than one leaped into the air and fell forward upon their faces. The fight was over, and, when they came to look round, Francis was the only man who had suffered.

Morning had dawned even whilst they had been fighting. Little wreaths of mist were curling upwards, and the sun shone down with a cloudless, golden light, every moment more clear as the vapours melted away. Francis was lying upon his face groaning heavily; the Kru boys, to whom he was well known, were gathered in a little circle around him. Trent brushed them on one side and made a brief examination. Then he had him carried carefully into one of the tents while he went for his medicine-chest.

Preparations for a start were made, but Trent was thoughtful. For the second time within a few hours this man, in whose power it was to ruin him, lay at his mercy. That he had saved his life went for nothing. In the heat of battle there had been no time for thought or calculation. Trent had simply obeyed the generous instinct of a brave man whose blood was warm with the joy of fighting. Now it was different. Trent was seldom sentimental, but from the first he had had an uneasy presentiment concerning this man who lay now within his power and so near to death. A mutual antipathy seemed to have been born between them from the first moment when they had met in the village of Bekwando. As though it were yesterday, he remembered that leave-taking and Francis's threatening words. Trent had always felt that the man was his enemy--certainly the power to do him incalculable harm, if not to altogether ruin him, was his now. And he would not hesitate about it. Trent knew that, although broadly speaking he was innocent of any desire to harm or desert Monty, no power on earth would ever convince Francis of that. Appearances were, and always must be, overwhelmingly against him. Without interference from any one he had already formulated plans for quietly putting Monty in his rightful position, and making over to him his share in the Bekwando Syndicate. But to arrange this without catastrophe would need skill and tact; interference from any outside source would be fatal, and Francis meant to interfere--nothing would stop him. Trent walked backwards and forwards with knitted brows, glancing every now and then at the unconscious man. Francis would certainly interfere if he were allowed to recover!

CHAPTER XXVII

A fortnight afterwards Trent rode into Attra, pale, gaunt, and hollow-eyed. The whole history of those days would never be known by another man! Upon Trent they had left their mark for ever. Every hour of his time in this country he reckoned of great value--yet he had devoted fourteen days to saving the life of John Francis. Such days too--and such nights! They had carried him sometimes in a dead stupor, sometimes a raving madman, along a wild bush-track across rivers and swamps into the town of Garba, where years ago a Congo trader, who had made a fortune, had built a little white-washed hospital! He was safe now, but surely never a man before had walked so near the "Valley of the Shadow of Death." A single moment's vigilance relaxed, a blanket displaced, a dose of brandy forgotten, and Trent might have walked this life a multi-millionaire, a peer, a little god amongst his fellows, freed for ever from all anxiety. But Francis was tended as never a man was tended before. Trent himself had done his share of the carrying, ever keeping his eyes fixed upon the death-lit face of their burden, every ready to fight off the progress of the fever and ague, as the twitching lips or shivering limbs gave warning of a change. For fourteen days he had not slept; until they had reached Garba his clothes had never been changed since they had started upon their perilous journey. As he rode into Attra he reeled a little in his saddle, and he walked into the office of the Agent more like a ghost than a man.

Two men, Cathcart and his assistant, who was only a boy, were lounging in low chairs. As he entered they looked up, exchanging quick, startled glances. Then Cathcart gave vent to a little exclamation.

"Great Heavens, Trent, what have you been doing?" Trent sank into a chair. "Get me some wine," he said. "I am all right but over-tired."

Cathcart poured champagne into a tumbler. Trent emptied it at a gulp and asked for biscuits. The man's recuperative powers were wonderful. Already the deathly whiteness was passing from his cheeks.

"Where is Da Souza?" he asked.

"Gone back to England," Cathcart answered, looking out of the open casement shaded from the sun by the sloping roof. "His steamer started yesterday."

Trent was puzzled. He scarcely understood this move.

"Did he give any reason?"

Cathcart smoked for a moment in silence. After all though a disclosure would be unpleasant, it was inevitable and as well now as any time. "I think," Cathcart said, "that he has gone to try and sell his shares in the Bekwando concessions."

"Gone--to--sell--his--shares!" Trent repeated slowly. "You mean to say that he has gone straight from here to put a hundred thousand Bekwando shares upon the market?"

Cathcart nodded.

He said so!

"And why? Did he tell you that?"

"He has come to the conclusion," Cathcart said, "that the scheme is impracticable altogether and the concessions worthless. He is going to get what he can for his shares while he has the chance."

Trent drained his tumbler and lit a cigar. "So much for Da Souza," he said. "And now I should like to know, Mr. Stanley Cathcart, what the devil you and your assistant are doing shacking here in the cool of the day when you are the servants of the Bekwando Company and there's work to be done of the utmost importance? The whole place seems to be asleep. Where's your labour? There's not a soul at work. We planned exactly when to start the road. What the mischief do you mean by wasting a fortnight?"

Cathcart coughed and was obviously ill-at-ease, but he answered with some show of dignity.

"I have come to the conclusion, Mr. Trent, that the making of the road is impracticable and useless. There is insufficient labour and poor tools, no satisfactory method of draining the swampy country, and further, I don't think any one would work with the constant fear of an attack from those savages."

"So that's your opinion, is it?" Trent said grimly.

"That is my opinion," Cathcart answered. "I have embodied it in a report which I despatched to the secretary of the Company by Mr. Da Souza."

Trent rose and opened the door which swung into the little room.

"Out you go!" he said fiercely.

Cathcart looked at him in blank astonishment.

"What do you mean?" he exclaimed. "These are my quarters!"

"They're nothing of the sort," Trent answered. "They are the headquarters in this country of the Bekwando Company, with which you have nothing to do! Out you go!"

"Don't talk rubbish!" Cathcart said angrily. "I'm the authorised and properly appointed surveyor here!"

"You're a liar!" Trent answered, "you've no connection at all with the Company! you're dismissed, sir, for incompetence and cowardice, and if you're not off the premises in three minutes it'll be the worse for you!"

"You--you--haven't the power to do this," Cathcart stuttered.

Trent laughed.

"We'll see about that," he said. "I never had much faith in you, sir, and I guess you only got the job by a rig. But out you go now, sharp. If there's anything owing you, you can claim it in London.

"There are all my clothes--" Cathcart began.

Trent laid his hands upon his shoulders and threw him softly outside.

"I'll send your clothes to the hotel," he said. "Take my advice, young man, and keep out of my sight till you can find a steamer to take you where they'll pay you for doing nothing. You're the sort of man who irritates me and it's a nasty climate for getting angry in!"

Cathcart picked himself up. "Well, I should like to know who's going to make your road," he said spitefully.

"I'll make it myself," Trent roared. "Don't you think a little thing like some stupid laws of science will stand in my way, or the way of a man who knows his own mind. I tell you I'll level that road from the tree there which we marked as the starting-point to the very centre of Bekwando."

He slammed the door and re-entered the room. The boy was there, sitting upon the office stool hard at work with a pair of compasses.

"What the devil are you doing there?" Trent asked. "Out you go with your master!"

The boy looked up. He had a fair, smooth face, but lips like Trent's own.

"I'm just thinking about that first bend by Kurru corner, sir," he said, "I'm not sure about the level."

Trent's face relaxed. He held out his hand.

"My boy," he said, "I'll make your fortune as sure as my name is Scarlett Trent!"

"We'll make that road anyway," the boy answered, with a smile.

$$* \quad * \quad * \quad * \quad *$$

After a rest Trent climbed the hill to the Basle Mission House. There was no sign of Monty on the potato patch, and the woman who opened the door started when she saw him.

"How is he?" Trent asked quickly.

The woman looked at him in wonder.

"Why, he's gone, sir--gone with the Jewish gentleman who said that you had sent him."

"Where to?" Trent asked quickly.

"Why, to England in the Ophir!" the woman answered.

Then Trent began to feel that, after all, the struggle of his life was only beginning.

CHAPTER XXVIII

It was then perhaps that Trent fought the hardest battle of his life. The start was made with only a dozen Kru boys, Trent himself, stripped to the shirt, labouring amongst them spade in hand. In a week the fishing boats were deserted, every one was working on the road. The labour was immense, but the wages were magnificent. Real progress was made and the boy's calculations were faultless. Trent used the cable freely.

"Have dismissed Cathcart for incompetence--road started--progress magnificent," he wired one week, and shortly afterwards a message came back--"Cathcart cables resigned--scheme impossible--shares dropping--wire reply."

Trent clenched his fist, and his language made the boy, who had never heard him violent, look up in surprise. Then he put on his coat and walked out to the cable station.

"Cathcart lies. I dismissed him for cowardice and incompetence. The road is being made and I pledge my word that it will be finished in six months. Let our friends sell no shares."

Then Trent went back and, hard as he had worked before, he surpassed it all now. Far and wide he sent ever with the same inquiry--for labour and stores. He spent money like water, but he spent from a bottomless purse. Day after day Kru boys, natives and Europeans down on their luck, came creeping in. Far away across the rolling plain the straight belt of flint-laid road-bed stretched to the horizon, one gang in advance cutting turf, another beating in the small stones. The boy grew thin and bronzed, Trent and he toiled as though their lives hung upon the work. So they went on till the foremost gang came close to the forests, beyond which lay the village of Bekwando.

Then began the period of the greatest anxiety, for Trent and the boy and a handful of the others knew what would have sent half of the natives flying from their work if a whisper had got abroad. A few soldiers were drafted down from the Fort, arms were given out to all those who could be trusted to use them and by night men watched by the great red fires which flared along the path of their labours. Trent and the boy took it by turns to watch, their revolvers loaded by their side, and their eyes ever turned towards that dark line of forest whence came nothing but the singing of night birds and the calling of wild animals. Yet Trent would have no caution relaxed, the more they progressed, the more vigilant the watch they kept. At last came signs of the men of Bekwando. In the small hours of the morning a burning spear came hurtling through the darkness and fell with a hiss and a quiver in the ground, only a few feet from where Trent and the boy lay. Trent stamped on it hastily and gave no alarm. But the boy stole round with a whispered warning to those who could be trusted to fight.

Yet no attack came on that night or the next; on the third Trent and the boy sat talking and the latter frankly owned that he was nervous.

"It's not that I'm afraid," he said, smiling. "You know it isn't that! But all day long I've had the same feeling--we're being watched! I'm perfectly certain that the beggars are skulking round the borders of the forest there. Before morning we shall hear from them."

"If they mean to fight," Trent said, "the sooner they come out the better. I'd send a messenger to the King only I'm afraid they'd kill him. Oom Sam won't come! I've sent for him twice."

The boy was looking backwards and forwards along the long line of disembowelled earth.

"Trent," he said suddenly, "you're a wonderful man. Honestly, this road is a marvellous feat for untrained labour and with such rotten odds and ends of machinery. I don't know what experience you'd had of road-making."

"None," Trent interjected.

"Then it's wonderful!"

Trent smiled upon the boy with such a smile as few people had ever seen upon his lips.

"There's a bit of credit to you, Davenant," he said. "I'd never have been able to figure out the levelling alone. Whether I go down or not, this shall be a good step up on the ladder for you."

The boy laughed.

"I've enjoyed it more than anything else in my life," he said. "Fancy the difference between this and life in a London office. It's been magnificent! I never dreamed what life was like before."

Trent looked thoughtfully into the red embers. "You had the mail to-day," the boy continued. "How were things in London?"

"Not so bad," Trent answered. "Cathcart has been doing all the harm he can, but it hasn't made a lot of difference. My cables have been published and our letters will be in print by now, and the photographs you took of the work. That was a splendid idea!"

"And the shares?"

"Down a bit--not much. Da Souza seems to be selling out carefully a few at a time, and my brokers are buying most of them. Pound shares are nineteen shillings to-day. They'll be between three and four pounds, a week after I get back."

"And when shall you go?" the boy asked.

"Directly I get a man out here I can trust and things are fixed with his Majesty the King of Bekwando! We'll both go then, and you shall spend a week or two with me in London."

The boy laughed.

"What a time we'll have!" he cried. "Say, do you know your way round?"

Trent shook his head.

"I'm afraid not," he said. "You'll have to be my guide."

"Right you are," was the cheerful answer. "I'll take you to Jimmy's, and the Empire, and down the river, and to a match at Lord's, and to Henley if we're in time, and I'll take you to see my aunt! You'll like her."

Trent nodded.

"I'll expect to," he said. "Is she anything like you?"

"Much cleverer," the boy said, "but we've been great chums all our life. She's the cleverest woman ever knew, earns lots of money writing for newspapers.

"Here, you've dropped your cigar, Trent."

Trent groped for it on the ground with shaking fingers.

"Writes for newspapers?" he repeated slowly. "I wonder--her name isn't Davenant, is it?"

The boy shook his head.

"No, she's my mother's cousin really--only I call her Aunty, we always got on so. She isn't really much older than me, her name is Wendermott--Ernestine Wendermott. Ernestine's a pretty name, don't you think?"

Trent rose to his feet, muttering something about a sound in the forest. He stood with his back to the boy looking steadily at the dark line of outlying scrub, seeing in reality nothing, yet keenly anxious that the red light of the dancing flames should not fall upon his face. The boy leaned on his elbow and looked in the same direction. He was puzzled by a fugitive something which he had seen in Trent's face.

Afterwards Trent liked sometimes to think that it was the sound of her name which had saved them all. For, whereas his gaze had been idle at first, it became suddenly fixed and keen. He stooped down and whispered something to the boy. The word was passed along the line of sleeping men and one by one they dropped back into the deep-cut trench. The red fire danced and crackled--only a few yards outside the flame-lit space came the dark forms of men creeping through the rough grass like snakes.

CHAPTER XXIX

The attack was a fiasco, the fighting was all over in ten minutes. A hundred years ago the men of Bekwando, who went naked and knew no drink more subtle than palm wine had one virtue--bravery. But civilisation pressing upon their frontiers had brought Oom Sam greedy for ivory and gold, and Oom Sam had bought rum and strong waters. The nerve of the savage had gone, and his muscle had become a flaccid thing. When they had risen from the long grass with a horrid yell and had rushed in upon the hated intruders with couched spears only to be met by a blinding fire of Lee-Metford and revolver bullets their bravery vanished like breath from the face of a looking-glass. They hesitated, and a rain of bullets wrought terrible havoc amongst their ranks. On every side the fighting-men of Bekwando went down like ninepins--about half a dozen only sprang forward for a hand-to-hand fight, the remainder, with shrieks of despair, fled back to the shelter of the forest, and not one of them again ever showed a bold front to the white man. Trent, for a moment or two, was busy, for a burly savage, who had marked him out by the light of the gleaming flames, had sprung upon him spear in hand, and behind him came others. The first one dodged Trent's bullet and was upon him, when the boy shot him through the cheek and he went rolling over into the fire, with a death-cry which rang through the camp high above the din of fighting, another behind him Trent shot himself, but the third was upon him before he could draw his revolver and the two rolled over struggling fiercely, at too close quarters for weapons, yet with the thirst for blood fiercely kindled in both of them. For a moment Trent had the worst of it--a blow fell upon his forehead (the scar of which he never lost) and the wooden club was brandished in the air for a second and more deadly stroke. But at that moment Trent leaped up, dashed his unloaded revolver full in the man's face and, while he staggered with the shock, a soldier from behind shot him through the heart. Trent saw him go staggering backwards and then himself sank down, giddy with the blow he had received. Afterwards he knew that he must have fainted, for when he opened his eyes the sun was up and the men were strolling about looking at the dead savages who lay thick in the grass. Trent sat up and called for water.

"Any one hurt?" he asked the boy who brought him some. The boy grinned, but shook his head.

"Plenty savages killed," he said, "no white man or Kru boy."

"Where's Mr. Davenant," Trent asked suddenly.

The boy looked round and shook his head.

"No seen Mr. Dav'nant," he said. "Him fight well though! Him not hurt!"

Trent stood up with a sickening fear at his heart. He knew very well that if the boy was about and unhurt he would have been at his side. Up and down the camp he strode in vain. At last one of the Kru boys thought he remembered seeing a great savage bounding away with some one on his back. He had thought that it was one of their wounded--it might have been the boy. Trent, with a sickening sense of horror, realised the truth. The boy had been taken prisoner.

Even then he preserved his self-control to a marvellous degree. First of all he gave directions for the day's work--then he called for volunteers to accompany him to the village. There was no great enthusiasm. To fight in trenches against a foe who had no cover nor any firearms was rather a different thing from bearding them in their own lair. Nevertheless, about twenty men came forward, including a guide, and Trent was satisfied.

They started directly after breakfast and for five hours fought their way through dense undergrowth and shrubs with never a sign of a path, though here and there were footsteps and broken boughs. By noon some of the party were exhausted and lagged behind, an hour later a long line of exhausted stragglers were following Trent and the native guide. Yet to all their petitions for a rest Trent was adamant. Every minute's delay might lessen the chance of saving the boy, even now they might have begun their horrible tortures. The thought inspired him with fresh vigour. He plunged on with long, reckless strides which soon placed a widening gap between him and the rest of the party.

By degrees he began to recollect his whereabouts. The way grew less difficult-

-occasionally there were signs of a path. Every moment the soft, damp heat grew more intense and clammy. Every time he touched his forehead he found it dripping. But of these things he recked very little, for every step now brought him nearer to the end of his journey. Faintly, through the midday silence he could hear the clanging of copper instruments and the weird mourning cry of the defeated natives. A few more steps and he was almost within sight of them. He slackened his pace and approached more stealthily until only a little screen of bushes separated him from the village and, peering through them, he saw a sight which made his blood run cold within him.

They had the boy! He was there, in that fantastic circle bound hand and foot, but so far as he could see, at present unhurt. His face was turned to Trent, white and a little scared, but his lips were close-set and he uttered no sound. By his side stood a man with a native knife dancing around and singing--all through the place were sounds of wailing and lamentation, and in front of his hut the King was lying, with an empty bottle by his side, drunk and motionless. Trent's anger grew fiercer as he watched. Was this a people to stand in his way, to claim the protection and sympathy of foreign governments against their own bond, that they might keep their land for misuse and their bodies for debauchery? He looked backwards and listened. As yet there was no sign of any of his followers and there was no telling how long these antics were to continue. Trent looked to his revolver and set his teeth. There must be no risk of evil happening to the boy. He walked boldly out into the little space and called to them in a loud voice.

There was a wild chorus of fear. The women fled to the huts--the men ran like rats to shelter. But the executioner of Bekwando, who was a fetish man and holy, stood his ground and pointed his knife at Trent. Two others, seeing him firm, also remained. The moment was critical.

"Cut those bonds!" Trent ordered, pointing to the boy.

The fetish man waved his hands and drew a step nearer to Trent, his knife outstretched. The other two backed him up. Already a spear was couched.

Trent's revolver flashed out in the sunlight.

"Cut that cord!" he ordered again.

The fetish man poised his knife. Trent hesitated no longer, but shot him deliberately through the heart. He jumped into the air and fell forward upon his face with a death-cry which seemed to find an echo from every hut and from behind every tree of Bekwando. It was like the knell of their last hope, for had he not told them that he was fetish, that his body was proof against those wicked fires and that if the white men came, he himself would slay them! And now he was dead! The last barrier of their superstitious hope was broken down. Even the drunken King sat up and made strange noises.

Trent stooped down and, picking up the knife, cut the bonds which had bound the boy. He staggered up to his feet with a weak, little laugh.

"I knew you'd find me," he said. "Did I look awfully frightened?"

Trent patted him on the shoulder. "If I hadn't been in time," he said, "I'd have shot every man here and burned their huts over their heads. Pick up the knife, old chap, quick. I think those fellows mean mischief."

The two warriors who had stood by the priest were approaching, but when they came within a few yards of Trent's revolver they dropped on their knees. It was their token of submission. Trent nodded, and a moment afterwards the reason for their non-resistance was made evident. The remainder of the expedition came filing into the little enclosure.

Trent lit a cigar and sat down on a block of wood to consider what further was best to be done. In the meantime the natives were bringing yams to the white men with timid gestures. After a brief rest Trent called them to follow him. He walked across to the dwelling of the fetish man and tore down the curtain of dried grass which hung before the opening. Even then it was so dark inside that they had to light a torch before they could see the walls, and the stench was horrible.

A little chorus of murmurs escaped the lips of the Europeans as the interior became revealed to them. Opposite the door was a life-size and hideous effigy of a grinning god, made of wood and painted in many colours. By its side were other more horrible images and a row of human skulls hung from the roof. The hand of a white man, blackened with age, was stuck to the wall by a spear-head, the stench and filth of the whole place were pestilential. Yet outside a number of women and several of the men were on their knees hoping still against hope for aid from their ancient gods. There was a cry of horror when Trent unceremoniously kicked over the nearest idol--a yell of panic when the boy, with a gleam of mischief in his eyes, threw out amongst them a worm-eaten, hideous effigy and with a hearty kick stove in its hollow side. It lay there bald and ugly in the streaming sunshine, a block of misshapen wood ill-painted in flaring daubs, the thing which they had worshipped in gloom and secret, they and a generation before them--all the mystery of its shrouded existence, the terrible fetish words of the dead priest, the reverence which an all-powerful and inherited superstition had kept alive within them, came into their minds as they stood there trembling, and then fled away to be out of the reach of the empty, staring eyes--out of reach of the vengeance which must surely fall from the skies upon these white savages. So they watched, the women beating their bosoms and uttering strange cries, the men stolid but scared. Trent and the boy came out coughing, and half-stupefied with the rank odour, and a little murmur went up from them. It was a device of the gods--a sort of madness with which they were afflicted. But soon their murmurs turned again into lamentation when they saw what was to come. Men were running backwards and forwards, piling up dried wood and branches against the idol-house, a single spark and the thing was done. A tongue of flame leaped up, a thick column of smoke stole straight up in the breathless air. Amazed, the people stood and saw the home of dreadful mystery, whence came the sentence of life and death, the voice of the King-maker, the omens of war and fortune, enveloped in flames, already a ruined and shapeless mass. Trent stood and watched it, smoking fiercely and felt himself a civiliser. But the boy seemed to feel some of the pathos of the moment and he looked curiously at the little crowd of wailing natives.

"And the people?" he asked.

"They are going to help me make my road," Trent said firmly. "I am going to teach them to work!"

CHAPTER XXX

MY DEAR AUNT ERNIE,--At last I have a chance of sending you a letter--and, this time at any rate, you won't have to complain about my sending you no news. I'll promise you that, before I begin, and you needn't get scared either, because it's all good. I've been awfully lucky, and all because that fellow Cathcart turned out such a funk and a bounder. It's the oddest thing in the world too, that old Cis should have written me to pick up all the news I could about Scarlett Trent and send it to you. Why, he's within a few feet of me at this moment, and I've been seeing him continually ever since I came here. But there, I'll try and begin at the beginning.

"You know Cathcart got the post of Consulting Surveyor and Engineer to the Bekwando Syndicate, and he was head man at our London place. Well, they sent me from Capetown to be junior to him, and a jolly good move for me too. I never did see anything in Cathcart! He's a lazy sort of chap, hates work, and I guess he only got the job because his uncle had got a lot of shares in the business. It seems he never wanted to come, hates any place except London, which accounts for a good deal.

"All the time when we were waiting, he wasn't a bit keen and kept on rotting about the good times he might have been having in London, and what a fearful country we were stranded in, till he almost gave me the blues, and if there hadn't been some jolly good shooting and a few nice chaps up at the Fort, I should have been miserable. As it was, I left him to himself a good deal, and he didn't like that either. I think Attra was a jolly place, and the landing in surf boats was no end of fun. Cathcart got beastly wet, and you should have seen what a stew he was in because he'd put on a beautiful white suit and it got spoilt. Well, things weren't very lively at Attra at first, I'm bound to admit. No one seemed to know much about the

Bekwando Land Company, and the country that way was very rough. However, we got sent out at last, and Cathcart, he simply scoffed at the whole thing from the first. There was no proper labour, not half enough machinery, and none of the right sort--and the gradients and country between Bekwando and the sea were awful. Cathcart made a few reports and we did nothing but kick our heels about until HE came. You'll see I've written that in big letters, and I tell you if ever a man deserved to have his name written in capitals Scarlett Trent does, and the oddest part of it is he knows you, and he was awfully decent to me all the time.

"Well, out he went prospecting, before he'd been in the country twenty-four hours, and he came back quite cheerful. Then he spoke to Cathcart about starting work, and Cathcart was a perfect beast. He as good as told him that he'd come out under false pretences, that the whole affair was a swindle and that the road could not be made. Trent didn't hesitate, I can tell you. There were no arguments or promises with him. He chucked Cathcart on the spot, turned him out of the place, and swore he'd make the road himself. I asked if I might stop, and I think he was glad, anyhow we've been ever such pals ever since, and I never expect to have such a time again as long as I live! But do you know, Auntie, we've about made that road. When I see what we've done, sometimes I can't believe it. I only wish some of the bigwigs who've never been out of an office could see it. I know I'll hate to come away.

"You'd never believe the time we had--leaving out the fighting, which I am coming to by and by. We were beastly short of all sorts of machinery and our labour was awful. We had scarcely any at first, but Trent found 'em somehow, Kru boys and native Zulus and broken-down Europeans--any one who could hold a pick. More came every day, and we simply cut our way through the country. I think I was pretty useful, for you see I was the only chap there who knew even a bit about engineering or practical surveying, and I'd sit up all night lots of times working the thing out. We had a missionary came over the first Sunday, and wanted to preach, but Trent stopped him. 'We've got to work here,' he said, 'and Sunday or no Sunday I can't let my men stop to listen to you in the cool of the day. If you want to preach, come and take a pick now, and preach when they're resting,' and he did and worked well too, and afterwards when we had to knock off, he preached, and Trent took the chair and made 'em all listen. Well, when we got a bit inland we had the natives to deal with, and if you ask me I believe that's one reason Cathcart hated the whole thing so. He's a beastly coward I think, and he told me once he'd never let off a revolver in his life. Well, they tried to surprise us one night, but Trent was up himself watching, and I tell you we did give 'em beans. Great, ugly-looking, black chaps they were. Aunt Ernie, I shall never forget how I felt when I saw them come creeping through the long, rough grass with their beastly spears all poised ready to throw. And now for my own special adventure. Won't you shiver when you read this! I was taken prisoner by one of those chaps, carried off to their beastly village and very nearly murdered by a chap who seemed to be a cross between an executioner and a high-priest, and who kept dancing round me, singing a lot of rot and pointing a knife at me. You see, I was right on the outside of the fighting and I got a knock on the head with the butt-end of a spear, and was a bit silly for a moment, and a great chap, who'd seen me near Trent and guessed I was somebody, picked me up as though I'd been a baby and carried me off. Of course I kicked up no end of a row as soon as I came to, but what with the firing and the screeching no one heard me, and Trent said it was half an hour before he missed me and an hour before they started in pursuit. Anyhow, there I was, about morning-time when you were thinking of having your cup of tea, trussed up like a fowl in the middle of the village, and all the natives, beastly creatures, promenading round me and making faces and bawling out things--oh, it was beastly I can tell you! Then just as they seemed to have made up their mind to kill me, up strode Scarlett Trent alone, if you please, and he walked up to the whole lot of 'em as bold as brass. He'd got a long way ahead of the rest and thought they meant mischief, so he wouldn't wait for the others but faced a hundred of them with a revolver in his hand, and I can tell you things were lively then. I'd never be able to describe the next few minutes--one man Trent knocked down with his fist, and you could hear his skull crack, then he shot the chap who had been threatening me, and cut my bonds, and then they tried to resist us, and I thought it was all over. They were horribly afraid of Trent though, and while they were closing round us the others came up and the natives chucked it at once. They used to be a very brave race, but since they were able to get rum for their timber and ivory, they're a lazy and drunken lot. Well, I must tell you what Trent did then. He went to the priest's house where the gods were kept--such a beastly hole--and he burned the place before the eyes of all the natives. I believe they thought every moment that we should be struck dead, and they stood round in a ring, making an awful row, but they never dared interfere. He burnt the place to the ground, and then what do you think he did? From the King downward he made every Jack one of them come and work on his road. You'll never believe it, but it's perfectly true. They looked upon him as their conqueror, and they came like lambs when he ordered it. They think they're slaves you know, and don't understand their pay, but they get it every week and same as all the other labourers--and oh, Aunt Ernie, you should see the King work with a pickaxe! He is fat and so clumsy and so furiously angry, but he's too scared of Trent to do anything but obey orders, and there he works hour after hour, groaning, and the perspiration rolls off him as though he were in a Turkish bath. I could go on telling you odd things that happen here for hours, but I must finish soon as the chap is starting with the mail. I am enjoying it. It is something like life I can tell you, and aren't I lucky? Trent made me take Cathcart's place. I am getting 800 pounds a year, and only fancy it, he says he'll see that the directors make me a special grant. Everything looks very different here now, and I do hope the Company will be a success. There's whole heaps of mining machinery landed and waiting for the road to be finished to go up, and people seem to be streaming into the place. I wonder what Cathcart will say when he knows that the road is as good as done, and that I've got his job!

"Chap called for mail. Goodbye.

"Ever your affectionate

"FRED.

"Trent is a brick."

Ernestine read the letter slowly, line by line, word by word. To tell the truth it was absorbingly interesting to her. Already there had come rumours of the daring and blunt, resistless force with which this new-made millionaire had confronted a gigantic task. His terse communications had found their way into the Press, and in them and in the boy's letter she seemed to discover something Caesaric. That night it was more than usually difficult for her to settle down to her own work. She read her nephew's letter more than once and continually she found her thoughts slipping away--traveling across the ocean to a tropical strip of country, where a heterogeneous crowd of men were toiling and digging under a blazing sun. And, continually too, she seemed to see a man's face looking steadily over the sea to her, as he stood upright for a moment and rested from his toil. She was very fond of the boy--but the face was not his!

CHAPTER XXXI

A special train from Southampton had just steamed into Waterloo with the passengers from the Royal Mail steamer Ophir. Little groups of sunburnt men were greeting old friends upon the platform, surrounded by piles of luggage, canvas trunks and steamer chairs. The demand for hansoms was brisk, cab after cab heavily loaded was rolling out of the yard. There were grizzled men and men of fair complexion, men in white helmets and puggarees, and men in silk hats. All sorts were represented there, from the successful diamond digger who was spasmodically embracing a lady in black jet of distinctly Jewish proclivities, to a sporting lord who had been killing lions. For a few minutes the platforms were given over altogether to a sort of pleasurable confusion, a vivid scene, full of colour and human interest. Then the people thinned away, and, very nearly last of all, a wizened-looking, grey-headed man, carrying a black bag and a parcel, left the platform with hesitating footsteps and turned towards the bridge. He was followed almost immediately by Hiram Da Souza, who, curiously enough, seemed to have been on the platform when the train came in and to have been much interested in this shabby, lonely old man, who carried himself like a waif stranded in an unknown land. Da Souza was gorgeous in frock coat and silk hat, a carnation in his buttonhole, a diamond in his black satin tie, yet he was not altogether happy. This little man hobbling along in front represented fate to him. On the platform at Waterloo he had heard him timidly ask a bystander the way to the offices of the Bekwando Land and Gold Exploration Company, Limited. If ever he got there, what would be the price of Bekwando shares on the morrow?

On the bridge Da Souza saw him accost a policeman, and brushing close by, heard him ask the same question. The man shook his head, but pointed eastwards.

"I can't say exactly, sir, but somewhere in the City, for certain," he answered.

"I should make for the Bank of England, a penny 'bus along that way will take you--and ask again there."

The old man nodded his thanks and stepped along Da Souza felt that his time had come. He accosted him with an urbane smile.

"Excuse me," he said, "but I think I heard you ask for the offices of the Bekwando Land Company."

The old man looked up eagerly. "If you can direct me there, sir," he said, "I shall be greatly obliged."

"I can do so," Da Souza said, falling into step, "and will with pleasure. I am going that way myself. I hope," he continued in a tone of kindly concern, "that you are not a shareholder in the Company."

The old man dropped his bag with a clatter upon the pavement, and his lips moved for a moment without any speech coming from them. Da Souza picked up the bag and devoutly hoped that none of his City friends were in the way.

"I don't exactly know about being a shareholder," the old man said nervously, "but I've certainly something to do with it. I am, or should have been, joint vendor. The Company is wealthy, is it not?"

Da Souza changed the bag into his other hand and thrust his arm through his companion's.

"You haven't seen the papers lately, have you?"

"No! I've just landed--to-day--from Africa!"

"Then I'm sorry to say there's some bad news for you," Da Souza said. "The Bekwando Land and Gold Company has gone into liquidation--smashed up altogether. They say that all the directors and the vendor will be arrested. It seems to have been a gigantic swindle."

Monty had become a dead weight upon his arm. They were in the Strand now, and he pushed open the swing-door of a public-house, and made his way into the private bar. When Monty opened his eyes he was on a cushioned seat, and before him was a tumbler of brandy half empty. He stared round him wildly. His lips were moist and the old craving was hot upon him. What did it mean? After all he had broken his vow, then! Had he not sworn to touch nothing until he had found his little girl and his fortune? yet the fire of spirits was in his veins and the craving was tearing him to pieces. Then he remembered! There was no fortune, no little girl! His dreams were all shattered, the last effort of his life had been in vain. He caught hold of the tumbler with fingers that shook as though an ague were upon him, lifted it to his lips and drank. Then there came the old blankness, and he saw nothing but what seemed to him the face of a satyr--dark and evil--mocking him through the shadows which had surely fallen now for ever. Da Souza lifted him up and conveyed him carefully to a four-wheel cab.

*   *   *   *   *

An hour afterwards Da Souza, with a grin of content upon his unshapely mouth, exchanged his frock coat for a gaudy smoking-jacket, and, with a freshly-lit cigar in his mouth, took up the letters which had arrived by the evening post. Seeing amongst them one with an African stamp he tore it open hastily, and read:--

"MY DEAR HIRAM,--You was in luck now or never, if you really want to stop that half--witted creature from doing mischief in London. I sometimes think, my brother, that you would do better to give me even more of your confidence. You are a very clever man, but you do keep yourself so secret. If I too were not clever, how would I know to send you this news, how would I know that it will make you glad? But there, you will go your way. I know it!

"Now for the news! Monty, as I cabled (I send the bill) has gone secretly to London. Since Scarlett Trent found our Hausa friend and the rum flask, there have been no means of getting liquor to him, so I suppose he has very near regained his senses, anyhow he shipped off very cunning, not even Missionary Walsh knowing, but he made a very big mistake, the news of which I send to you knowing it will be good. Hiram, he stole the money to pay for his passage from the missionary's cash-box! All one day he stood under a tree looking out to sea, and a steamer from Capetown called, and when he heard the whistle and saw the surf boats he seemed to wake up. He walked up and down restlessly for a long time, muttering to himself. Mrs. Walsh came out to him and he was still staring at the steamer. She told him to come in out of the sun, which was very hot, but he shook his head. 'She's calling me,' he kept on saying, 'calling me!' She heard him in the room where the money was and then saw no more of him. But others saw him running to the shore, and he paid to be taken out to the steamer. They wouldn't take him on at first, because he hadn't secured a passage, but he laid down and wouldn't move. So, as he had the money, they took him, and when I heard I cabled to you. But what harm can he do, for you are his master? He is a thief and you know it. Surely you can do with him what you will.

"Trent was here yesterday and heard for the first time of his flight. How he took it I cannot tell you, for I was not the one to tell him, but this I know for a fact. He cabled to Capetown offering 100 pounds if the Star Line steamer leaving to-morrow would call for him here. Hiram, he is a great man, this Trent. I hate him, for he has spoilt much trade for me, and he treats me as though I were the dirt under his feet, but never a man before who has set foot upon the Coast could have done what he has done. Without soldiers he has beaten the Bekwando natives, and made them even work for him. He has stirred the whole place here into a state of fever! A thousand men are working upon his road and sinking shafts upon the Bekwando hills. Gold is already coming down, nuggets of it, and he is opening a depot to buy all the mahogany and ivory in the country. He spends money like water, he never rests, what he says must be done is done! The authorities are afraid of him, but day by day they become more civil! The Agent here called him once an adventurer, and threatened him with arrest for his fighting with the Bekwandos. Now they go to him cap in hand, for they know that he will be a great power in this country. And Hiram, my brother, you have not given me your trust though I speak to you so openly, but here is the advice of a brother, for blood is blood, and I would have you make monies. Don't you put yourself against Trent. Be on his side, for his is the winning side. I don't know what you got in your head about that poor scarecrow Monty, but I tell you, Hiram, Trent is the man to back right through. He has the knack of success, and he is a genius. My! he's a great man, and he's a king out here. You be on his side, Hiram, and you're all right.

"Now goodbye, but send me the money for the cable when you write, and remember--Monty is a thief and Trent is the man to back, which reminds me that Trent repaid to Missionary Walsh all the money which Monty took, which it seems was left with Walsh by him for Monty's keep. But Monty does not know that, so you have the string to make him dance.

"Which comes from your brother

"SAMUEL.

"P.S.--Do not forget the small account for disbursements."

Da Souza folded up the letter, and a look of peace shone in his face. Presently he climbed the stairs to a little back-room and noiselessly unlocked the door. Monty, with pale face and bloodshot eyes, was walking up and down, mumbling to himself. He addressed Da Souza eagerly.

"I think I will go away now," he said. "I am very much obliged to you for looking after me."

Da Souza gazed at him with well-affected gravity. "One moment first," he said, "didn't I understand you that you had just come from Africa?"

Monty nodded.

"The Gold Coast?"

Monty nodded again, but with less confidence.

"By any chance--were you called Monty there?"

Monty turned ghastly pale. Surely his last sin had not found him out. He was silent, but there was no need for speech. Da Souza motioned him to sit down.

"I am very sorry," he said, "of course it's true. The police have been here."

"The police!" Monty moaned.

Da Souza nodded. Benevolence was so rare a part for him to play, that he rather enjoyed it.

"Don't be scared," he said. "Yes, your description is out, and you are wanted for stealing a few pounds from a man named Walsh. Never mind. I won't give you up. You shall lie snug here for a few days!"

Monty fell on his knees. "You won't let any one know that I am here!" he pleaded.

"Not I," Da Souza answered fervently.

Monty rose to his feet, his face full of dumb misery.

"Now," he muttered, "I shall never see her--never--never--never!"

There was a bottle half full of spirits upon the table and a tumbler as yet unused. A gleam flashed in his eyes. He filled the tumbler and raised it to his lips. Da Souza watched him curiously with the benevolent smile still upon his face.

CHAPTER XXXII

Y ou are very smart, Ernestine," he said, looking her admiringly.

"One must be smart at Ascot," she answered, "or stay away."

"I've just heard some news," he continued.

"Yes?"

"Who do you think is here?"

She glanced at him sideways under her lace parasol. "Every one I should think."

"Including," he said, "Mr. Scarlett Trent!" She grew a shade paler, and leaned for a moment against the rail of the paddock in which they were lounging.

"I thought," she said, "that the Mazetta Castle was not due till to-day."

"She touched at Plymouth in the night, and he had a special train up. He has some horses running, you know."

"I suppose," she remarked, "that he is more of a celebrity than ever now!"

"Much more," he answered. "If he chooses he will be the lion of the season! By the by, you had nothing of interest from Fred?"

She shook her head impatiently.

"Nothing but praises! According to Fred, he's a hero!"

"I hate him," Davenant said sulkily.

"And so," she answered softly, "do I! Do you see him coming, Cecil?"

"In good company too," the young man laughed bitterly.

A little group of men, before whom every one fell back respectfully, were strolling through the paddock towards the horses. Amongst them was Royalty, and amongst them also was Scarlett Trent. But when he saw the girl in the white foulard smile at him from the paling he forgot etiquette and everything else. He walked straight across to her with that keen, bright light in his eyes which Fred had described so well in his letter.

"I am very fortunate," he said, taking the delicately gloved hand into his fingers, "to find you so soon. I have only been in England a few hours."

She answered him slowly, subjecting him the while to a somewhat close examination. His face was more sunburnt than ever she had seen a man's, but there was a wonderful force and strength in his features, which seemed to have become refined instead of coarsened by the privations through which he had passed. His hand, as she had felt, was as hard as iron, and it was not without reluctance that she felt compelled to take note of his correct attire and easy bearing. After all he must be possessed of a wonderful measure of adaptability.

"You have become famous," she said. "Do you know that you are going to be made a lion?"

"I suppose the papers have been talking a lot of rot," he answered bluntly. "I've had a fairly rough time, and I'm glad to tell you this, Miss Wendermott--I don't believe I'd ever have succeeded but for your nephew Fred. He's the pluckiest boy I ever knew."

"I am very pleased to hear it," she answered. "He's a dear boy!"

"He's a brick," Trent answered. "We've been in some queer scrapes together--I've lots of messages for you! By the by, are you alone?"

"For the moment," she answered; "Mr. Davenant left me as you came up. I'm with my cousin, Lady Tresham. She's on the lawn somewhere."

He looked down the paddock and back to her.

"Walk with me a little way," he said, "and I will show you Iris before she starts."

"You!" she exclaimed.

He pointed to the card. It was surely an accident that she had not noticed it before. Mr. Trent's Iris was amongst the entries for the Gold Cup.

"Why, Iris is the favourite!"

He nodded.

"So they tell me! I've been rather lucky haven't I, for a beginner? I found a good trainer, and I had second call on Cannon, who's riding him. If you care to back him for a trifle, I think you'll be all right, although the odds are nothing to speak of."

She was walking by his side now towards the quieter end of the paddock.

"I hear you have been to Torquay," he said, looking at her critically, "it seems to have agreed with you. You are looking well!"

She returned his glance with slightly uplifted eyebrows, intending to convey by that and her silence a rebuke to his boldness. He was blandly unconscious, however, of her intent, being occupied just then in returning the greetings of passersby. She bit her lip and looked straight ahead.

"After all," he said, "unless you are very keen on seeing Iris, I think we'd better give it up. There are too many people around her already."

"Just as you like," she answered, "only it seems a shame that you shouldn't look over your own horse before the race if you want to. Would you like to try alone?"

"Certainly not," he answered. "I shall see plenty of her later. Are you fond of horses?"

"Very."

"Go to many race-meetings?"

"Whenever I get the chance!--I always come here."

"It is a great sight," he said thoughtfully, looking around him. "Are you here just for the pleasure of it, or are you going to write about it?"

She laughed.

"I'm going to write about some of the dresses," she said. "I'm afraid no one would read my racing notes."

"I hope you'll mention your own," he said coolly. "It's' quite the prettiest here."

She scarcely knew whether to be amused or offended.

"You are a very downright person, Mr. Trent," she said.

"You don't expect me to have acquired manners yet, do you?" he answered drily.

"You have acquired a great many things," she said, "with surprising facility. Why not manners?"

He shrugged his shoulders.

"No doubt they will come, but I shall want a lot of polishing. I wonder--"

"Well?"

"Whether any one will ever think it worth while to undertake the task."

She raised her eyes and looked him full in the face. She had made up her mind exactly what to express--and she failed altogether to do it. There was a fire and a strength in the clear, grey eyes fixed so earnestly upon hers which disconcerted her altogether. She was desperately angry with herself and desperately uneasy.

"You have the power," she said with slight coldness, "to buy most things. By the by, I was thinking only just now, how sad it was that your partner did not live. He shared the work with you, didn't he? It seems such hard lines that he could not have shared the reward!"

He showed no sign of emotion such as she had expected, and for which she had been narrowly watching him. Only he grew at once more serious, and he led her a little further still from the crush of people. It was the luncheon interval, and though the next race was the most important of the day, the stream of promenaders had thinned off a little.

"It is strange," he said, "that you should have spoken to me of my partner. I have been thinking about him a good deal lately."

"In what way?"

"Well, first of all, I am not sure that our agreement was altogether a fair one," he said. "He had a daughter and I am very anxious to find her! I feel that she is entitled to a certain number of shares in the Company, and I want her to accept them."

"Have you tried to find her?" she asked.

He looked steadily at her for a moment, but her parasol had dropped a little upon his side and he could not see her face.

"Yes, I have tried," he said slowly, "and I have suffered a great disappointment. She knows quite well that I am searching for her, and she prefers to remain undiscovered."

"That sounds strange," she remarked, with her eyes fixed upon the distant Surrey hills. "Do you know her reason?"

"I am afraid," he said deliberately, "that there can be only one. It's a miserable thing to believe of any woman, and I'd be glad--"

He hesitated. She kept her eyes turned away from him, but her manner denoted impatience.

"Over on this side," he continued, "it seems that Monty was a gentleman in his day, and his people were--well, of your order! There was an Earl I believe in the family, and no doubt they are highly respectable. He went wrong once, and of course they never gave him another chance. It isn't their way--that sort of people! I'll admit he was pretty low down when I came across him, but I reckon that was the fault of those who sent him adrift--and after all there was good in him even then. I am going to tell you something now, Miss Wendermott, which I've often wanted to--that is, if you're interested enough to care to hear it!"

All the time she was asking herself how much he knew. She motioned him to proceed.

"Monty had few things left in the world worth possessing, but there was one which he had never parted with, which he carried with him always. It was the picture of his little girl, as she had been when his trouble happened."

He stooped a little as though to see over the white rails, but she was too adroit. Her face remained hidden from him by that little cloud of white lace.

"It is an odd thing about that picture," he went on slowly, "but he showed it to me once or twice, and I too got very fond of it! It was just a little girl's face, very bright and very winsome, and over there we were lonely, and it got to mean a good deal to both of us. And one night Monty would gamble--it was one of his faults, poor chap--and he had nothing left but his picture, and I played him for it--and won!"

"Brute!" she murmured in an odd, choked tone.

"Sounds so, doesn't it? But I wanted that picture. Afterwards came our terrible journey back to the Coast, when I carried the poor old chap on my back day by day, and stood over him at night potting those black beasts when they crept up too close--for they were on our track all the time. I wouldn't tell you the whole story of those days, Miss Wendermott for it would keep you awake at night; but I've a fancy for telling you this. I'd like you to believe it, for it's gospel truth. I didn't leave him until I felt absolutely and actually certain that he couldn't live an hour. He was passing into unconsciousness, and a crowd of those natives were close upon our heels. So I left him and took the picture with me--and I think since then that it has meant almost as much to me as ever it had been to him."

"That," she remarked, "sounds a little far-fetched--not to say impossible."

"Some day," he answered boldly, "I shall speak to you of this again, and I shall try to convince you that it is truth!"

He could not see her face, but he knew very well in some occult manner that she had parted with some at least of her usual composure. As a matter of fact she was nervous and ill-at-ease.

"You have not yet told me," she said abruptly, "what you imagine can be this girl's reasons for remaining unknown."

"I can only guess them," he said gravely; "I can only suppose that she is ashamed of her father and declines to meet any one connected with him. It is very wrong and very narrow of her. If I could talk to her for ten minutes and tell her how the poor old chap used to dream about her and kiss her picture, I can't think but she'd be sorry."

"Try and think," she said, looking still away from him, "that she must have another reason. You say that you liked her picture! Try and be generous in your thoughts of her for its sake."

"I will try," he answered, "especially--"

"Yes?"

"Especially--because the picture makes me think--sometimes--of you!"

CHAPTER XXXIII

Trent had done many brave things in his life, but he had never been conscious of such a distinct thrill of nervousness as he experienced during those few minutes' silence. Ernestine, for her part, was curiously exercised in her mind. He had shaken her faith in his guilt--he had admitted her to his point of view. She judged herself from his standpoint, and the result was unpleasant. She had a sudden impulse to tell him the truth, to reveal her identity, tell him her reasons for concealment. Perhaps her suspicions had been hasty. Then the personal note in his last speech had produced a serious effect on her, and all the time she felt that her silence was emboldening him, as indeed it was.

"The first time I saw you," he went on, "the likeness struck me. I felt as though I were meeting some one whom I had known all my life."

She laughed a little uneasily. "And you found yourself instead the victim of an interviewer! What a drop from the romantic to the prosaic!"

"There has never been any drop at all," he answered firmly, "and you have always seemed to me the same as that picture--something quite precious and apart from my life. It's been a poor sort of thing perhaps. I came from the people, I never had any education, I was as rough as most men of my sort, and I have done many things which I would sooner cut off my right hand than do again. But that was when I lived in the darkness. It was before you came."

"Mr. Trent, will you take me back to Lady Tresham, please?"

"In a moment," he answered gravely. "Don't think that I am going to be too rash. I know the time hasn't come yet. I am not going to say any more. Only I want you to know this. The whole success of my life is as nothing compared with the hope of one day--"

"I will not hear another word," she interrupted hastily, and underneath her white veil he could see a scarlet spot of colour in her cheeks; in her speech, too, there was a certain tremulousness. "If you will not come with me I must find Lady Tresham alone."

They turned round, but as they neared the middle of the paddock progress became almost impossible. The bell had rung for the principal race of the day and the numbers were going up. The paddock was crowded with others beside loiterers, looking the horses over and stolidly pushing their way through the little groups to the front rank. From Tattersall's came the roar of clamorous voices. All around were evidences of that excitement which always precedes a great race.

"I think," he said, "that we had better watch the race from these railings. Your gown will be spoilt in the crowd if we try to get out of the paddock, and you probably wouldn't get anywhere in time to see it."

She acquiesced silently, recognising that, although he had not alluded to it in words, he had no intention of saying anything further at present. Trent, who had been looking forward to the next few minutes with all the eagerness of a man who, for the first time in his life, runs the favourite in a great race, smiled as he realised how very content he was to stay where nothing could be seen until the final struggle was over. They took up their places side by side and leaned over the railing.

"Have you much money on Iris?" she asked.

"A thousand both ways," he answered. "I don't plunge, but as I backed her very early I got 10 to 1 and 7 to 2. Listen! They're off!"

There was a roar from across the course, followed by a moment's breathless silence. The clamour of voices from Tattersall's subsided, and in its place rose the buzz of excitement from the stands, the murmur of many voices gradually growing in volume. Far away down the straight Ernestine and Trent, leaning over the rail, could see the little coloured specks come dancing into sight. The roar of voices once more beat upon the air.

"Nero the Second wins!"

"The favourite's done!"

"Nero the Second for a monkey!"

"Nero the Second romps in!"

"Iris! Iris! Iris wins!"

It was evident from the last shout and the gathering storm of excitement that, after all, it was to be a race They were well in sight now; Nero the Second and Iris, racing neck-and-neck, drawing rapidly away from the others. The air shook with the sound of hoarse and fiercely excited voices.

"Nero the Second wins!"

"Iris wins!"

Neck-and-neck they passed the post. So it seemed at least to Ernestine and many others, but Trent shook his head and looked at her with a smile.

"Iris was beaten by a short neck," he said. "Good thing you didn't back her. That's a fine horse of the Prince's, though!"

"I'm so sorry," she cried. "Are you sure?"

He nodded and pointed to the numbers which were going up. She flashed a sudden look upon him which more than compensated him for his defeat. At least he had earned her respect that day, as a man who knew how to accept defeat gracefully. They walked slowly up the paddock and stood on the edge of the crowd, whilst a great person went out to meet his horse amidst a storm of cheering. It chanced that he caught sight of Trent on the way, and, pausing for a moment, he held out his hand.

"Your horse made a magnificent fight for it, Mr. Trent," he said. "I'm afraid I only got the verdict by a fluke. Another time may you be the fortunate one!"

Trent answered him simply, but without awkwardness. Then his horse came in and he held out his hand to the crestfallen jockey, whilst with his left he patted Iris's head.

"Never mind, Dick," he said cheerfully, "you rode a fine race and the best horse won. Better luck next time."

Several people approached Trent, but he turned away at once to Ernestine.

"You will let me take you to Lady Tresham now," he said.

"If you please," she answered quietly.

They left the paddock by the underground way. When they emerged upon the lawn the band was playing and crowds of people were strolling about under the trees.

"The boxes," Trent suggested, "must be very hot now!"

He turned down a side-walk away from the stand towards an empty seat under an elm-tree, and, after a moment's scarcely perceptible hesitation, she followed his lead. He laughed softly to himself. If this was defeat, what in the world was better?

"This is your first Ascot, is it not?" she asked.

"My first!"

"And your first defeat?"

"I suppose it is," he admitted cheerfully. "I rather expected to win, too."

"You must be very disappointed, I am afraid."

"I have lost," he said thoughtfully, "a gold cup. I have gained--"

She half rose and shook out her skirts as though about to leave him. He stopped short and found another conclusion to his sentence.

"Experience!"

A faint smile parted her lips. She resumed her seat.

"I am glad to find you," she said, "so much of a philosopher. Now talk to me for a few minutes about what you have been doing in Africa."

He obeyed her, and very soon she forgot the well dressed crowd of men and women by whom they were surrounded, the light hum of gay conversation, the band which was playing the fashionable air of the moment. She saw instead the long line of men of many races, stripped to the waist and toiling as though for their lives under a tropical sun, she saw the great brown water-jars passed down the line, men fainting beneath the burning sun and their places taken by others. She heard the shrill whistle of alarm, the beaten drum; she saw the spade exchanged for the rifle, and the long line of toilers disappear behind the natural earthwork which their labours had created. She saw black forms rise stealthily from the long, rank grass, a flight of quivering spears, the horrid battle-cry of the natives rang in her ears. The whole drama of the man's great past rose up before her eyes, made a living and real thing by his simple but vigorous language. That he effaced himself from it went for nothing; she saw him there perhaps more clearly than anything else, the central and domineering figure, a man of brains and nerve who, with his life in his hands, faced with equal immovability a herculean task and the chances of death. Certain phrases in Fred's letter had sunk deep into her mind, they were recalled very vividly by the presence of the man himself, telling his own story. She sat in the sunlight with the music in her ears, listening to his abrupt, vivid speech, and a fear came to her which blanched her cheeks and caught at her throat. The hand which held her dainty parasol of lace shook, and an indescribable thrill ran through her veins. She could no more think of this man as a clodhopper, a coarse upstart without manners or imagination. In many ways he fell short of all the usual standards by which the men of her class were judged, yet she suddenly realised that he possessed a touch of that quality which lifted him at once far over their heads, The man had genius. Without education or culture he had yet achieved greatness. By his side the men who were passing about on the lawn became suddenly puppets. Form and style, manners and easy speech became suddenly stripped of their significance to her. The man at her side had none of these things, yet he was of a greater world. She felt her enmity towards him suddenly weakened. Only her pride now could help her. She called upon it fiercely. He was the man whom she had deliberately believed to be guilty of her father's death, the man whom she had set herself to entrap. She brushed all those other thoughts away and banished firmly that dangerous kindness of manner into which she had been drifting.

And he, on his part, felt a glow of keen pleasure When he realised how the events of the day had gone in his favour. If not yet of her world, he knew now that his becoming so would be hereafter purely a matter of time. He looked up through the green leaves at the blue sky, bedappled with white, fleecy clouds, and wondered whether she guessed that his appearance here, his ownership of Iris, the studious care with which he had placed himself in the hands of a Seville Row tailor were all for her sake. It was true that she had condescended to Bohemianism, that he had first met her as a journalist, working for her living in a plain serge suit and a straw hat. But he felt sure that this had been to a certain extent a whim with her. He stole a sidelong glance at her--she was the personification of daintiness from the black patent shoes showing beneath the flouncing of her skirt, to the white hat with its clusters of roses. Her foulard gown was as simple as genius could make it, and she wore no ornaments, save a fine clasp to her waistband of dull gold, quaintly fashioned, and the fine gold chain around her neck, from which hung her racing-glasses. She was to him the very type of everything aristocratic. It might be, as she had told him, that she chose to work for her living, but he knew as though by inspiration that her people and connections were of that world to which he could never belong, save on sufferance. He meant to belong to it, for her sake--to win her! He admitted the presumption, but then it would be presumption of any man to lift his eyes to her. He estimated his chances with common sense; he was not a man disposed to undervalue himself. He knew the power of his wealth and his advantage over the crowd of young men who were her equals by birth. For he had met some of them, had inquired into their lives, listened to their jargon, and had come in a faint sort of way to understand them. It had been an encouragement to him. After all it was only serious work, life lived out face to face with the great realities of existence which could make a man. In a dim way he realised that there were few in her own class likely to satisfy Ernestine. He even dared to tell himself that those things which rendered him chiefly unfit for her, the acquired vulgarities of his rougher life, were things which he could put away; that a time would come when he would take his place confidently in her world, and that the end would be success. And all the while from out of the blue sky Fate was forging a thunderbolt to launch against him!

CHAPTER XXXIV

A nd now," she said, rising, "you really must take me to Lady Tresham! They will think that I am lost."

"Are you still at your rooms?" he asked.

She nodded.

"Yes, only I'm having them spring-cleaned for a few days. I am staying at Tresham House."

"May I come and see you there?"

The man's quiet pertinacity kindled a sort of indignation in her. The sudden weakness in her defences was unbearable.

"I think not," she answered shortly. "You don't know Lady Tresham, and they might not approve. Lady Tresham is rather old-fashioned."

"Oh, Lady Tresham is all right," he answered. "I suppose I shall see you to-night if you are staying there. They have asked me to dinner!"

She was taken aback and showed it. Again he had the advantage. He did not tell her that on his return he had found scores of invitations from people he had never heard of before.

"You are by way of going into society, then," she answered insolently.

"I don't think I've made any particular efforts," he answered.

"Money," she murmured, "is an everlasting force!"

"The people of your world," he answered, with a flash of contempt, "are the people who find it so."

She was silent then, and Trent was far from being discouraged by her momentary irritability. He was crossing the lawn now by her side, carrying himself well, with a new confidence in his air and bearing which she did not fail to take note of. The sunlight, the music, and the pleasant air of excitement were all in his veins.

He was full of the strong joy of living. And then, in the midst of it all, came a dull, crashing blow. It was as though all his castles in the air had come toppling about his ears, the blue sky had turned to stony grey and the sweet waltz music had become a dirge. Always a keen watcher of men's faces, he had glanced for a second time at a gaunt, sallow man who wore a loose check suit and a grey Homburg hat. The eyes of the two men met. Then the blood had turned to ice in Trent's veins and the ground had heaved beneath his feet. It was the one terrible chance which Fate had held against him, and she had played the card.

Considering the nature and suddenness of the blow which had fallen upon him, Trent's recovery was marvellous. The two men had come face to face upon the short turf, involuntarily each had come to a standstill. Ernestine looked from one to the other a little bewildered.

"I should like a word with you, Trent," Captain Francis said quietly.

Trent nodded.

"In five minutes," he said, "I will return here--on the other side of the band-stand, say."

Francis nodded and stood aside. Trent and Ernestine continued their progress towards the stand.

"Your friend," Ernestine remarked, "seemed to come upon you like a modern Banquo!"

Trent, who did not understand the allusion, was for once discreet.

"He is a man with whom I had dealings abroad," he said, "I did not expect him to turn up here."

"In West Africa?" she asked quickly.

Trent smiled enigmatically.

"There are many foreign countries besides Africa," he said, "and I've been in most of them. This is box No. 13, then. I shall see you this evening."

She nodded, and Trent was free again. He did not make his way at once to the band-stand. Instead he entered the small refreshment-room at the base of the building and called for a glass of brandy. He drank it slowly, his eyes fixed upon the long row of bottles ranged upon the shelf opposite to him, he himself carried back upon a long wave of thoughts to a little West African station where the moist heat rose in fever mists and where an endless stream of men passed backward and forward to their tasks with wan, weary faces and slowly dragging limbs. What a cursed chance which had brought him once more face to face with the one weak spot in his life, the one chapter which, had he the power, he would most willingly seal for ever! From outside came the ringing of a bell, the hoarse shouting of many voices in the ring, through the open door a vision of fluttering waves of colour, lace parasols and picture hats, little trills of feminine laughter, the soft rustling of muslins and silks. A few moments ago it had all seemed so delightful to him--and now there lay a hideous blot upon the day.

It seemed to him when he left the little bar that he had been there for hours, as a matter of fact barely five minutes had passed since he had left Ernestine. He stood for a moment on the edge of the walk, dazzled by the sunlight, then he stepped on to the grass and made his way through the throng. The air was full of soft, gay music, and the skirts and flounces of the women brushed against him at every step. Laughter and excitement were the order of the day. Trent, with his suddenly pallid face and unseeing eyes, seemed a little out of place in such a scene of pleasure. Francis, who was smoking a cigar, looked up as he approached and made room for him upon the seat.

"I did not expect to see you in England quite so soon, Captain Francis," Trent said.

"I did not expect," Francis answered, "ever to be in England again. I am told that my recovery was a miracle. I am also told that I owe my Life to you!"

Trent shrugged his shoulders.

"I would have done as much for any of my people," he said, "and you don't owe me any thanks. To be frank with you, I hoped you'd die."

"You could easily have made sure of it," Francis answered.

"It wasn't my way," Trent answered shortly. "Now what do you want with me?"

Francis turned towards him with a curious mixture of expressions in his face.

"Look here," he said, "I want to believe in you! You saved my life and I'm not over-anxious to do you a mischief. But you must tell me what you have done with Vill--Monty."

"Don't you know where he is?" Trent asked quickly.

"I? Certainly not! How should I?"

"Perhaps not," Trent said, "but here's the truth. When I got back to Attra Monty had disappeared--ran away to England, and as yet I've heard never a word of him. I'd meant to do the square thing by him and bring him back myself. Instead of that he gave us all the slip, but unless he's a lot different to what he was last time I saw him, he's not fit to be about alone."

"I heard that he had left," Francis said, "from Mr. Walsh."

"He either came quite alone," Trent said, "in which case it is odd that nothing has been heard of him, or Da Souza has got hold of him."

"Oom Sam's brother?"

Trent nodded.

"And his interest?" Francis asked.

"Well, he is a large shareholder in the Company," Trent said. "Of course he could upset us all if he liked. I should say that Da Souza would try all he could to keep him in the background until he had disposed of his shares."

"And how does your stock hold?"

"I don't know," Trent said. "I only landed yesterday. I'm pretty certain though that there's no market for the whole of Da Souza's holding."

"He has a large interest, then?"

"A very large one," Trent answered drily.

"I should like," Francis said, "to understand this matter properly. As a matter of fact I suppose that Monty is entitled to half the purchase-money you received for the Company."

Trent assented.

"It isn't that I grudge him that," he said, "although, with the other financial enterprises I have gone into, I don't know how I should raise half a million of money to pay him off. But don't you see my sale of the charter to the Company is itself, Monty being alive, an illegal act. The title will be wrong, and the whole affair might drift into Chancery, just when a vigorous policy is required to make the venture a success. If Monty were here and in his right mind, I think we could come to terms, but, when I saw him last at any rate, he was quite incapable, and he might become a tool to anything. The Bears might get hold of him and ruin us all. In short, it's a beastly mess!"

Francis looked at him keenly.

"What do you expect me to do?" he asked.

"I have no right to expect anything," Trent said. "However, I saved your life and you may consider yourself therefore under some obligation to me. I will tell you then what I would have you do. In the first place, I know no more where he is than you do. He may be in England or he may not. I shall go to Da Souza, who probably knows. You can come with me if you like. I don't want to rob the man of a penny. He shall have all he is entitled to--only I do want to arrange terms with him quietly, and not have the thing talked about. It's as much for the others' sake as my own. The men who came into my Syndicate trusted me, and I don't want them left."

Francis took a little silver case from his pocket, lit a cigarette, and smoked for a moment or two thoughtfully.

"It is possible," he said at last, "that you are an honest man. On the other hand you must admit that the balance of probability from my point of view is on the other side. Let us travel backwards a little way--to my first meeting with you. I witnessed the granting of this concession to you by the King of Bekwando. According to its wording you were virtually Monty's heir, and Monty was lying drunk, in a climate where strong waters and death walk hand-in-hand. You leave him in the bush, proclaim his death, and take sole possession. I find him alive, do the best I can for him, and here the first act ends. Then what afterwards? I hear of you as an empire-maker and a millionaire. Nevertheless, Monty was alive and you knew he was alive, but when I reach Attra he has been spirited away! I want to know where! You say you don't know. It may be true, but it doesn't sound like it."

Trent's under-lip was twitching, a sure sign of the tempest within, but he kept himself under restraint and said never a word.

Francis continued, "Now I do not wish to be your enemy, Scarlett Trent, or to do you an ill turn, but this is my word to you. Produce Monty within a week and open reasonable negotiations for treating him fairly, and I will keep silent. But if you can't produce him at the end of that time I must go to his relations and lay all these things before them."

Trent rose slowly to his feet.

"Give me your address," he said, "I will do what I can."

Francis tore a leaf from his pocket-book and wrote a few words upon it.

"That will find me at any time," he said. "One moment, Trent. When I saw you first you were with--a lady."

"Well!"

"I have been away from England so long," Francis continued slowly, "that my memory has suffered. Yet that lady's face was somehow familiar. May I ask her name?"

"Miss Ernestine Wendermott," Trent answered slowly.

Francis threw away his cigarette and lit another.

"Thank you," he said.

CHAPTER XXXV

Da Souza's office was neither furnished nor located with the idea of impressing casual visitors. It was in a back-street off an alley, and although within a stone's throw of Lothbury its immediate surroundings were not exhilarating. A blank wall faced it, a green-grocer's shop shared with a wonderful, cellar-like public-house the honour of its more immediate environment. Trent, whose first visit it was, looked about him with surprise mingled with some disgust.

He pushed open the swing door and found himself face to face with Da Souza's one clerk--a youth of unkempt appearance, shabbily but flashily dressed, with sallow complexion and eyes set close together. He was engaged at that particular moment in polishing a large diamond pin upon the sleeve of his coat, which operation he suspended to gaze with much astonishment at this unlooked-for visitor. Trent had come straight from Ascot, straight indeed from his interview with Francis, and was still wearing his racing-glasses.

"I wish to see Mr. Da Souza," Trent said. "Is he in?"

"I believe so, sir," the boy answered. "What name?"

"Trent! Mr. Scarlett Trent!"

The door of an inner office opened, and Da Souza, sleek and curled, presented himself. He showed all his white teeth in the smile with which he welcomed his visitor. The light of battle was in his small, keen eyes, in his cringing bow, his mock humility.

"I am most honoured, Mr. Trent, sir," he declared. "Welcome back to England. When did you return?"

"Yesterday," Trent said shortly.

"And you have come," Da Souza continued, "fresh from the triumphs of the race-course. It is so, I trust?"

"I have come straight from Ascot," Trent replied, "but my horse was beaten if that is what you mean. I did not come here to talk about racing though. I want a word with you in private."

"With much pleasure, sir," Da Souza answered, throwing open with a little flourish the door of his sanctum. "Will you step in? This way! The chair is dusty. Permit me!"

Trent threw a swift glance around the room in which he found himself. It was barely furnished, and a window, thick with dust, looked out on the dingy back-wall of a bank or some public building. The floor was uncovered, the walls were hung with yellow maps of gold-mines all in the West African district. Da Souza himself, spick and span, with glossy boots and a flower in his buttonhole, was certainly the least shabby thing in the room.

"You know very well," Trent said, "what I have come about. Of course you'll pretend you don't, so to save time I'll tell you. What have you done with Monty?"

Da Souza spread outwards the palms of his hands. He spoke with well-affected impatience.

"Monty! always Monty! What do I want with him? It is you who should look after him, not I."

Trent turned quietly round and locked the door. Da Souza would have called out, but a paroxysm of fear had seized him. His fat, white face was pallid, and his knees were shaking. Trent's hand fell upon his shoulder, and Da Souza felt as though the claws of a trap had gripped him.

"If you call out I'll throttle you," Trent said. "Now listen. Francis is in England and, unless Monty is produced, will tell the whole story. I shall do the best I can for all of us, but I'm not going to have Monty done to death. Come, let's have the truth."

Da Souza was grey now with a fear greater even than a physical one. He had been so near wealth. Was he to lose everything?

"Mr. Trent," he whispered, "my dear friend, have reason. Monty, I tell you, is only half alive, he hangs on, but it is a mere thread of life. Leave it all to me! To-morrow he shall be dead!--oh, quite naturally. There shall be no risk! Trent, Trent!"

His cry ended in a gurgle, for Trent's hand was on his throat.

"Listen, you miserable hound," he whispered. "Take me to him this moment, or I'll shake the life out of you. Did you ever know me go back from my word?"

Da Souza took up his hat with an ugly oath and yielded. The two men left the office together.

*   *   *   *   *

"Listen!"

The two women sat in silence, waiting for some repetition of the sound. This time there was certainly no possibility of any mistake. From the room above their heads came the feeble, quavering sobbing of an old man. Julie threw down her book and sprang up.

"Mother, I cannot bear it any longer," she cried. "I know where the key is, and I am going into that room."

Mrs. Da Souza's portly frame quivered with excitement.

"My child," she pleaded, "don't Julie, do remember! Your father will know, and then--oh, I shall be frightened to death!"

"It is nothing to do with you, mother," the girl said, "I am going."

Mrs. Da Souza produced a capacious pocket-handkerchief, reeking with scent, and dabbed her eyes with it. From the days when she too had been like Julie, slim and pretty, she had been every hour in dread of her husband. Long ago her spirit had been broken and her independence subdued. To her friend and confidants no word save of pride and love for her husband had ever passed her lips, yet now as she watched her daughter she was conscious of a wild, passionate wish that her fate at least might be a different one. And while she mopped her eyes and looked backward, Julie disappeared.

Even Julie, as she ascended the stairs with the key of the locked room in her hand, was conscious of unusual tremors. If her position with regard to her father was not the absolute condition of serfdom into which her mother had been ground down, she was at least afraid of him, and she remembered the strict commands he had laid upon them all. The room was not to be open save by himself. All cries and entreaties were to be disregarded, every one was to behave as though that room did not exist. They had borne it already for days, the heart-stirring moans, the faint, despairing cries of the prisoner, and she could bear it no longer. She had a tender little heart, and from the first it had been moved by the appearance of the pitiful old man, leaning so heavily upon her father's arm, as they had come up the garden walk together. She made up her mind to satisfy herself at least that his isolation was of his own choice. So she went boldly up the stairs and thrust the key into the lock. A moment's hesitation, then she threw it open.

Her first impulse, when she had looked into the face of the man who stumbled up in fear at her entrance, was to then and there abandon her enterprise--for Monty just then was not a pleasant sight to look upon. The room was foul with the odour of spirits and tobacco smoke. Monty himself was unkempt and unwashed, his eyes were bloodshot, and he had fallen half across the table with the gesture of a drunken man. At the sight of him her pity died away. After all, then, the sobbing they had heard was the maudlin crying of a drunken man. Yet he was very old, and there was something about the childish, breathless fear with which he was regarding her which made her hesitate. She lingered instead, and finding him tongue-tied, spoke to him.

"We heard you talking to yourself downstairs," she said, "and we were afraid that you might be in pain."

"Ah," he muttered, "That is all, then! There is no one behind you--no one who wants me!"

"There is no one in the house," she assured him, "save my mother and myself."

He drew a little breath which ended in a sob. "You see," he said vaguely, "I sit up here hour by hour, and I think that I fancy things. Only a little while ago I fancied that I heard Mr. Walsh's voice, and he wanted the mission-box, the wooden box with the cross, you know. I keep on thinking I hear him. Stupid, isn't it?"

He smiled weakly, and his bony fingers stole round the tumbler which stood by his side. She shook her head at him smiling, and crossed over to him. She was not afraid any more.

"I wouldn't drink if I were you," she said, "it can't be good for you, I'm sure!"

"Good," he answered slowly, "it's poison--rank poison."

"If I were you," she said, "I would put all this stuff away and go for a nice walk.

It would do you much more good."

He shook his head.

"I daren't," he whispered. "They're looking for me now. I must hide--hide all the time!"

"Who are looking for you?" she asked.

"Don't you know? Mr. Walsh and his wife! They have come over after me!"

"Why?"

"Didn't you know," he muttered, "that I am a thief?"

She shook her head.

"No, I certainly didn't. I'm very sorry!"

He nodded his head vigorously a great many times.

"Won't you tell me about it?" she asked. "Was it anything very bad?"

"I don't know," he said. "It's so hard to remember! It is something like this! I seem to have lived for such a long time, and when I look back I can remember things that happened a very long time ago, but then there seems a gap, and everything is all misty, and it makes my head ache dreadfully to try and remember," he moaned.

"Then don't try," she said kindly. "I'll read to you for a little time if you like, and you shall sit quite quiet."

He seemed not to have heard her. He continued presently--

"Once before I died, it was all I wanted. Just to have heard her speak, to have seen my little girl grown into a woman, and the sea was always there, and Oom Sam would always come with that cursed rum. Then one day came Trent and talked of money and spoke of England, and when he went away it rang for ever in my ears, and at night I heard her calling for me across the sea. So I stole out, and the great steamer was lying there with red fires at her funnel, and I was mad. She was crying for me across the sea, so I took the money!"

She patted his hand gently. There was a lump in her throat, and her eyes were wet.

"Was it your daughter you wanted so much to see?" she asked softly.

"My daughter! My little girl," he answered! "And I heard her calling to me with her mother's voice across the sea. So I took the money."

"No one would blame you very much for that, I am sure," she said cheerfully.

"You are frightening yourself needlessly. I will speak to Father, and he shall help you."

He held up his hand.

"He is hiding me," he whispered. "It is through him I knew that they were after me. I don't mind for myself, but she might get to know, and I have brought disgrace enough upon her. Listen!"

There were footsteps upon the stairs. He clung to her in an agony of terror.

"They are coming!" he cried. "Hide me! Oh, hide me!"

But she too was almost equally terrified, for she had recognised her father's tread. The door was thrown open and De Souza entered, followed by Scarlett Trent.

CHAPTER XXXVI

The old man and the girl were equally terrified, both without cause. Da Souza forgot for a moment to be angry at his daughter's disobedience; and was quick to see that her presence there was all to his advantage. Monty, as white as death, was stricken dumb to see Trent. He sank back gasping into a chair. Trent came up to him with outstretched hands and with a look of keen pity in his hard face.

"Monty, old chap," he said, "what on earth are you scared at? Don't you know I'm glad to see you! Didn't I come to Attra to get you back to England? Shake hands, partner. I've got lots of money for you and good news."

Monty's hand was limp and cold, his eyes were glazed and expressionless. Trent looked at the half-empty bottle by his side and turned savagely to Da Souza.

"You blackguard!" he said in a low tone, "you wanted to kill him, did you? Don't you know that to shut him up here and ply him with brandy is as much murder as though you stood with a knife at his throat?"

"He goes mad without something to drink," Da Souza muttered.

"He'll go mad fast enough with a bottle of brandy within reach, and you know it," Trent answered fiercely. "I am going to take him away from here."

Da Souza was no longer cringing. He shrugged his shoulders and thrust his fat little hands into his trousers pockets.

"Very well," he said darkly, "you go your own way. You won't take my advice. I've been a City man all my life, and I know a thing or two. You bring Monty to the general meeting of the Bekwando Company and explain his position, and I tell you, you'll have the whole market toppling about your ears. No concern of mine, of course. I have got rid of a few of my shares, and I'll work a few more off before the crash. But what about you? What about Scarlett Trent, the millionaire?"

"I can afford to lose a bit," Trent answered quietly, "I'm not afraid."

Da Souza laughed a little hysterically.

"You think you're a financial genius, I suppose," he said, "because you've brought a few things off. Why, you don't know the A B C of the thing. I tell you this, my friend. A Company like the Bekwando Company is very much like a woman's reputation, drop a hint or two, start just a bit of talk, and I tell you the flames'll soon do the work."

Trent turned his back upon him.

"Monty," he said, "you aren't afraid to come with me?"

Monty looked at him, perplexed and troubled.

"You've nothing to be afraid of," Trent continued. "As to the money at Mr. Walsh's house, I settled that all up with him before I left Attra. It belonged to you really, for I'd left more than that for you."

"There is no one, then," Monty asked in a slow, painful whisper, "who will put me in prison?"

"I give you my word, Monty," Trent declared, "that there is not a single soul who has any idea of the sort."

"You see, it isn't that I mind," Monty continued in a low, quivering voice, "but there's my little girl! My real name might come out, and I wouldn't have her know what I've been for anything."

"She shall not know," Trent said, "I'll promise you'll be perfectly safe with me."

Monty rose up weakly. His knees were shaking, and he was in a pitiful state. He cast a sidelong glance at the brandy bottle by his side, and his hand stole out towards it. But Trent stopped him gently but firmly.

"Not now, Monty," he said, "you've had enough of that!"

The man's hand dropped to his side. He looked into Trent's face, and the years seemed to fade away into a mist.

"You were always a hard man, Scarlett Trent," he said. "You were always hard on me!"

"Maybe so," Trent answered, "yet you'd have died in D.T. before now but for me! I kept you from it as far as I could. I'm going to keep you from it now!"

Monty turned a woebegone face around the little room.

"I don't know," he said; "I'm comfortable here, and I'm too old, Trent, to live your life. I'd begin again, Trent, I would indeed, if I were ten years younger. It's too late now! I couldn't live a day without something to keep up my strength!"

"He's quite right, Trent," Da Souza put in hastily. "He's too old to start afresh now. He's comfortable here and well looked after; make him an allowance, or give him a good lump sum in lieu of all claims. I'll draw it out; you'll sign it, won't you, Monty? Be reasonable, Trent! It's the best course for all of us!"

But Trent shook his head. "I have made up my mind," he said. "He must come with me. Monty, there is the little girl!

"Too late," Monty moaned; "look at me!"

"But if you could leave her a fortune, make her magnificent presents?"

Monty wavered then. His dull eyes shone once more!

"If I could do that," he murmured.

"I pledge my word that you shall," Trent answered. Monty rose up.

"I am ready," he said simply. "Let us start at once."

Da Souza planted himself in front of them.

"You defy me!" he said. "You will not trust him with me or take my advice. Very well, my friend! Now listen! You want to ruin me! Well, if I go, the Bekwando Company shall go too, you understand! Ruin for me shall mean ruin for Mr. Scarlett Trent--ah, ruin and disgrace. It shall mean imprisonment if I can bring it about, and I have friends! Don't you know that you are guilty of fraud? You sold what wasn't yours and put the money in your pocket! You left your partner to rot in a fever swamp, or to be done to death by those filthy blacks. The law will call that swindling! You will find yourself in the dock, my friend, in the prisoners' dock, I say! Come, how do you like that, Mr. Scarlett Trent? If you leave this room with him, you are a ruined man. I shall see to it."

Trent swung him out of the way--a single contemptuous turn of the wrist, and Da Souza reeled against the mantelpiece. He held out his hand to Monty and they left the room together.

CHAPTER XXXVII

From a conversational point of view," Lady Tresham remarked, "our guest to-night seems scarcely likely to distinguish himself."

Ernestine looked over her fan across the drawing-room.

"I have never seen such an alteration in a man," she said, "in so short a time. This morning he amazed me. He knew the right people and did the right things--carried himself too like a man who is sure of himself. To-night he is simply a booby."

"Perhaps it is his evening clothes," Lady Tresham remarked, "they take some getting used to, I believe."

"This morning," Ernestine said, "he had passed that stage altogether. This is, I suppose, a relapse! Such a nuisance for you!"

Lady Tresham rose and smiled sweetly at the man who was taking her in.

"Well, he is to be your charge, so I hope you may find him more amusing than he looks," she answered.

It was an early dinner, to be followed by a visit to a popular theatre. A few hours ago Trent was looking forward to his evening with the keenest pleasure--now he was dazed--he could not readjust his point of view to the new conditions. He knew very well that it was his wealth, and his wealth only, which had brought him as an equal amongst these people, all, so far as education and social breeding was concerned, of so entirely a different sphere. He looked around the table. What would they say if they knew? He would be thrust out as an interloper. Opposite to him was a Peer who was even then engaged in threading the meshes of the Bankruptcy Court, what did they care for that?--not a whit! He was of their order though he was a beggar. But as regards himself, he was fully conscious of the difference. The measure of his wealth was the measure of his standing amongst them. Without it he would be thrust forth--he could make no claim to association with them. The thought filled him with a slow, bitter anger. He sent away his soup untasted, and he could not find heart to speak to the girl who had been the will-o'-the-wisp leading him into this evil plight.

Presently she addressed him.

"Mr. Trent!"

He turned round and looked at her.

"Is it necessary for me to remind you, I wonder," she said, "that it is usual to address a few remarks--quite as a matter of form, you know--to the woman whom you bring in to dinner?"

He eyed her dispassionately.

"I am not used to making conversation," he said. "Is there anything in the world which I could talk about likely to interest you?"

She took a salted almond from a silver dish by his side and smiled sweetly upon him. "Dear me!" she said, "how fierce! Don't attempt it if you feel like that, please! What have you been doing since I saw you last?--losing your money or your temper, or both?"

He looked at her with a curiously grim smile.

"If I lost the former," he said, "I should very soon cease to be a person of interest, or of any account at all, amongst your friends."

She shrugged her shoulders.

"You do not strike one," she remarked, "as the sort of person likely to lose a fortune on the race-course."

"You are quite right," he answered, "I think that I won money. A couple of thousand at least."

"Two thousand pounds!" She actually sighed, and lost her appetite for the oyster patty with which she had been trifling. Trent looked around the table.

"At the same time," he continued in a lower key, "I'll make a confession to you, Miss Wendermott, I wouldn't care to make to any one else here. I've been pretty lucky as you know, made money fast--piled it up in fact. To-day, for the first time, I have come face to face with the possibility of a reverse."

"Is this a new character?" she murmured. "Are you becoming faint-hearted?"

"It is no ordinary reverse," he said slowly. "It is collapse--everything!"

"O--oh!"

She looked at him attentively. Her own heart was beating. If he had not been engrossed by his care lest any one might over-hear their conversation, he would have been astonished at the change in her face.

"You are talking in enigmas surely," she said. "Nothing of that sort could possibly happen to you. They tell me that the Bekwando Land shares are priceless, and that you must make millions."

"This afternoon," he said, raising his glass to his lips and draining it, "I think that I must have dozed upon the lawn at Ascot. I sat there for some time, back amongst the trees, and I think that I must have fallen to sleep. There was a whisper in my ears and I saw myself stripped of everything. How was it? I forget now! A concession repudiated, a bank failure, a big slump--what does it matter? The money was gone, and I was simply myself again, Scarlett Trent, a labourer, penniless and of no account."

"It must have been an odd sensation," she said thoughtfully.

"I will tell you what it made me realise," he said. "I am drifting into a dangerous position. I am linking myself to a little world to whom, personally, I am as nothing and less than nothing. I am tolerated for my belongings! If by any chance I were to lose these, what would become of me?"

"You are a man," she said, looking at him earnestly; "you have the nerve and wits of a man, what you have done before you might do again."

"In the meantime I should be ostracised."

"By a good many people, no doubt."

He held his peace for a time, and ate and drank what was set before him. He was conscious that his was scarcely a dinner-table manner. He was too eager, too deeply in earnest. People opposite were looking at them, Ernestine talked to her vis-a-vis. It was some time before he spoke again, when he did he took up the thread of their conversation where he had left it.

"By the majority, of course," he said. "I have wondered sometimes whether there might be any one who would be different."

"I should be sorry," she said demurely.

"Sorry, yes; so would the tradespeople who had had my money and the men who call themselves my friends and forget that they are my debtors."

"You are cynical."

"I cannot help it," he answered. "It is my dream. To-day, you know, I have stood face to face with evil things."

"Do you know," she said, "I should never have called you a dreamer, a man likely to fancy things. I wonder if anything has really happened to make you talk like this?"

He flashed a quick glance at her underneath his heavy brows. Nothing in her face betrayed any more than the most ordinary interest in what he was saying. Yet somehow, from that moment, he had uneasy doubts concerning her, whether there might be by any chance some reason for the tolerance and the interest with which she had regarded him from the first. The mere suspicion of it was a shock to him. He relapsed once more into a state of nervous silence. Ernestine yawned, and her hostess threw more than one pitying glance towards her.

Afterwards the whole party adjourned to the theatre, altogether in an informal manner. Some of the guests had carriages waiting, others went down in hansoms. Ernestine was rather late in coming downstairs and found Trent waiting for her in the hall. She was wearing a wonderful black satin opera cloak with pale green lining, her maid had touched up her hair and wound a string of pearls around her neck. He watched her as she came slowly down the stairs, buttoning her gloves, and looking at him with eyebrows faintly raised to see him waiting there alone. After all, what folly! Was it likely that wealth, however great, could ever make him of her world, could ever bring him in reality one degree nearer to her? That night he had lost all confidence. He told himself that it was the rankest presumption to even think of her.

"The others," he said, "have gone on. Lady Tresham left word that I was to take you."

She glanced at the old-fashioned clock which stood in the corner of the hall.

"How ridiculous to have hurried so!" she said. "One might surely be comfortable here instead of waiting at the theatre."

She walked towards the door with him. His own little night-brougham was waiting there, and she stepped into it.

"I am surprised at Lady Tresham," she said, smiling. "I really don't think that I am at all properly chaperoned. This comes, I suppose, from having acquired a character for independence."

Her gown seemed to fill the carriage--a little sea of frothy lace and muslin. He hesitated on the pavement.

"Shall I ride outside?" he suggested. "I don't want to crush you."

She gathered up her skirt at once and made room for him. He directed the driver and stepped in beside her.

"I hope," she said, "that your cigarette restored your spirits. You are not going to be as dull all the evening as you were at dinner, are you?"

He sighed a little wistfully. "I'd like to talk to you," he said simply, "but somehow to-night... you know it was much easier when you were a journalist from the 'Hour'."

"Well, that is what I am now," she said, laughing. "Only I can't get away from all my old friends at once. The day after to-morrow I shall be back at work."

"Do you mean it?" he asked incredulously.

"Of course I do! You don't suppose I find this sort of thing particularly amusing, do you? Hasn't it ever occurred to you that there must be a terrible sameness about people who have been brought up amongst exactly the same surroundings and taught to regard life from exactly the same point of view?"

"But you belong to them--you have their instincts."

"I may belong to them in some ways, but you know that I am a revolted daughter. Haven't I proved it? Haven't I gone out into the world, to the horror of all my relatives, for the sole purpose of getting a firmer grip of life? And yet, do you know, Mr. Trent, I believe that to-night you have forgotten that. You have remembered my present character only, and, in despair of interesting a fashionable young lady, you have not talked to me at all, and I have been very dull."

"It is quite true," he assented. "All around us they were talking of things of which I knew nothing, and you were one of them."

"How foolish! You could have talked to me about Fred and the road-making in Africa and I should have been more interested than in anything they could have said to me."

They were passing a brilliantly-lit corner, and the light flashed upon his strong, set face with its heavy eyebrows and firm lips. He leaned back and laughed hoarsely. Was it her fancy, she wondered, or did he seem not wholly at his ease.

"Haven't I told you a good deal? I should have thought that Fred and I between us had told you all about Africa that you would care to hear."

She shook her head. What she said next sounded to him, in a certain sense, enigmatic.

"There is a good deal left for you to tell me," she said. "Some day I shall hope to know everything."

He met her gaze without flinching.

"Some day," he said, "I hope you will."

CHAPTER XXXVIII

The carriage drew up at the theatre and he handed her out--a little awkwardly perhaps, but without absolute clumsiness. They found all the rest of the party already in their seats and the curtain about to go up. They took the two end stalls, Trent on the outside. One chair only, next to him, remained unoccupied.

"You people haven't hurried," Lady Tresham remarked, leaning forward.

"We are in time at any rate," Ernestine answered, letting her cloak fall upon the back of the stall.

The curtain was rung up and the play began. It was a modern society drama, full of all the most up-to-date fashionable jargon and topical illusions. Trent grew more and more bewildered at every moment. Suddenly, towards the end of the first act, a fine dramatic situation leaped out like a tongue of fire. The interest of the whole audience, up to then only mildly amused, became suddenly intense. Trent sat forward in his seat. Ernestine ceased to fan herself. The man and the woman stood face to face--the light badinage which had been passing between them suddenly ended--the man, with his sin stripped bare, mercilessly exposed, the woman, his accuser, passionately eloquent, pouring out her scorn upon a mute victim. The audience knew what the woman in the play did not know, that it was for love of her that the man had sinned, to save her from a terrible danger which had hovered very near her life. The curtain fell, the woman leaving the room with a final taunt flung over her shoulder, the man seated at a table looking steadfastly into the fire with fixed, unseeing eyes. The audience drew a little breath and then applauded; the orchestra struck up and a buzz of conversation began.

It was then that Ernestine first noticed how absorbed the man at her side had become. His hands were gripping the arms of the stall, his eyes were fixed upon the spot somewhere behind the curtain where this sudden little drama had been played out, as though indeed they could pierce the heavy upholstery and see beyond into the room where the very air seemed quivering still with the vehemence of the woman's outpoured scorn. Ernestine spoke to him at last, the sound of her voice brought him back with a start to the present.

"You like it?"

"The latter part," he answered. "What a sudden change! At first I thought it rubbish, afterwards it was wonderful!"

"Hubert is a fine actor," she remarked, fanning herself. "It was his first opportunity in the play, and he certainly took advantage of it."

He turned deliberately round in his seat towards her, and she was struck with the forceful eagerness of his dark, set face.

"The man," he whispered hoarsely, "sinned for the love of the woman. Was he right? Would a woman forgive a man who deceived her for her own sake--when she knew?"

Ernestine held up her programme and studied it deeply.

"I cannot tell," she said, "it depends."

Trent drew a little breath and turned away. A quiet voice from his other side whispered in his ear--"The woman would forgive if she cared for the man."

*   *   *   *   *

Trent turned sharply and the light died out of his voice. Surely it was an evil omen, this man's coming; for it was Captain Francis who had taken the vacant seat and who was watching his astonishment with a somewhat saturnine smile.

"Rather a stupid play, isn't it? By the by, Trent, I wish you would ask Miss Wendermott's permission to present me. I met her young cousin out at Attra."

Ernestine heard and leaned forward smiling. Trent did as he was asked, with set teeth and an ill grace. From then, until the curtain went up for the next act, he had only to sit still and listen.

Afterwards the play scarcely fulfilled the promise of its commencement. At the third act Trent had lost all interest in it. Suddenly an idea occurred to him. He drew a card from his pocket and, scribbling a word or two on it, passed it along to Lady

Tresham. She leaned forward and smiled approval upon him.

"Delightful!"

Trent reached for his hat and whispered in Ernestine's ear.

"You are all coming to supper with me at the 'Milan,'" he said; "I am going on now to see about it."

She smiled upon him, evidently pleased.

"What a charming idea! But do you mean all of us?"

"Why not?"

He found his carriage outside without much difficulty and drove quickly round to the Milan Restaurant. The director looked doubtful.

"A table for eighteen, sir! It is quite too late to arrange it, except in a private room."

"The ladies prefer the large room," Trent answered decidedly, "and you must arrange it somehow. I'll give you carte blanche as to what you serve, but it must be of the best."

The man bowed. This must be a millionaire, for the restaurant was the "Milan."

"And the name, sir?"

"Scarlett Trent--you may not know me, but Lady Tresham, Lord Colliston, and the Earl of Howton are amongst my guests."

The man saw no more difficulties. The name of Scarlett Trent was the name which impressed him. The English aristocrat he had but little respect for, but a millionaire was certainly next to the gods.

"We must arrange the table crossways, sir, at the end of the room," he said. "And about the flowers?"

"The best, and as many as you can get," Trent answered shortly. "I have a 100 pound note with me. I shall not grumble if I get little change out of it, but I want value for the money."

"You shall have it, sir!" the man answered significantly--and he kept his word.

Trent reached the theatre only as the people were streaming out. In the lobby he came face to face with Ernestine and Francis. They were talking together earnestly, but ceased directly they saw him.

"I have been telling Captain Francis," Ernestine said, "of your delightful invitation."

"I hope that Captain Francis will join us," Trent said coldly.

Francis stepped behind for a moment to light a cigarette.

"I shall be delighted," he answered.

*   *   *   *   *

The supper party was one of those absolute and complete successes which rarely fall to the lot of even the most carefully thought out of social functions. Every one of Lady Tresham's guests had accepted the hurried invitation, every one seemed in good spirits, and delighted at the opportunity of unrestrained conversation after several hours at the theatre. The supper itself, absolutely the best of its kind, from the caviare and plovers' eggs to the marvellous ices, and served in one of the handsomest rooms in London, was really beyond criticism. To Trent it seemed almost like a dream, as he leaned back in his chair and looked down at the little party--the women with their bare shoulders and jewels, bathed in the soft glow of the rose-shaded electric lights, the piles of beautiful pink and white flowers, the gleaming silver, and the wine which frothed in their glasses. The music of the violins on the balcony blended with the soft, gay voices of the women. Ernestine was by his side, every one was good-humoured and enjoying his hospitality. Only one face at the table was a reminder of the instability of his fortunes--a face he had grown to hate during the last few hours with a passionate, concentrated hatred. Yet the man was of the same race as these people, his connections were known to many of them, he was making new friends and reviving old ties every moment. During a brief lull in the conversation his clear, soft voice suddenly reached Trent's ears. He was telling a story.

"Africa," he was saying, "is a country of surprises. Attra seems to be a city of hopeless exile for all white people. Last time I was there I used to notice every day a very old man making a pretence of working in a kitchen garden attached to a little white mission-house--a Basle Society depot. He always seemed to be leaning on his spade, always gazing out seawards in the same intent, fascinated way. Some one told me his history at last. He was an Englishman of good position who had got into trouble in his younger days and served a term of years in prison. When he came out, sooner than disgrace his family further, he published a false account of his death and sailed under a disguised name for Africa. There he has lived ever since, growing older and sinking lower, often near fortune but always missing it, a slave to bad habits, weak and dissolute if you like, but ever keeping up his voluntary sacrifice, ever with that unconquerable longing for one last glimpse of his own country and his own people. I saw him, not many months ago, still there, still with his eyes turned seawards and with the same wistful droop of the head. Somehow I can't help thinking that that old man was also a hero."

The tinkling of glasses and the sort murmuring of whispered conversation had ceased during Francis' story. Every one was a little affected--the soft throbbing of the violins upon the balcony was almost a relief. Then there was a little murmur of sympathetic remarks--but amongst it all Trent sat at the head of the table with white, set face but with red fire before his eyes. This man had played him false. He dared not look at Ernestine--only he knew that her eyes were wet with tears and that her bosom was heaving.

The spirits of men and women who sup are mercurial things, and it was a gay leave-taking half an hour or so later in the little Moorish room at the head of the staircase. But Ernestine left her host without even appearing to see his outstretched hand, and he let her go without a word. Only when Francis would have followed her Trent laid a heavy hand upon his shoulder.

"I must have a word with you, Francis," he said.

"I will come back," he said. "I must see Miss Wendermott into her carriage."

But Trent's hand remained there, a grip of iron from which there was no escaping. He said nothing, but Francis knew his man and had no idea of making a scene. So he remained till the last had gone and a tall, black servant had brought their coats from the cloak-room.

"You will come with me please," Trent said, "I have a few words to say to you."

Francis shrugged his shoulders and obeyed.

CHAPTER XXXIX

Scarcely a word passed between the two men until they found themselves in the smoking-room of Trent's house. A servant noiselessly arranged decanters and cigars upon the sideboard, and, in response to an impatient movement of Trent's, withdrew. Francis lit a cigarette. Trent, contrary to his custom, did not smoke. He walked to the door and softly locked it. Then he returned and stood looking down at his companion.

"Francis," he said, "you have been my enemy since the day I saw you first in Bekwando village."

"Scarcely that," Francis objected. "I have distrusted you since then if you like."

"Call it what you like," Trent answered. "Only to-night you have served me a scurvy trick. You were a guest at my table and you gave me not the slightest warning. On the contrary, this morning you offered me a week's respite."

"The story I told," Francis answered, "could have had no significance to them."

"I don't know whether you are trying to deceive me or not," Trent said, "only if you do not know, let me tell you--Miss Wendermott is that old man's daughter!"

The man's start was real. There was no doubt about that. "And she knew?"

"She knew that he had been in Africa, but she believed that he had died there. What she believes at this moment I cannot tell. Your story evidently moved her. She will probably try to find out from you the truth."

Francis nodded.

"She has asked me to call upon her to-morrow."

"Exactly. Now, forgive my troubling you with personal details, but you've got to understand. I mean Miss Wendermott to be my wife."

Francis sat up in his chair genuinely surprised. Something like a scowl was on his dark, sallow face.

"Your wife!" he exclaimed, "aren't you joking, Trent?"

"I am not," Trent answered sharply. "From the moment I saw her that has been my fixed intention. Every one thinks of me as simply a speculator with the money fever in my veins. Perhaps that was true once. It isn't now! I must be rich to give her the position she deserves. That's all I care for money.'"

"I am very much interested," Francis said slowly, "to hear of your intentions. Hasn't it occurred to you, however, that your behaviour toward Miss Wendermott's father will take a great deal of explanation?"

"If there is no interference," Trent said, "I can do it. There is mystery on her part too, for I offered a large reward and news of him through my solicitor, and she actually refused to reply. She has refused any money accruing to her through her father, or to be brought into contact with any one who could tell her about him."

"The fact," Francis remarked drily, "is scarcely to her credit. Monty may have been disreputable enough, I've no doubt he was; but his going away and staying there all these years was a piece of noble unselfishness."

"Monty has been hardly used in some ways," Trent said. "I've done my best by him, though."

"That," Francis said coldly, "is a matter of opinion."

"I know very well," Trent answered, "what yours is. You are welcome to it. You can blackguard me all round London if you like in a week--but I want a week's grace."

"Why should I grant it you?"

Trent shrugged his shoulders.

"I won't threaten," he said, "and I won't offer to bribe you, but I've got to have that week's grace. We're both men, Francis, who've been accustomed to our own way, I think. I want to know on what terms you'll grant it me."

Francis knocked the ash off his cigarette and rose slowly to his feet.

"You want to know," he repeated meditatively, "on what terms I'll hold my tongue for a week. Well, here's my answer! On no terms at all!"

"You don't mean that," Trent said quietly.

"We shall see," Francis answered grimly. "I'll be frank with you, Trent. When we came in here you called me your enemy. Well, in a sense you were right. I distrusted and disliked you from the moment I first met you in Bekwando village with poor old Monty for a partner, and read the agreement you had drawn up and the clause about the death of either making the survivor sole legatee. In a regular fever swamp Monty was drinking poison like water--and you were watching. That may have seemed all right to you. To me it was very much like murder. It was my mistrust of you which made me send men after you both through the bush, and, sure enough, they found poor Monty abandoned, left to die while you had hastened off to claim your booty. After that I had adventures enough of my own for a bit and I lost sight of you until I came across you and your gang road-making, and I am bound to admit that you saved my life. That's neither here nor there. I asked about Monty and you told me some plausible tale. I went to the place you spoke of--to find him of course spirited away. We have met again in England, Scarlett Trent, and I have asked once more for Monty. Once more I am met with evasions. This morning I granted you a week--now I take back my word. I am going to make public what I know to-morrow morning."

"Since this morning, then," Trent said, "your ill-will toward me has increased."

"Quite true," Francis answered. "We are playing with the cards upon the table, so I will be frank with you. What you told me about your intentions towards Miss Wendermott makes me determined to strike at once!"

"You yourself, I fancy," Trent said quietly, "admired her?"

"More than any woman I have ever met," Francis answered promptly, "and I consider your attitude towards her grossly presumptuous."

Trent stood quite still for a moment--then he unlocked the door.

"You had better go, Francis," he said quietly. "I have a defence prepared but I will reserve it. And listen, when I locked that door it was with a purpose. I had no mind to let you leave as you are leaving. Never mind. You can go--only be quick."

Francis paused upon the threshold. "You understand," he said significantly.

"I understand," Trent answered.

*   *   *   *   *

An hour passed, and Trent still remained in the chair before his writing-table, his head upon his hand, his eyes fixed upon vacancy. Afterwards he always thought of that hour as one of the bitterest of his life. A strong and self-reliant man, he had all his life ignored companionship, had been well content to live without friends, self-contained and self-sufficient. To-night the spectre of a great loneliness sat silently by his side! His heart was sore, his pride had been bitterly touched, the desire and the whole fabric of his life was in imminent and serious danger.

The man who had left him was an enemy and a prejudiced man, but Trent knew that he was honest. He was the first human being to whom he had ever betrayed the solitary ambition of his life, and his scornful words seemed still to bite the air. If--he was right! Why not? Trent looked with keen, merciless eyes through his past, and saw never a thing there to make him glad. He had started life a workman, with a few ambitions' all of a material nature--he had lived the life of a cold, scheming money-getter, absolutely selfish, negatively moral, doing little evil perhaps, but less good. There was nothing in his life to make him worthy of a woman's love, most surely there was nothing which could ever make it possible that such a woman as Ernestine Wendermott should ever care for him. All the wealth of Africa could never make him anything different from what he was. And yet, as he sat and realised this, he knew that he was writing down his life a failure. For, beside his desire for her, there were no other things he cared for in life. Already he was weary of financial warfare--the City life had palled upon him. He looked around the magnificent room in the mansion which his agents had bought and furnished for him. He looked at the pile of letters waiting for him upon his desk, little square envelopes many of them, but all telling the same tale, all tributes to his great success, and the mockery of it all smote hard upon the walls of his fortitude. Lower and lower his head drooped until it was buried in his folded arms--and the hour which followed he always reckoned the bitterest of his life.

CHAPTER XL

A little earlier than usual next morning Trent was at his office in the City, prepared for the worst, and in less than half an hour he found himself face to face with one of those crises known to most great financiers at some time or other during their lives. His credit was not actually assailed, but it was suspended. The general public did not understand the situation, even those who were in a measure behind the scenes found it hard to believe that the attack upon the Bekwando Gold and Land shares was purely a personal one. For it was Da Souza who had fired the train, who had flung his large holding of shares upon the market, and, finding them promptly taken up, had gone about with many pious exclamations of thankfulness and sinister remarks. Many smaller holders followed suit, and yet never for a moment did the market waver. Gradually it leaked out that Scarlett Trent was the buyer, and public interest leaped up at once. Would Trent be able to face settling-day without putting his vast holdings upon the market? If so the bulls were going to have the worst knock they had had for years--and yet--and yet--the murmur went round from friend to friend--"Sell your Bekwandos."

At midday there came an urgent message from Trent's bankers, and as he read it he cursed. It was short but eloquent.

"DEAR SIR,--We notice that your account to-day stands 119,000 pounds overdrawn, against which we hold as collateral security shares in the Bekwando Land Company to the value of 150,000 pounds. As we have received certain very disquieting information concerning the value of these shares, we must ask you to adjust the account before closing hours to-day, or we shall be compelled to place the shares upon the market.

"Yours truly,

"A. SINCLAIR, General Manager."

Trent tore the letter into atoms, but he never quailed. Telegraph and telephone worked his will, he saw all callers, a cigar in his mouth and flower in his buttonhole, perfectly at his ease, sanguine and confident. A few minutes before closing time he strolled into the bank and no one noticed a great bead of perspiration which stood out upon his forehead. He made out a credit slip for 119,000 pounds, and, passing it across the counter with a roll of notes and cheques, asked for his shares.

They sent for the manager. Trent was ushered with much ceremony into his private room. The manager was flushed and nervous.

"I am afraid you must have misunderstood my note, Mr. Trent," he stammered. But Trent, remembering all that he had gone through to raise the money, stopped him short.

"This is not a friendly call, Mr. Sinclair," he said, "but simply a matter of business. I wish to clear my account with you to the last halfpenny, and I will take my shares away with me. I have paid in the amount I owe. Let one of your clerks make out the interest account."

The manager rang the bell for the key of the security safe. He opened it and took out the shares with fingers which trembled a good deal.

"Did I understand you, Mr. Trent, that you desired to absolutely close the account?" he asked.

"Most decidedly," Trent answered.

"We shall be very sorry to lose you."

"The sorrow will be all on your side, then," Trent answered grimly. "You have done your best to ruin me, you and that blackguard Da Souza, who brought me here. If you had succeeded in lumping those shares upon the market to-day or to-morrow, you know very well what the result would have been. I don't know whose game you have been playing, but I can guess!"

"I can assure you, Mr. Trent," the manager declared in his suavest and most professional manner, "that you are acting under a complete misapprehension. I will admit that our notice was a little short. Suppose we withdraw it altogether, eh? I am quite satisfied. We will put back the shares in the safe and you shall keep your money."

"No, I'm d--d if you do!" Trent answered bluntly. "You've had your money and I'll have the shares. I don't leave this bank without them, and I'll be shot if ever I enter it again."

So Trent, with his back against the wall and not a friend to help him, faced for twenty-four hours the most powerful bull syndicate which had ever been formed against a single Company. Inquiries as to his right of title had poured in upon him, and to all of them he had returned the most absolute and final assurances. Yet he knew when closing-time came, that he had exhausted every farthing he possessed in the world--it seemed hopeless to imagine that he could survive another day. But with the morning came a booming cable from Bekwando. There had been a great find of gold before ever a shaft had been sunk; an expert, from whom as yet nothing had been heard, wired an excited and wonderful report. Then the men who had held on to their Bekwandos rustled their morning papers and walked smiling to their offices. Prices leaped up. Trent's directors ceased to worry him and wired invitations to luncheon at the West End. The bulls were the sport of everybody. When closing-time came Trent had made 100,000 pounds, and was looked upon everywhere as one of the rocks of finance.

Only then he began to realise what the strain had been to him. His hard, impassive look had never altered, he had been seen everywhere in his accustomed City haunts, his hat a little better brushed than usual, his clothes a little more carefully put on, his buttonhole more obvious and his laugh readier. No one guessed the agony through which he had passed, no one knew that he had spent the night at a little inn twelve miles away, to which he had walked after nine o'clock at night. He had not a single confidant, even his cashier had no idea whence came the large sums of money which he had paid away right and left. But when it was all over he left the City, and, leaning back in the corner of his little brougham, was driven away to Pont Street. Here he locked himself in his room, took off his coat and threw himself upon a sofa with a big cigar between his teeth.

"If you let any one in to see me, Miles," he told the footman, "I'll kick you out of the house." So, though the bell rang often, he remained alone. But as he lay there with half-closed eyes living again through the tortures of the last few hours, he heard a voice that startled him. It was surely hers--already! He sprang up and opened the door. Ernestine and Captain Francis were in the hall.

He motioned them to follow him into the room. Ernestine was flushed and her eyes were very bright. She threw up her veil and faced him haughtily. "Where is he?" she asked. "I know everything. I insist upon seeing him at once."

"That," he said coolly, "will depend upon whether he is fit to see you!"

He rang the bell.

"Tell Miss Fullagher to step this way a moment," he ordered.

"He is in this house, then," she cried. He took no notice. In a moment a young woman dressed in the uniform of one of the principal hospitals entered.

"Miss Fullagher," he asked, "how is the patient?"

"We've had a lot of trouble with him, sir," she said significantly. "He was terrible all last night, and he's very weak this morning. Is this the young lady, sir?"

"This is the young lady who I told you would want to see him when you thought it advisable."

The nurse looked doubtful. "Sir Henry is upstairs, sir," she said. "I had better ask his advice."

Trent nodded and she withdrew. The three were left alone, Ernestine and Francis remained apart as though by design. Trent was silent.

She returned in a moment or two.

"Sir Henry has not quite finished his examination, sir," she announced. "The young lady can come up in half an hour."

Again they were left alone. Then Trent crossed the room and stood between them and the door.

"Before you see your father, Miss Wendermott," he said, "I have an explanation to make to you!"

CHAPTER XLI

He looked at him calmly, but in her set, white face he seemed to read already his sentence!

"Do you think it worth while, Mr. Trent? There is so much, as you put it, to be explained, that the task, even to a man of your versatility, seems hopeless!"

"I shall not trouble you long," he said. "At least one man's word should be as good as another's--and you have listened to what my enemy"--he motioned towards Francis--"has to say."

Francis shrugged his shoulders.

"I can assure you," he interrupted, "that I have no feeling of enmity towards you in the slightest. My opinion you know. I have never troubled to conceal it. But I deny that I am prejudiced by any personal feeling."

Trent ignored his speech.

"What I have to say to you," he continued addressing Ernestine, "I want to say before you see your father. I won't take up your time. I won't waste words. I take you back ten years to when I met him at Attra and we became partners in a certain enterprise. Your father at that time was a harmless wreck of a man who was fast killing himself with brandy. He had some money, I had none. With it we bought the necessary outfit and presents for my enterprise and started for Bekwando. The whole of the work fell to my share, and with great trouble I succeeded in obtaining the concessions we were working for. Your father spent all his time drinking, and playing cards, when I would play with him. The agreement as to the sharing of the profits was drawn up, it is true, by me, but at that time he made no word of complaint. I had no relations, he described himself as cut off wholly from his. It was here Francis first came on the scene. He found your father half drunk, and when he read the agreement it was plain what he thought. He thought that I was letting your father kill himself that the whole thing might be mine. He has probably told you so. I deny it. I did all I could to keep him sober!

"On our homeward way your father was ill and our bearers deserted us. We were pursued by the natives, who repented their concession, and I had to fight them more than once, half a dozen strong, with your father unconscious at my feet. It is true that I left him in the bush, but it was at his bidding and I believed him dying. It was my only chance and I took it. I escaped and reached Attra. Then, to raise money to reach England, I had to borrow from a man named Da Souza, and afterwards, in London, to start the Company, I had to make him my partner in the profits of the concession. One day I quarrelled with him--it was just at the time I met you--and then, for the first time, I heard of your father's being alive. I went out to Africa to bring him back and Da Souza followed me in abject fear, for as my partner he lost half if your father's claim was good. I found your father infirm and only half sane. I did all I could for him whilst I worked in the interior, and meant to bring him back to England with me when I came, unfortunately he recovered a little and suddenly seized upon the idea of visiting England. He left before me and fell into the hands of Da Souza, who had the best possible reasons in the world for keeping him in the background. I rescued him from them in time to save him from death and brought him to my own house, sent for doctors and nurses, and, when he was fit for you to see, I should have sent for you. I did not, I'll admit, make any public declaration of his existence, for the simple reason that it would have crippled our Company, and there are the interests of the shareholders to be considered, but I executed and signed a deed of partnership days ago which makes him an equal sharer in every penny I possess. Now this is the truth, Miss Wendermott, and if it is not a story I am particularly proud of, I don't very well see what else I could have done. It is my story and it is a true one. Will you believe it or will you take his word against mine?"

She would have spoken, but Francis held up his hand.

"My story," he said coolly, "has been told behind your back. It is only fair to repeat it to your face. I have told Miss Wendermott this--that I met you first in the village of Bekwando with a concession in your hand made out to you and her father jointly, with the curious proviso that in the event of the death of one the other was his heir. I pointed out to Miss Wendermott that you were in the prime of life and in magnificent condition, while her father was already on the threshold of the grave and drinking himself into a fever in a squalid hut in a village of swamps. I told her that I suspected foul play, that I followed you both and found her father left to the tender mercies of the savages, deserted by you in the bush. I told her that many months afterwards he disappeared, simultaneously with your arrival in the country, that a day or two ago you swore to me you had no idea where he was. That has been my story, Trent, let Miss Wendermott choose between them."

"I am content," Trent cried fiercely. "Your story is true enough, but it is cunningly linked together. You have done your worst. Choose!"

For ever afterwards he was glad of that single look of reproach which seemed to escape her unwittingly as her eyes met his. But she turned away and his heart was like a stone.

"You have deceived me, Mr. Trent. I am very sorry, and very disappointed."

"And you," he cried passionately, "are you yourself so blameless? Were you altogether deceived by your relations, or had you never a suspicion that your father might still be alive? You had my message through Mr. Cuthbert; I met you day by day after you knew that I had been your father's partner, and never once did you give yourself away! Were you tarred with the same brush as those canting snobs who doomed a poor old man to a living death? Doesn't it look like it? What am I to think of you?"

"Your judgment, Mr. Trent," she answered quietly, "is of no importance to me! It does not interest me in any way. But I will tell you this. If I did not disclose myself, it was because I distrusted you. I wanted to know the truth, and I set myself to find it out."

"Your friendship was a lie, then!" he cried, with flashing eyes. "To you I was nothing but a suspected man to be spied upon and betrayed."

She faltered and did not answer him. Outside the nurse was knocking at the door. Trent waved them away with an imperious gesture.

"Be off," he cried, "both of you! You can do your worst! I thank Heaven that I am not of your class, whose men have flints for hearts and whose women can lie like angels."

They left him alone, and Trent, with a groan, plucked from his heart the one strong, sweet hope which had changed his life so wonderfully. Upstairs, Monty was sobbing, with his little girl's arms about him.

CHAPTER XLII

With the darkness had come a wind from the sea, and the boy crept outside in his flannels and planter's hat and threw himself down in a cane chair with a little murmur of relief. Below him burned the white lights of the town, a little noisier than usual to-night, for out in the bay a steamer was lying-to, and there had been a few passengers and cargo to land. The boy had had a hard day's work, or he would have been in the town himself to watch for arrivals and wait for the mail. He closed his eyes, half asleep, for the sun had been hot and the murmurs of the sea below was almost like a lullaby. As he lay there a man's voice from the path reached him. He sprang up, listening intently. It must have been fancy--and yet! He leaned over the wooden balcony. The figure of a man loomed out through the darkness, came nearer, became distinct. Fred recognised him with a glad shout.

"Trent!" he cried. "Scarlett Trent, by all that's amazing!"

Trent held out his hand quickly. Somehow the glad young voice, quivering with excitement, touched his heart in an unexpected and unusual manner. It was pleasant to be welcomed like this--to feel that one person in the world at least was glad of his coming. For Trent was a sorely stricken man and the flavour of life had gone from him. Many a time he had looked over the steamer's side during that long, lonely voyage and gazed almost wishfully into the sea, in whose embrace was rest. It seemed to him that he had been a gambler playing for great stakes, and the turn of the wheel had gone against him.

"Fred!"

They stood with hands locked together, the boy breathless with surprise. Then he saw that something was wrong.

"What is it, Trent?" he asked quickly. "Have we gone smash after all, or have you been ill?"

Trent shook his head and smiled gravely.

"Neither," he said. "The Company is booming, I believe. Civilised ways didn't agree with me, I'm afraid. That's all! I've come back to have a month or two's hard work--the best physic in the world."

"I am delighted to see you," Fred said heartily. "Everything's going A1 here, and they've built me this little bungalow, only got in it last week--stunning, isn't it? But--just fancy your being here again so soon! Are your traps coming up?"

"I haven't many," Trent answered. "They're on the way. Have you got room for me?"

"Room for you!" the boy repeated scornfully. "Why, I'm all alone here. It's the only thing against the place, being a bit lonely. Room for you! I should think there is! Here, Dick! Dinner at once, and some wine!"

Trent was taken to see his room, the boy talking all the time, and later on dinner was served and the boy did the honours, chaffing and talking lightly. But later on when they sat outside, smoking furiously to keep off the mosquitoes and watching the fireflies dart in and out amongst the trees, the boy was silent. Then he leaned over and laid his hand on Trent's arm.

"Tell me all about it--do," he begged.

Trent was startled, touched, and suddenly filled with a desire for sympathy such as he had never before in his life experienced. He hesitated, but it was only for a moment.

"I never thought to tell any one," he said slowly, "I think I'd like to!"

And he did. He told his whole story. He did not spare himself. He spoke of the days of his earlier partnership with Monty, and he admitted the apparent brutality of his treatment of him on more than one occasion. He spoke of Ernestine too--of his strange fancy for the photograph of Monty's little girl, a fancy which later on when he met her became almost immediately the dominant passion of his life. Then he spoke of the coming of Francis, of the awakening of Ernestine's suspicions, and of that desperate moment when he risked everything on her faith in him--and lost. There was little else to tell and afterwards there was a silence. But presently the boy's hand fell upon his arm almost caressingly and he leaned over through the darkness.

"Women are such idiots," the boy declared, with all the vigour and certainty of long experience. "If only Aunt Ernestine had known you half as well as I do, she would have been quite content to have trusted you and to have believed that what you did was for the best. But I say, Trent, you ought to have waited for it. After she had seen her father and talked with him she must have understood you better. I shall write to her."

But Trent shook his head.

"No," he said sternly, "it is too late now. That moment taught me all I wanted to know. It was her love I wanted, Fred, and--that--no use hoping for that, or she would have trusted me. After all I was half a madman ever to have expected it--a rough, coarse chap like me, with only a smattering of polite ways! It was madness! Some day I shall get over it! We'll chuck work for a bit, soon, Fred, and go for some lions. That'll give us something to think about at any rate."

But the lions which Trent might have shot lived in peace, for on the morrow he was restless and ill, and within a week the deadly fever of the place had him in its clutches. The boy nursed him and the German doctor came up from Attra and, when he learnt who his patient was, took up his quarters in the place. But for all his care and the boy's nursing things went badly with Scarlett Trent.

To him ended for a while all measure of days--time became one long night, full of strange, tormenting flashes of thought, passing like red fire before his burning eyes. Sometimes it was Monty crying to him from the bush, sometimes the yelling of those savages at Bekwando seemed to fill the air, sometimes Ernestine was there, listening to his passionate pleading with cold, set face, In the dead of night he saw her and the still silence was broken by his hoarse, passionate cries, which they strove in vain to check. And when at last he lay white and still with exhaustion, the doctor looked at the boy and softly shook his head. He had very little hope.

Trent grew worse. In those rare flashes of semi-consciousness which sometimes come to the fever-stricken, he reckoned himself a dying man and contemplated the end of all things without enthusiasm and without regret. The one and only failure of his life had eaten like canker into his heart. It was death he craved for in the hot, burning nights, and death came and sat, a grisly shadow, at his pillow. The doctor and the boy did their best, but it was not they who saved him.

There came a night when he raved, and the sound of a woman's name rang out from the open windows of the little bungalow, rang out through the drawn mosquito netting amongst the palm-trees, across the surf-topped sea to the great steamer which lay in the bay. Perhaps she heard it--perhaps after all it was a fancy. Only, in the midst of his fever, a hand as soft as velvet and as cool as the night sea-wind touched his forehead, and a voice sounded in his ears so sweetly that the blood burned no longer in his veins, so sweetly that he lay back upon his pillow like a man under the influence of a strong narcotic and slept. Then the doctor smiled and the boy sobbed.

"I came," she said softly, "because it was the only atonement I could make. I ought to have trusted you. Do you know, even my father told me that."

"I have made mistakes," he said, "and of course behaved badly to him."

"Now that everything has been explained," she said, "I scarcely see what else you could have done. At least you saved him from Da Souza when his death would have made you a freer man. He is looking forward to seeing you, you must make haste and get strong."

"For his sake," he murmured.

She leaned over and caressed him lightly. "For mine, dear."

The Codes Of Hammurabi And Moses
W. W. Davies

QTY

The discovery of the Hammurabi Code is one of the greatest achievements of archaeology, and is of paramount interest, not only to the student of the Bible, but also to all those interested in ancient history...

Religion   ISBN: *1-59462-338-4*   Pages:132
MSRP $12.95

The Theory of Moral Sentiments
Adam Smith

QTY

This work from 1749. contains original theories of conscience amd moral judgment and it is the foundation for systemof morals.

Philosophy ISBN: *1-59462-777-0*   Pages:536
MSRP $19.95

Jessica's First Prayer
Hesba Stretton

QTY

In a screened and secluded corner of one of the many railway-bridges which span the streets of London there could be seen a few years ago, from five o'clock every morning until half past eight, a tidily set-out coffee-stall, consisting of a trestle and board, upon which stood two large tin cans, with a small fire of charcoal burning under each so as to keep the coffee boiling during the early hours of the morning when the work-people were thronging into the city on their way to their daily toil...

Childrens   ISBN: *1-59462-373-2*   Pages:84
MSRP $9.95

My Life and Work
Henry Ford

QTY

Henry Ford revolutionized the world with his implementation of mass production for the Model T automobile. Gain valuable business insight into his life and work with his own auto-biography... "We have only started on our development of our country we have not as yet, with all our talk of wonderful progress, done more than scratch the surface. The progress has been wonderful enough but..."

Biographies/   ISBN: *1-59462-198-5*   Pages:300
MSRP $21.95

The Art of Cross-Examination
Francis Wellman

QTY

I presume it is the experience of every author, after his first book is published upon an important subject, to be almost overwhelmed with a wealth of ideas and illustrations which could readily have been included in his book, and which to his own mind, at least, seem to make a second edition inevitable. Such certainly was the case with me; and when the first edition had reached its sixth impression in five months, I rejoiced to learn that it seemed to my publishers that the book had met with a sufficiently favorable reception to justify a second and considerably enlarged edition. ..

Reference   **ISBN: *1-59462-647-2***

Pages:412

MSRP $19.95

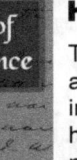

On the Duty of Civil Disobedience
Henry David Thoreau

QTY

Thoreau wrote his famous essay, On the Duty of Civil Disobedience, as a protest against an unjust but popular war and the immoral but popular institution of slave-owning. He did more than write—he declined to pay his taxes, and was hauled off to gaol in consequence. Who can say how much this refusal of his hastened the end of the war and of slavery ?

Law   **ISBN: *1-59462-747-9***

Pages:48

MSRP $7.45

Dream Psychology Psychoanalysis for Beginners
Sigmund Freud

QTY

Sigmund Freud, born Sigismund Schlomo Freud (May 6, 1856 - September 23, 1939), was a Jewish-Austrian neurologist and psychiatrist who co-founded the psychoanalytic school of psychology. Freud is best known for his theories of the unconscious mind, especially involving the mechanism of repression; his redefinition of sexual desire as mobile and directed towards a wide variety of objects; and his therapeutic techniques, especially his understanding of transference in the therapeutic relationship and the presumed value of dreams as sources of insight into unconscious desires.

Pages:196

Psychology   **ISBN: *1-59462-905-6***

MSRP $15.45

The Miracle of Right Thought
Orison Swett Marden

QTY

Believe with all of your heart that you will do what you were made to do. When the mind has once formed the habit of holding cheerful, happy, prosperous pictures, it will not be easy to form the opposite habit. It does not matter how improbable or how far away this realization may see, or how dark the prospects may be, if we visualize them as best we can, as vividly as possible, hold tenaciously to them and vigorously struggle to attain them, they will gradually become actualized, realized in the life. But a desire, a longing without endeavor, a yearning abandoned or held indifferently will vanish without realization.

Pages:360

Self Help   **ISBN: *1-59462-644-8***

MSRP $25.45

The Rosicrucian Cosmo-Conception Mystic Christianity by *Max Heindel*   ISBN: *1-59462-188-8*   **$38.95**
The Rosicrucian Cosmo-conception is not dogmatic, neither does it appeal to any other authority than the reason of the student. It is: not controversial, but is: sent forth in the, hope that it may help to clear...   New Age/Religion Pages 646

Abandonment To Divine Providence by *Jean-Pierre de Caussade*   ISBN: *1-59462-228-0*   **$25.95**
"The Rev. Jean Pierre de Caussade was one of the most remarkable spiritual writers of the Society of Jesus in France in the 18th Century. His death took place at Toulouse in 1751. His works have gone through many editions and have been republished...   Inspirational/Religion Pages 400

Mental Chemistry by *Charles Haanel*   ISBN: *1-59462-192-6*   **$23.95**
Mental Chemistry allows the change of material conditions by combining and appropriately utilizing the power of the mind. Much like applied chemistry creates something new and unique out of careful combinations of chemicals the mastery of mental chemistry...   New Age Pages 354

The Letters of Robert Browning and Elizabeth Barret Barrett 1845-1846 vol II   ISBN: *1-59462-193-4*   **$35.95**
by Robert Browning and Elizabeth Barrett   Biographies Pages 596

Gleanings In Genesis (volume I) by *Arthur W. Pink*   ISBN: *1-59462-130-6*   **$27.45**
Appropriately has Genesis been termed "the seed plot of the Bible" for in it we have, in germ form, almost all of the great doctrines which are afterwards fully developed in the books of Scripture which follow...   Religion/Inspirational Pages 420

The Master Key by *L. W. de Laurence*   ISBN: *1-59462-001-6*   **$30.95**
In no branch of human knowledge has there been a more lively increase of the spirit of research during the past few years than in the study of Psychology, Concentration and Mental Discipline. The requests for authentic lessons in Thought Control, Mental Discipline and...   New Age/Business Pages 422

The Lesser Key Of Solomon Goetia by *L. W. de Laurence*   ISBN: *1-59462-092-X*   **$9.95**
This translation of the first book of the "Lernegton" which is now for the first time made accessible to students of Talismanic Magic was done, after careful collation and edition, from numerous Ancient Manuscripts in Hebrew, Latin, and French...   New Age/Occult Pages 92

Rubaiyat Of Omar Khayyam by *Edward Fitzgerald*   ISBN:*1-59462-332-5*   **$13.95**
Edward Fitzgerald, whom the world has already learned, in spite of his own efforts to remain within the shadow of anonymity, to look upon as one of the rarest poets of the century, was born at Bredfield, in Suffolk, on the 31st of March, 1809. He was the third son of John Purcell...   Music Pages 172

Ancient Law by *Henry Maine*   ISBN: *1-59462-128-4*   **$29.95**
The chief object of the following pages is to indicate some of the earliest ideas of mankind, as they are reflected in Ancient Law, and to point out the relation of those ideas to modern thought.   Religiom/History Pages 452

Far-Away Stories by *William J. Locke*   ISBN: *1-59462-129-2*   **$19.45**
"Good wine needs no bush, but a collection of mixed vintages does. And this book is just such a collection. Some of the stories I do not want to remain buried for ever in the museum files of dead magazine-numbers an author's not unpardonable vanity..."   Fiction Pages 272

Life of David Crockett by *David Crockett*   ISBN: *1-59462-250-7*   **$27.45**
"Colonel David Crockett was one of the most remarkable men of the times in which he lived. Born in humble life, but gifted with a strong will, an indomitable courage, and unremitting perseverance...   Biographies/New Age Pages 424

Lip-Reading by *Edward Nitchie*   ISBN: *1-59462-206-X*   **$25.95**
Edward B. Nitchie, founder of the New York School for the Hard of Hearing, now the Nitchie School of Lip-Reading, Inc, wrote "LIP-READING Principles and Practice". The development and perfecting of this meritorious work on lip-reading was an undertaking...   How-to Pages 400

A Handbook of Suggestive Therapeutics, Applied Hypnotism, Psychic Science   ISBN: *1-59462-214-0*   **$24.95**
by Henry Munro   Health/New Age/Health/Self-help Pages 376

A Doll's House: and Two Other Plays by *Henrik Ibsen*   ISBN: *1-59462-112-8*   **$19.95**
Henrik Ibsen created this classic when in revolutionary 1848 Rome. Introducing some striking concepts in playwriting for the realist genre, this play has been studied the world over.   Fiction/Classics/Plays 308

The Light of Asia by *sir Edwin Arnold*   ISBN: *1-59462-204-3*   **$13.95**
In this poetic masterpiece, Edwin Arnold describes the life and teachings of Buddha. The man who was to become known as Buddha to the world was born as Prince Gautama of India but he rejected the worldly riches and abandoned the reigns of power when...   Religion/History/Biographies Pages 170

The Complete Works of Guy de Maupassant by *Guy de Maupassant*   ISBN: *1-59462-157-8*   **$16.95**
"For days and days, nights and nights, I had dreamed of that first kiss which was to consecrate our engagement, and I knew not on what spot I should put my lips..."   Fiction/Classics Pages 240

The Art of Cross-Examination by *Francis L. Wellman*   ISBN: *1-59462-309-0*   **$26.95**
Written by a renowned trial lawyer, Wellman imparts his experience and uses case studies to explain how to use psychology to extract desired information through questioning.   How-to/Science/Reference Pages 408

Answered or Unanswered? by *Louisa Vaughan*   ISBN: *1-59462-248-5*   **$10.95**
Miracles of Faith in China   Religion Pages 112

The Edinburgh Lectures on Mental Science (1909) by *Thomas*   ISBN: *1-59462-008-3*   **$11.95**
This book contains the substance of a course of lectures recently given by the writer in the Queen Street Hail, Edinburgh. Its purpose is to indicate the Natural Principles governing the relation between Mental Action and Material Conditions...   New Age/Psychology Pages 148

Ayesha by *H. Rider Haggard*   ISBN: *1-59462-301-5*   **$24.95**
Verily and indeed it is the unexpected that happens! Probably if there was one person upon the earth from whom the Editor of this, and of a certain previous history, did not expect to hear again...   Classics Pages 380

Ayala's Angel by *Anthony Trollope*   ISBN: *1-59462-352-X*   **$29.95**
The two girls were both pretty, but Lucy who was twenty-one who supposed to be simple and comparatively unattractive, whereas Ayala was credited, as her Bombwhat romantic name might show, with poetic charm and a taste for romance. Ayala when her father died was nineteen...   Fiction Pages 484

The American Commonwealth by *James Bryce*   ISBN: *1-59462-286-8*   **$34.45**
An interpretation of American democratic political theory. It examines political mechanics and society from the perspective of Scotsman James Bryce   Politics Pages 572

Stories of the Pilgrims by *Margaret P. Pumphrey*   ISBN: *1-59462-116-0*   **$17.95**
This book explores pilgrims religious oppression in England as well as their escape to Holland and eventual crossing to America on the Mayflower, and their early days in New England...   History Pages 268

QTY

The Fasting Cure *by Sinclair Upton*   ISBN: *1-59462-222-1*   **$13.95**
In the Cosmopolitan Magazine for May, 1910, and in the Contemporary Review (London) for April, 1910, I published an article dealing with my experiences in fasting. I have written a great many magazine articles, but never one which attracted so much attention... New Age/Self Help/Health Pages 164

Hebrew Astrology *by Sepharial*   ISBN: *1-59462-308-2*   **$13.45**
In these days of advanced thinking it is a matter of common observation that we have left many of the old landmarks behind and that we are now pressing forward to greater heights and to a wider horizon than that which represented the mind-content of our progenitors... Astrology Pages 144

Thought Vibration or The Law of Attraction in the Thought World   ISBN: *1-59462-127-6*   **$12.95**

by William Walker Atkinson   *Psychology/Religion Pages 144*

Optimism *by Helen Keller*   ISBN: *1-59462-108-X*   **$15.95**
Helen Keller was blind, deaf, and mute since 19 months old, yet famously learned how to overcome these handicaps, communicate with the world, and spread her lectures promoting optimism. An inspiring read for everyone... Biographies/Inspirational Pages 84

Sara Crewe *by Frances Burnett*   ISBN: *1-59462-360-0*   **$9.45**
In the first place, Miss Minchin lived in London. Her home was a large, dull, tall one, in a large, dull square, where all the houses were alike, and all the sparrows were alike, and where all the door-knockers made the same heavy sound... Childrens/Classic Pages 88

The Autobiography of Benjamin Franklin *by Benjamin Franklin*   ISBN: *1-59462-135-7*   **$24.95**
The Autobiography of Benjamin Franklin has probably been more extensively read than any other American historical work, and no other book of its kind has had such ups and downs of fortune. Franklin lived for many years in England, where he was agent... Biographies/History Pages 332

Name	
Email	
Telephone	
Address	
City, State ZIP	

☐ **Credit Card**   ☐ **Check / Money Order**

Credit Card Number	
Expiration Date	
Signature	

Please Mail to: Book Jungle
                            PO Box 2226
                            Champaign, IL 61825
or Fax to: 630-214-0564

ORDERING INFORMATION

web: *www.bookjungle.com*
email: *sales@bookjungle.com*
fax: *630-214-0564*
mail: *Book Jungle PO Box 2226 Champaign, IL 61825*
or PayPal *to sales@bookjungle.com*

Please contact us for bulk discounts

DIRECT-ORDER TERMS

**20% Discount if You Order
Two or More Books**
Free Domestic Shipping!
Accepted: Master Card, Visa,
Discover, American Express

www.ingramcontent.com/pod-product-compliance
Lightning Source LLC
Chambersburg PA
CBHW080902020726
47502CB00008B/2321